THE CHRONICLES OF LIBRON

THE ADVENTURES OF ZEPH

TOLU SAJOBI

Brandives.

Published by Brandives
www.brandives.com

ISBN: 978-1-7773270-6-4

Dedication

For Tolutoyosi and Tolutofunmi – may you
become all that you are born to be.

TABLE OF CONTENT

CHAPTER 1: PROLOGUE

It was the start of the rainy season in Buhen, the capital city of the Nubian Kingdom. I had gone to bed earlier that evening hoping to get some much-needed sleep. After hours of tossing and turning in bed, staring at the ceiling in silence that was intermittently punctuated by thunderous lightning and rushing sounds of winds blowing against my windows, I managed to get up. I groped around in darkness a bit before finding my bedside lamp. Shortly after, it began to rain. It was first a gentle shower that grazed off the roof and the windows of my quarters, but it was not long before the rain grew in intensity until it was deafening. I got up and walked towards the window overlooking the city to inspect the heavy downpour. As I watched the runoffs meander into nearby underground drainage, I reminisced about my life's journey filled with twists and turns. The journey from the country hills of Shalaptonia, to the banks of the Nubia River, to the corridors of power negotiating deals with several kings and kingdoms, and now as a retired public servant.

After decades of public service to three generations of
Nubian kings, King Nobiin IV (the grandson of Nobiin II
who appointed me as the prime minister) still consults me on
economic issues and matters of national security despite my
retirement. What a journey, I muttered to myself as I trudged
towards my study desk. Then I remembered the national
report that was delivered to my home by His Highness's
emissaries the previous day. It contained expert assessment
and data on several sectors of the Nubian kingdom, including
economy, national defense, and agriculture. I had promised
his aides that I would read the report and give my feedback
later. Since sleep wasn't forthcoming, I resolved to review it
right away.

I gazed into the horizon, at the dashing lights of the
capital city from the window of my room while reflecting on
the report. A slight ache coursed through my head. Of greater
concern were some of the emerging economic and social issues
from the national report and the data that was presented.
Even though the Nubian kingdom is predominantly Black,
the nation's net immigration rate has tripled in the last
decade and immigrant communities now account for 60% of
all live births. The income inequality gap, an ever-growing
chasm between the "haves" and "have nots", remains a thorny
issue for the kingdom. Eighty-five percent of Nubia's wealth
is concentrated in the royal family and a select few. During
the last four decades, the Nubian kingdom has risen from the
abyss of racism and oppression to become a beacon of hope

and haven for people from diverse kingdoms and tongues who have come to seek refuge within her borders. But income inequality and the recent economic crisis have pushed the kingdom back to the edge. The rising racial violence and anti-immigrant rhetoric being promoted by the mainstream Nubians was becoming unsettling. As I reflected on these issues, I was worried that some of the progress we have made as a kingdom with respect to anti-racism legislations might just be eroded with the re-emergence of these hate groups. Hours later, after pacing up and down in my study room to reflect on possible solutions, I was ready to write my strategic recommendations for the current administration.

Limnea and Eran barged into my room after chasing each other around the house, startling me, and distracting me from my work. A somewhat warm but annoying intrusion. "Why are you two up this early?" I asked. Limnea could not be more different from Eran both in personality and mannerism, it is probably why they get at each other a lot. I am always somehow caught in the middle when one, after the other, reports each other's actions to me. My negotiation skills which once served me well in the corridors of power comes handy when dealing with these two, at least to buy me enough time to focus on the task at hand daily. I would not have it any other way though, these two bring so much joy to my world, they remind me of my childhood, oh what would I give to be a child again. I was still lost in my thoughts when their nanny showed up to get a hold of them.

"I am very sorry, your excellency. I need to prepare them for school, but they have been running all over the place since they got up," she explained in frustration.

"Time flies by so fast," I mumbled to myself while rearranging the scrolls of reports I have been poring through in the last few hours. I wanted to attend to the boys, who by now were playing hide-and-seek in my office.

"Catch us if you can grandpa!" Eran called out from under my desk and giggled.

I smiled amusedly. "It's time for school, children. Let's continue this game when you get back."

"No, we want to stay with you grandpa," Eran resisted.

"Eran, you know too well that I cannot get under the desk because of my long-term back problem. Come out here and let's talk about school."

By this time, the Nanny had already gotten hold of the boys and brought them to me. Although they were both upset, I promised to make it up to them if they would just listen and comply with their Nanny's instructions. Despite their disapproval, I planted kisses on their cheeks before she took them back to their quarters.

Just before I settled into my seat to continue writing my report, I overheard other aides pleading with Philia to open the door.

"Go away!" I heard her yell. Wondering what was going on, I stepped out of my office to investigate. As I stood up, my legs felt a little stiff. Then I remembered I had been seated in the same spot for most of the night and not moved an inch. I thought to myself, I really need to remind myself to move about every hour or so, even if it is just for a quick stretch. My doctor has been advising this, but once I get engrossed in my work, it literally seems like time flies. I was still deliberating on this when I stepped out of my quarters to check to see what the issue is.

"What's going on here, people?"

The aides appeared flustered and fumbled with their hands nervously.

"It's Lady Philia." One of the servants offered.

"She has been acting rather sad and unlike herself since last night. She even refused to eat her dinner and has locked herself up in her chambers. We don't know what's wrong." The servant said in one breath with a look in her eyes that silently beseeched me to help them out. So, I approached and knocked on Philia's door.

"Darling Philia, could you open?"

There was a slight rustling from the other side of the door and then the soft padding of feet in the room.

"Grandpa, is that you?"

"Yes, my dear. Are you okay? What is going on with you?" I probed a bit further.

She was silent for a long time and I was beginning to think she had gone back to bed.

"I am not fine grandpa…please, go away. You won't understand," she said eventually.

I heard her sigh, the slight tremor in her voice, and the sniffle she tried to mask by clearing her throat. Why would she be so distraught anyway? What problems could a teenager of her caliber possibly have?

I sought to find the right words.

"You are right that I may not understand, but you can

share your troubles with me, I promise to listen."

"No, you adults are all the same." She snapped, and I winced. Something was really wrong with her.

"You don't listen, you just want to shove your ideas down our throats as though they would solve every of our problems." She sniffed more loudly now.

I pursed my lips grimly. Hearing her so distraught broke my heart, many thoughts were running through my mind to see if I could get a clue to what the problem might be by running through the conversations we might have had recently or something she had mentioned in passing but nothing particularly stood out. That sound coming from Philia does not sound like her at all, I have never heard her speak or act this way. All I want to do is to get to the bottom of this and hopefully help her feel better again, my heart really went out to her.

"Alright, I hear you my darling. I will sit here until you are done processing your thoughts." I replied while asking my aides to bring my rocking chair.

"No, grandpa," she protested.

"You cannot sit by my door all day. You should go back to your quarters. I will come out when I am ready."

Unfazed, I took my seat.

"I'm just as stubborn as you are. I am going nowhere, Philia. I will be here if you need anything." I scraped my rocking chair across the floor noisily for effect.

Philia heaved a sigh of resignation. Resignation was a good sign, I quietly chuckled to myself.

"Alright, grandpa. I will open the door soon. Give me a

few minutes to put on my robe." She replied after a long pause. I exhaled loudly with relief; glad we were making progress.

After about twenty minutes, Philia finally opened the door and gave me a big hug as she sobbed uncontrollably.

"Let's go into my office, Philia." I gently patted her on the back as I led her into my quarters.

"My darling, I don't want you to cry anymore. I need you to tell me what or who upsets you."

I gently prodded as I invited her to take a seat on the couch near my office window. The sun was out, shining brightly into the office. I could see the morning hustle and bustle going on in the streets at a distance. I took a seat on the brown leather sofa next to her, sinking in and placing a cushion behind me to help balance my back nicely as I am not sure how long this conversation would take.

My gaze turned to Philia, and I noticed that she's calmed a little. I probed further in my attempt to understand her sadness. Wiping her face with her hands, she leaned gently on my shoulder and started to cry again. I held her hand and looked straight into her eyes reassuring her of my love and support.

"I am always here for you, Philia. Always." She smiled a little and gently raised her head and straightened her shoulders.

"Thank you, grandpa. I don't understand why we are different from everyone else. I just want to be a normal kid, like all my friends." My brow was raised with a confused look on my face as I tried to make sense of the statement.

"Why do we live a lie?" She asked after seeing the

confusion on my face. Amazed, and at the same time confused at the gravity of those words from my thirteen-year-old granddaughter, I gently asked her to elaborate further.

"We are neither Nubian nor Libronian. My school mates believe I am not black enough because my parents are not "truly" of Nubian descent. They always taunt me in school for being a brown girl. They claim brown people are ugly and that people who are not truly of Nubian stock are less intelligent. Why do Nubians think less of us, yet they worship the ground you walk on, grandpa? On the other hand, my cousins and uncles here in Buhen often deride my cousins and me that we are not brown enough because grandma is a black Nubian. Why do my great-grand uncles and aunties often think that we are less Libronian than others? Why are you more 'Nubian' than the rest of us? Am I wrong grandpa?"

As I watched her grapple with these questions about her identity, I sat there heartbroken that my descendants are still experiencing the same racial discrimination I had experienced decades after I arrived in Nubia. I understood her frustration and confusion. The Nubians consider brown people, such as Philia, and those from other races as not truly Nubian even if they have spent their entire lives in Nubia. My Libronian community in Buhen, on the other hand, consider mixed-race children, like Philia, and those born in diaspora as half-Libronian because they are born in Nubia and had never experienced the "undiluted" Libronian culture. Philia had carefully observed my routine and watched closely as international dignitaries, aristocrats, and royal officials frequently visited my home for networking, mentorship, and advice on matters of national security and foreign policy, long after I had retired from public life. She had seen me host my brothers, nephews, and nieces and their families to lunches and dinners where we reminisced about my father and life in Libron. She was right to be confused by the racial discrimination she had experienced from both native Nubians and her people.

Yet, like every descendant of immigrants, she's confused and trying to make sense of the "double life" and, sometimes, contrasting cultures we live in.

As I reflected on the situation, I stared into the horizon through my office window, my gaze go in g far beyond the towering pyramids across Nubia to the countryside of Libron where I grew up. I wondered how much my life had changed from the simple peasant shepherd family life we lived in the countryside of Shalaptonia to being a man of influence in Nubia. I reflected on my journey and my accomplishments in the Nubian kingdom. But I felt powerless that the progress we had made in successfully passing equal rights and anti-racism legislations across Nubia and internationally have been in vain since my grand- and great-grandchildren are still experiencing such levels of racial discrimination. The most heartbreaking part of this was that the discrimination Philia was experiencing was from members of our community who think she's not Libronian enough!

"Yes, we are different," I whispered after what seemed like an eternity.

"Pardon me, grandpa. Did you just say we are different? " Philia asked, her eyebrows raised.

"Yes, we are different," I concluded.

As I watched her try to make sense of my response, it dawned on me that our children, born here in Nubia, must have been struggling with the same issues in silence - struggling to reconcile two different cultures, fit in with friends, wade off discrimination, while craving for acceptance from family relatives. As the only surviving son of my father at this time, I counted myself fortunate to have lived long enough to see three generations of my people born and raised in Nubia. However, most of them, except for my children and the third generation, have led isolationist lives in Upper Buhen, an upper-class neighborhood in Nubia, growing their livestock businesses while mingling with the Nubians for business reasons only. To them, I was a respected elder statesman who brought the entire family to Nubia when I became the prime minister, but I was not a role model of what a "godly" Libronian man should be. I was the right-hand man of secular Nubian kings, my economic policies saved Nubia but enslaved many Nubians to the royal family forever, and I married a black Nubian who was the daughter of a disgraced grandmaster of a religious order. In their conservative ideology, a true Libronian should not "mix" as much as I have done.

"Grandpa, why did you conclude that we are different?" Philia asked again as she tapped me on the shoulders.

"My child, I'm so sorry to hear that you are experiencing discrimination. I understand how frustrating this can be for you."

"Grandpa, I don't think you understand. You are considered a Nubian but not us."

"I do, my child. I have had my share of racial discrimination for being different. When I arrived here in Nubia as a teenager, I had even worse treatment from many who thought being different means you are inferior or that you don't belong."

"Are you serious, grandpa?"

"Oh yes. I want you to know that it is alright to be different."

"It is not easy to be different, you know. It makes you the butt of all jokes and an easy target for their taunts."

"My dear, you are different and unique in every sense of the word. I don't mean that in the negative sense, but in a positive sense. Being different is a strength. Those who call you names for being different are threatened by your uniqueness and unconsciously try to project their insecurities on you by making you feel inadequate."

"Wait, grandpa. Are you saying that people that make me feel bad and inferior are deliberately trying to push their inferiority on me?"

"Yes, my child. Don't let anyone rob you of identity or make you feel less adequate. Do you know how lucky you are? Less than one out of every five Nubians have the rare privilege of intimately experiencing two cultures in their lifetimes like you do. You have a rich heritage that is partly Nubian and partly Libronian."

"That's not a medal that makes others accept you right

away. They will still taunt me anyways, grandpa." Philia dismissed the idea.

"Of course, it is not a medal, but it is your heritage and an identity that is fundamental to your core as an individual. Why would you allow some student in your school to make you feel inferior because of how you look while they get to bask in their own identity. Who judges one race to be better, by the way? "

"Grandpa, you adults do. The society makes us think that other non-black people are inferior." She argued.

"The society? What if the society is wrong, ignorant, and afraid of people that are different? Why do you believe what a few ignorant people think about you? If they get to believe what they believe, what's stopping you from sticking to your beliefs?"

"Okay, that's a different way of looking at it, grandpa," she admitted while reflecting on that line of thought.

"I think this perspective is helpful, grandpa. It's really empowering. Racial discrimination is rooted in fear and ignorance. I should not allow someone's belief about me, or my kind, to define who I am or how I see myself. Next time someone tries to play the race card, I should point out their ignorance and refuse to let them project their insecurities on me. Is that right?"

"You are right, my dear. You are beautiful and of a rich heritage. Don't let anyone make you feel inferior."

"Thank you, grandpa. I can go to school today confident and able to stand up for what I believe. You have empowered me not to tolerate that nonsense anymore."

"That's right, my darling."

"One more thing, grandpa. I must share this discussion with my cousins, Adrianna and Lilia. The three of us are being called names in school for being Libronian Nubian kids. On the other hand, some of our uncles often make derogatory remarks about us and our moms, unaware that we understand the Libronian language even though we are not as fluent as our other cousins and uncles.

I clenched my jaw in frustration.

One would expect adults to have half the sense and know better but these ones… I was disappointed to say the least.

"I am sorry that you children are dealing with this, even from our family too. Please go ahead and speak to them about this. You should bring them here one of these days. Perhaps, I can share some words of wisdom with them."

"Alright, grandpa. I love you; you are simply the best! I need to go get ready for school." She replied with a big grin after giving me a big hug. Seeing her smile was a lot more than I had hoped when she walked into the office earlier, a sense of joy and relief washed over me. However, this joy was short lived as the issues we had just discussed came back to mind and a sense of sadness started to well up within me.

After Philia left, I reflected on our conversation and was saddened by the growing discrimination against mixed race children and those born in diaspora by members of our community and the discrimination immigrant families experience in Nubia. It brought the painful memories of my late wife's experience with my family. Also, my mind was flooded by the bad experiences I have had as an immigrant in Nubia. No one should continue to experience this, I thought to myself. Having helped Philia, I thought about the possibility of helping many other members of my community in Nubia. That morning, I resolved to be more involved in my community by helping them navigate their daily realities and challenges of being a Libronian Nubian. I felt a renewed purpose to help them come to terms with their identity, while teaching them important principles about integration into Nubian society without compromising their values and identities.

So, I wanted to run the idea by Philia who was about heading out of the door.

"Hey, Philia, I want to quickly run something by you."

"Grandpa, I am almost late for school. Can it wait?"

"It won't take long, my dear."

"Ok grandpa, I'm all ears."

"What do you think about having a broader discussion on race with our entire community?"

"That is a great idea grandpa, but they won't change." She casually dismissed the idea.

"Why? Who won't change?"

"Some of my uncles and first cousins have warned their children not to hang out with us again," she shrugged at first but later changed her mind.

"Perhaps, they will listen to you as the family patriarch."

"That's okay if they will listen to me. Alright, I will send word to everyone in our community for a meeting."

"I need to go now, papa."

"Have a great day my dear." I waved as I watched her

leave for school.

Then I returned to my study to complete drafting my report for the king. I spent the rest of the day drafting letters to each family head and elders of my people. Also, I sent word to all my children and their families. I wanted to speak with all of them one last time.

About a month later, my family and members of the Libronian community and their families visited me in my countryside home. The visit was more of a family reunion as I got to see family members I have not seen for years. We hugged, kissed, and exchanged pleasantries and then headed to the villa chapel to worship. The senior members of our community inquired afterwards about the reason I had sent for everyone, but I was over joyous and distracted by all that was going on to even give a reply. The sights of grand and great-grandchildren running all over the villa, teenage grandsons and daughters playing board games, and older sons and daughters of Libron helping around the villa filled me with joy. As we sat for lunch after worship, I noticed major absences. Notably, some of my nephews and nieces and their descendants stayed away, but others came out of respect for me. I was disappointed that those who stayed away would miss the opportunity to the misconceptions they had held on to for years. I had hoped that they would hear my story and correct their erroneous philosophy.

After a few moments of clinking wine glasses, I welcomed them all to my home and explained the reason for the invitation. "My children, I am happy to see all of you and your children in good health. Seeing you and your family abound in prosperity fills me with great joy and gratitude to God who has helped us in this kingdom. More importantly, seeing your little ones run over this villa warms my heart today." I said with invigorating excitement.

"I have watched with pride how many of you have conducted your businesses and raised happy families in this land. You continue to walk in faith and love for all just like our ancestors commanded. I am proud of all that you have continued to accomplish in this land."

"Thank you, grandpa. We love you too. It's always fun visiting your villa." One of the grandsons hollered from the audience after which everyone applauded.

"Thank you, my children. God bless you all." I was serenaded with applause, then I motioned for some silence to allow me to finish my speech.

"My people and elders of our community, I have sent for you for an important reason. A few weeks ago, Philia, one of my granddaughters, asked me a series of questions that made me reevaluate my purpose after several decades of public service. She was exasperated by the differential treatment she receives from black Nubians who see her as Libronian even though she was born and raised here in Nubia."

"She's not alone, grandpa, many of us have faced similar discrimination from Nubians. They are racists." One of my grandnephews interjected.

A wave of murmurs accompanied his admission, and one could not quite tell if they were for or against. My raised hand quelled them briefly.

"I hear you, son." I scanned their faces across the room, seeing that I had their attention, I proceeded with my speech.

"That morning, Philia and I discussed a wide range of issues including managing dual identity, handling racial discrimination, educating ignorant racists, and so on. As someone who arrived here as a teenager, I could relate to the burden of living with two identities and juggling the realities of two cultures while facing all manners of discrimination. Also, I am not oblivious to the conservative opinions many of your uncles, fathers, and cousins have embraced, thinking that complete segregation from the Nubian society is the only way to realize our destiny. After helping Philia to deal with these issues, it dawned on me that this would be a common issue for many of our children and grandchildren."

"Oh yes, our children also struggle with this identity crisis as well," another elder in the audience retorted. A louder wave of murmur followed. This time, I let them rave their incoherent agitations. I caught the indifference some of them had to the noise around them; they were not bothered in the slightest, and it made me wonder if they weren't the actual culprits I was worried about. I raised both hands and the din died down.

"My children, I understand that many of you have been warned to stay away from me because I represent everything that is pagan. I have intentionally kept a low profile in our community to allow you to deal with the challenges of your generation as I cheer you on. As someone who also had a first-hand experience of this situation, I feel qualified to discuss these issues and help you understand how to be correctly grounded in your identity while properly managing the realities of living with dual cultures without being overwhelmed. Once brunch is over, I would like to share with you my journey and experience in Nubia and to give you a unique perspective about the important roles that you play as immigrants in this kingdom. Through my life stories, I hope to help you realize that your destiny is to influence and contribute to this nation through integration into this society."

"Will this be of interest to you, today?" I asked.

"We are excited grandpa; we can't wait to hear your stories." Eran, Limnea, and their little cousins exclaimed in unison as everyone laughed.

After the meal, we moved to the backyard lawn. The seats were arranged in an arc pattern to capture a better look at the city while my rocking chair was placed at the center. Water, fruits, and snacks were placed at different positions near the audience. After everyone had settled into their seats, I joined them and settled comfortably in my chair.

"My children, I appreciate you all for willing to listen to an old man's story at this time of the day. Having retired from public life, I feel a renewed sense of purpose and urgency to address the various challenges you face as an immigrant. I don't know how much of our history you know. It is important for you all to know our history so that you can have a proper perspective of the present and be prepared to take on the future. I understand that most you of hold the belief that we were better off living in Shalaptonia, the land of our ancestors, rather than living with people who don't necessarily view us as equals. As you would see from my life's story, the past was not as rosy as it had been painted to you, even though we lived simple nomad lives in those days."

"Alright, grandpa. Can I sit beside you?" Eran asked.

"Of course, my son. You can bring your seat over."

"How about us, grandpa?" my other grandchildren queried in unison.

"Alright, all of you can bring your stools near me."

When all the little ones were fully seated near my feet, I was ready to begin.

"Please don't forget to help yourself to some snacks, water, and food any time through our discussion."

CHAPTER 2

It was spring in our country home in Shalaptonia region. The surrounding hills were adorned with snow patches, like black dots on a white canvas. The Shalaptonia River, sandwiched among the hills, overflowed its banks from thawed mountain snow, transforming the withered vegetation in the valley into a luscious green vegetation. The gradual, but seemingly sudden, transformation of the landscape after a brutal winter that depleted our stored livestock feed and family resources, was not lost on me as I reflected on the deep waters of austerity my family had to wade through. So, the changing natural scenery that accompanies the spring season filled us with a sense of hope and new beginning. My father and brothers were keen to take advantage of the early spring season to find natural grazing areas for the livestock and to make some sales to replenish the family's finances. On the other hand, my development from a tween into a teenager with deep voice, growing stubble, and break out acne heralded the new season that filled me with a new sense of responsibility. I am no longer a child, I must find a way to help the family through these challenging times, I thought to myself, but father was rather overprotective and still treated me as a child.

Weeks after my brothers travelled with the family livestock, the family was eager to welcome them back. Since they were supposed to return in two months, everyone unconsciously checked the horizon during the eighth week of their travel, as we awaited their return. However, the entire family grew apprehensive a month later. Father grew more anxious every day and would soliloquize when he was alone. He embarked on long fasts and hardly slept at night as he anxiously prayed for their safe return. He experienced significant mood swings with some days better than the others. Sometimes he would start the day confident assuring his wife, daughters-in-law, and their children that my brothers are well and will return in peace. On other days, he would be depressed, paralyzed by fear and panic attacks that kept him in bed for days. "What if they don't return alive? I don't think I can survive a day if the worst happens. God, please keep them safe and let them return in peace." He would soliloquize at length as my step-mother and sisters try to lift his spirit that all will be well.

After three months of being away, my brothers finally returned to Libron. It was Bennia, my younger brother, who sighted them first afar off. He ran as fast as he could, joyously screaming, to inform everyone that he has sighted my brothers' caravan. The entire family was ecstatic as children ran into the embrace of their fathers and wives reunited with their husbands. Father got down on his knees, in tears and with his hands raised to the heavens, praised God for the safe return of his sons. "Thank you, God, for bringing them back to me safely."

After about an hour of hugs and kisses, he demanded an explanation for the delayed return of my brothers.

"What took you young men so long to return home? Don't you know how precious you all are to me?"

Zebdi wondered what the fuss was all about as he played with his daughters who were all too excited to see their dad after months of being away.

"I don't know why you were all worried about us. This is not the first time we would travel with the flock. We are no longer children that need to be tracked. We are grown men these days." Samaan whispered loudly while rocking his newborn baby girl in his bosom.

"But you all are still my children, no matter how old you are. As a parent, I am meant to worry about you and ensure that you are safe."

"Alright father, you are right. We are still your children." Uwe grimaced.

"We were delayed because we did not find a proper grazing area in Astra. We travelled eastwards towards Mistra valley where we found a well-watered grazing area."

But father would have none of their explanations.

"You should have sent someone home to inform us of the change in your travel plans."

Frustrated by his incessant queries, my brothers quietly excused themselves from the conversation by deliberately exchanging pleasantries with everyone else.

"What am I going to do with these children? None of them would even answer my questions. Anyways, I am glad you are all home safely," he murmured to himself when he was left alone.

After my brothers retreated to their quarters to freshen up for the welcome feast, father turned his attention to supervise the domestic servants as they unloaded the caravan, stored the grain in the barn, and got the herds back into the pen. It wasn't long before my stepmom and my sisters-in-law also switched gears to prepare the meal for the welcome feast. I was jealous of the attention the entire family devoted to welcoming my brothers. I wished to join my brothers on their trips to receive such a "celebrity" welcome, as they always do.

"I want to be a good shepherd like Lamore when I grow up." I whispered to Lazar, my father's personal aide.

"I hope so too… as long as you don't grow up to be like Charmoun, your hot-headed brother." He quipped while nodding in agreement. We chuckled to ourselves.

"Be your own man, you are unique." Father interjected having overheard our conversation as he went about overseeing the feast preparation for my brothers.

"Wait…wait…father, how do you mean?" I asked as I was walking briskly to catch up with him.

"All of you are special and unique sons who will, one day, become great men. My God has assured me that all will be well with all of you." He explained while inspecting the dinner foods and dining area being set up.

"Uwe, summon your brothers; it is time for your welcome feast."

At the dinner, the business minded Lamore gave a detailed account of their trip, including the new additions to the flock, the number of animals lost to marauders and wild animals, sales of rams, the challenges of finding free grazing areas, and other accounting details. Father was quite impressed with his report and the state of the family business. But Uwe, my eldest brother, was bored with the business discussion.

"Oh my…," he yawned noisily.

"This entire conversation about the business is just so boring. Can we discuss something else?" He quipped as others roared in laughter.

"Hey brother, could you be serious for at least an hour. Life isn't all about pleasure. Your future and the future of this family lies in our undivided focus and ability to grow this business." Lamore shot back as he continued the discussion.

"Don't mind him, Lamore! Uwe only cares about wine and the girls of Astra." Charmoun replied with a big grin.

Uwe often acts like the family clown, although he is the oldest son, he hardly ever acts like one and is quite frivolous in his ways. My father was embarrassed by his unprofessional attitude when it comes to business.

"Uwe, it's disappointing that you would display this level of indiscipline. As the first-born son, one would expect that you should be the one to oversee my business affairs and explore new business opportunities, but all you ever care about are wine and women. It's Lamore, your younger brother, who is now running the show."

As father publicly rebuked Uwe for his behavior, he rolled his eyes as he acquiescently nodded in agreement.

"Alright, there is no need to prolong this public dress down tonight. I will get serious during business meetings and will always close my eyes when next beautiful girls pass by." Everyone burst into laughter at Uwe's response after which Lamore continued his business discussions.

While the dinner went on, I asked father if I could join my brothers on their next grazing trip, but he swiftly turned down my request on the basis that I was too young to accompany them on such a trip. My brothers, who have for a long time accused him of being overprotective, grew furious.

"You are spoiling Zeph, father. At his age, we were already fetching water for the camels at the city entrance! Zeph cannot even milk the goats early because he does not get up until mid-morning. It's unfair that you overpamper him while you accuse us of not working hard to grow the livestock." Saman snarled in exasperation.

As they all ranted about the unfair treatment they have received from father, I just cried on his shoulders.

"Father, why are they being so mean to me? they must all hate me."

"Your brothers don't hate you; they just want you to take more responsibilities." Father calmly reassured me.

"Poor Zeph, the best you could do right now is to cry.

What a way to confirm Saman' claims." Uwe interjected.

"Enough! Zeph is my son, although he might not learn and grow at the same pace; he is different. You all know how much I love him, his brother, and their late mother." he tearfully explained but my brothers still won't give up.

"Oh, not again, father! We've heard this story and excuses countless times now. Stop making excuses for his immaturity." Charmoun rebuked father's theatrics as he requested more wine.

As the merriment went far into the night, my brothers retreated to their quarters one by one until I was left alone with father. The criticisms about me brought him painful memories of my mother whom he loved very much. Also, Uwe's lack of discipline and his irresponsible behaviors as the heir apparent and the criticism about him bother father, bringing him memories of the painful loss of my mother.

"I miss your mother. My love for her made me marry Lillia, your stepmother, because your mom wanted to have children for me through her friend. Now she's not here to hold things together as she used to. When she was alive, she treated all her stepchildren as her own even before she ever conceived you. But in her absence, your stepmom and her sons criticize me for treating you special. They are more focused on claiming the family business and my inheritance."

"Don't worry father, I know you love Bennia and me. You know I love them, and they love me too, in their own way...I guess. We will get along someday."

"I worry that they might get rid of you or leave you with no inheritance after my demise."

His pessimistic words hung in the air like an ominous spider web. I shivered slightly, not from cold but from the likely reality of his words. Assuming it was the former, father drew me close and covered me with his big robe.

I sought to change the tense air.

"On another note, father, I have been wondering where did we originally come from? Have we always lived as nomads?" I asked as he cuddled me next to him that night.

"Son, that's a very good question. Our ancestors came from the land of Babylonia centuries ago, but the last four generations of our people have always led a nomad life. In particular, my grandfather once had a dream where he was asked to relocate from our ancestral land to the new land. My grandfather believed his dream and decided to leave his family and friends and travel eastward. We have since lived as nomads until now." He explained.

That night, he shared with me several stories of our ancestors, their conquests, and the tragedies that they experienced.

As a kid, I found those stories intriguing but too good to be true. I was too afraid to even disagree with him. As I laid beside him later that night, I meditated on those stories and imagined what life as a nomad might look like. It was not long before I fell asleep.

I looked up and saw a big shining city with fancy high-rise edifices, in a beautiful city surrounded by mountains. The people of this city dressed differently from any other kingdoms I know. The city had chariots, grinding mills, well-paved highways, and other modern technologies I had not seen until then. The mode of dressing of citizens in this kingdom was something I had not seen anywhere before then. When I turned northward, I saw a palace that seemed to be the seat of government for this kingdom. The royal complex had an exquisite throne hall; the furniture, wall artifacts, and floors in this hall were cast in gold and precious stones. The hall had a golden throne seat which was north of the main entrance where I stood. The throne hall was surrounded by a massive sprawl of high-rise buildings with a breath-taking aerial view. The order and arrangement of these buildings around the throne hall were patterned according to the revolution of the planetary bodies around the sun.

Then I was clothed in a royal regalia and started walking down the aisle of the golden throne hall where I found a congregation of about five hundred well-dressed men and women from different tribes being addressed by the head of that kingdom. He was a grey-haired, old man, about six feet tall with a well-built frame. He was dressed in a purple robe and wore a golden crown and was adorned with a special chain that was made from twenty-two different precious stones. The man spoke about the greatness of his kingdom and his vision for the years to come. His speech was intermittently interrupted by applause from his elated audience. When I got near the throne where he was speaking, he paused and then turned his gaze towards me as if he had been expecting me.

"Welcome, son. You are the embodiment of the solution we have been waiting for. Can't you see? All things have been prepared for you."

"He must have mistaken me for someone else," I mumbled to myself.

When the man realized I was not stepping out, he pointed towards me.

"Do you mean me?"

"Of course, son. Step forward and pay obeisance."

I looked around the entire hall with trepidation wondering what others would think since I was a stranger. To my surprise, everyone in the audience applauded in excitement. When I, finally, stepped forward and made obeisance, the man made some proclamations about my role in saving the kingdom, but I had no idea of what he was talking about.

"Son, arise and take your rightful place." He gleefully announced as he pointed to the golden throne next to him.

As I walked towards the throne, I reflect on those events, but I could not fathom how I got there and why these people confuse me for a royal.

"Don't be bewildered, son. We are pleased to have you here in our kingdom," the man whispered to me. Then I saw everyone in the throne hall and everywhere in that kingdom bow in honor and then rose to their feet to give me a big applause in unison that resonated from earth into the heavens.

"Zeph…Zeph…Zeph!" Charmoun furiously shouted.

As his voice grew louder, I jumped out of my sleep only

to realize that he had poured cold rainwater on my face.

"When are you going to get up, lazy bone? It's past 10:00 am and you are still overcome with sleep!"

"Father, can you see how Charmoun is maltreating me? This is not fair!" I cried, beckoning him to intervene.

Disappointed and embarrassed at the same time, father came and gently kneeled by my side.

"Zeph, you cannot wake up this late and still hope you can be a great shepherd." He said while caressing my wet hairs and checking for any bruises on my body. Shepherds are self-driven entrepreneurs who require little or no supervision. They are well motivated and excellent time managers."

"I understand, father; I have been a good shepherd to the five lambs you asked me to manage." I protested as I sought to deflect the blame.

"Come on, son. Those lambs are so malnourished since I assigned them to you nine months ago. You forget to feed them most of the time. For example, your lambs have been bleating all morning with no one to feed them. Lazar stepped in when he realized you were still asleep. You need to learn how to own up to your failures." In the end, I apologized for my inconsistencies and promised to take more responsibilities for my little flock.

"Alright, why don't you join your brothers as they build a new pen for the growing lambs?" He suggested as he shuffled away, embarrassed he had been caught red-handed overprotecting me.

"Alright, Papa, I need to go freshen up and have breakfast first. Then, I can join them later." I replied as he disappeared to the backyard. My fathers and my stepbrothers stared at each other in utter surprise at my lackadaisical attitude, wondering if father's half-hour lecture about hard work and time management ever made any sense to me.

When I was left alone, I reflected on my dream and wondered what it might mean.

"Zeph, you are royalty. Don't let anyone treat you less than that," I affirmed to myself.

By the time I finished breakfast, my brothers had already completed building the pen. I arrived at the site and met father and my brothers discussing other business matters.

"Dear brothers and my highly esteemed father, I can see that you have done an excellent job building this pen. But I had expected that you will build a bigger pen than this one. It's a bit disappointing."

This show of arrogance further infuriated my brothers, but they kept their cool because of father's presence.

"Oh Zeph, not again." he sighed.

"By the way, my dream is to become the most celebrated shepherd and a royal in the future. All of you will soon come to visit me in my kingdom."

"Your dream is to become a royal even though you were not born as one? Uwe asked."

"Yes, brother."

"This is what happens when an overpampered teenager sleeps too much." Charmoun and the rest of my brothers jeered.

"What insolence! You are just an arrogant, spoilt brat! You had better get out of here before I descend on you!" My disgruntled brothers threatened.

Even father was so annoyed at my arrogance.

Seeing that my brothers' aggression towards me was increasing, he quickly intervened.

"He is only a teenager; he will outgrow these childish tendencies someday." He answered while trying to douse the palpable tension in the pen.

Disgusted by father's staunch defense of my behavior even when I am wrong, they all excused themselves from the pen.

After my brothers departed, father sternly rebuked me for my arrogance.

"Zeph, I am concerned by your arrogance these past few months. You nearly got yourself into trouble out there with your brothers. You know how hot-tempered they can be".

"I have not done anything wrong, father. I was just sharing my vision with them. They just hate me for no reason."

"No, your brothers don't hate you. They are encouraging you to step and stop being childish and arrogant. Also, it's alright to share your aspirations with others, but you need to learn how to communicate your ideas without hurting others."

During the following months, my father and stepbrothers stressed the importance of hard work and embracing responsibilities. As much as I paid attention to their advice, I was more interested in going on the grazing trips. I kept nagging my father every day about going on the trips with my brothers. I argued that I cannot learn the tricks of the trade while sitting at home, but he wouldn't even budge. He was worried that my immaturity and my brothers' impatience could lead to a major fiasco.

It was a memorable afternoon when father sent for Uwe, to inform him of his decision to allow me to join them for the next grazing trip. Unaware of his intention, I was away playing near the Shalaptonian waterfalls with Bennia and my nephews when he sent for me.

"Your brothers will be heading out on their next grazing trip next month; I want you to join them. You must be of best behavior and respect your brothers." he reluctantly concluded.

"You mean I can go with my brothers?"

"Yes, son." He hesitantly replied.

I was so over joyous as I jumped up and down the front porch of our house in excitement. Although father and Lazar were happy for me, they were worried about the type of reception I would receive from my brothers and how things will turn out since this will be my first time being away from home. But their concerns really did not bother me.

"Uwe, take care of the kid and be patient with him". Father tersely instructed.

After thanking him, I sprinted back to the waterfalls to share the news with Bernnia and my nephews about the good news.

And so it was, on the D-day, that I led my flock of five lambs out with my brothers. Like gladiators, we all marched out of the shed with the flock. I wore my multicolored shepherd's coat, proudly held my little staff, and slung my leather skin bag across my chest while lining my flock alongside my brothers'. Father, Lazar, and the whole household came out and were all impressed to see me lineup as a shepherd alongside my brothers. He addressed us about important business matters and the need to be a good representative of the family. Most of his speech eluded me as I was too busy basking in the gladiatorial honor of being a shepherd.

As we headed out into the countryside, leading my flock of five lambs became awkward and wobbly as my animals continued to stray away from the group. In attempt to guide my lambs, I could not keep pace with the entire group. "You cannot even properly guide a flock of five lambs in spite of all your arrogance!" Dambi sneered while waiting for me to catch up with the group. The more my animals strayed away, the more frustrated I became, and the more I lagged. By late afternoon, I was already frustrated and wanted to head back home. Finally, I decided to ask my brothers for help to include my sheep in their flock. They all jeered for a while but agreed to help. Seeing that I had no choice, I had to live with their taunts and bullying all day. Aside from a few taunts here and there, the first day was not as bad as I had expected. Later that night, I assisted my brothers to set up the camp, which proved to be a good learning experience for me. Lamore and Zebdi taught me some tips for setting up a camp for short stays and long stays. The next day Uwe acted as my tour guide, showing me different grazing areas, they had previously visited. Even the hot-headed Charmoun taught me how to recognize a good grazing area. When we finally arrived at Mistra valley, I joined my brothers and their servants to set up camp for our entourage and the flock. After we finished, the servants began organizing for dinner. Although it was late afternoon, the sun set showed off the beauty of the valley. All you see was miles and miles of green land and luscious trees, it all looked so picturesque as the sun started to set, casting a different shade of light over the horizon. There was a stream further down south from where we were camping and a small waterfall east of the field. I took a moment to drink in the beauty of the scenery all around us as I breathe in the fresh clean air. Nature is truly beautiful, I said to myself.

"Zeph, Uwe and I are going to scout the surrounding fields for wild animals that might attack our flock. It should not take that long. Do you want to come along?" Lamore asked, his question jolting me back to the moment.

"Of course, I'd be delighted to learn how to scout and hunt."

By the time we got back, the dinner was ready. At the dinner, I realized that roasted lamb was prepared for dinner. But I was too hungry to even bother to ask for the reason for the change in plans. After the dinner, I wondered why we did not have barley for dinner as originally planned. "We decided to treat ourselves to a roasted lamb dinner using one of your straying lambs." Saman replied.

"You must be joking right?"

"Take it easy little brother. You still have four more lambs." Charmoun entreated.

When I realized I had been fed my own lamb, my hands trembled, and my body shook with rage.

"This is my lamb. This is so unfair…. what do you want me to tell father?" I yelled in exasperation.

As tears freely flowed down my cheeks, I hurled insults

and expletives at my brothers, but they only laughed me to scorn while they enjoyed a sumptuous dinner with their servants. I abandoned the dinner, went into the tent, and I cried myself to sleep that night.

Over the following days, my brothers taunted and bullied me as being too soft for an aspiring shepherd. They later slaughtered my remaining lambs for food. Seeing that I could no longer put up with them, I made the difficult decision to return home. When I informed my brothers about my decision, Uwe sought to handle the situation, but he could not even convince any of them to stop. So, I left them and returned home.

Two days later, I arrived in Libron in tears with soiled clothes. Everyone came out of their tents scared that some disaster had happened. But when they learned that I left my brothers because they killed my lambs for food, they returned to their tents relieved that all is well and shrugged their shoulders at what they considered a spoilt brat's show for attention. Father and Lazar were the only one that genuinely cared. I explained the situation and reported my brothers' maltreatment. Even though he was disappointed, he wasn't too surprised at how things turned out. "Obviously, the relationship is not working. You should stay here with me and raise your flocks at home." But I was not interested in his suggestions, I wanted to prove myself to my brothers. I was determined to show him that I can work successfully with my stepbrothers. When they finally returned two months later, they received the usual heroes' welcome, but father upbraided them for how they maltreated me.

The next time my brothers left for another grazing trip. I was determined to travel with them again. Even though father was worried, he entrusted me to Uwe to be responsible for my safety. I was determined, this time, to help my brothers as much as I could without ruffling their feathers. Despite having no sheep, I still marched out alongside my brothers with pride and hope that things will improve this time. The travel went very well, we all got along well for almost the entire trip. But I observed that my brothers had been living double lives for a while. They held parties with girls from the area, pocketed some of the proceeds from the sales of weak animals, and cooked up the accounts to satisfy father. When I queried some of the accounting practices, they asked me to keep their secrets if I ever want to get along with them. Also, I confronted them about their partying and affairs even though most of them were married with children.

"You are too young to understand." They would joke while sternly warning me against snitching on them.

We later returned home to heroes' welcome. Upon seeing my father from afar, I ran as fast as I could into his embrace. He was over joyous to see that I returned safely.

"How did it go? I hope there was no quarrel with your brothers."

"I am fine papa, my brothers and I got along well throughout the trip."

As customary, Lamore presented the business report, which I know was falsified. When I looked at my brothers, I could tell from their facial expressions that I could not contradict what Lamore had presented.

I was between a rock and a hard place – lying to father to avoid the wrath of my brothers. As everyone enjoyed the dinner, I was not my usual self. My younger brother and nephews asked me for juicy stories about the trip, but I found it hard to explain without revealing my brothers' secrets. It was not long before he also noticed my taciturn mood and secretiveness.

"What's eating you up, son? You had always dreamt about this type of welcome."

My brothers became apprehensive when they overheard his inquiry about my feelings.

"Zeph is probably too tired from the trip." Uwe suggested as he sought to change the discussion. While we all had a good night, Father was not convinced that all went well on our trip, but he could not explain the bad feeling he had. During the following year, I continued to keep my brothers' secrets, but lived with the guilt of lying to my father. During that time, I learned a lot about the flock business.

After returning from my fourth grazing trip with my brothers, we received the usual heroes' welcome. Father was excited to hear about my adventure with my brothers, but I was not as excited as I used to be. Living with my brothers' secret while lying to him was too much for me to bear. After observing the non-verbal communications between my brothers and me for a few days, he concluded that something was wrong. After the dinner, he pressed me for the truth and I, eventually, confessed that my brothers had threatened to kill me if I snitch on them. After assuring me that all was going to be okay, I spilled the beans. That afternoon, he sent for my brothers and took out his anger on them, giving them a public dress down for their shameful activities and financial dishonesty. He even threatened to disown them and cut them out of his will. Unfortunately, his angry outbursts exacerbated an already strained relationship with my brothers who now labeled me a snitch and would have nothing to do with me afterward. They did not see the actual lesson father was trying to pass across.

"You cannot cut us out of your will. We are your legitimate sons even though you have not shown us any love or attention. You maltreated us and our mother at the expense of these spoilt kids and their late mom," Uwe vituperated.

"I did not maltreat your mother, I loved her, but she has continued to sow seeds of discord in this family."

Then, Lillia, my stepmother, flew into a rage when she overheard father threaten to cut my brothers out of his will.

"You dare not do that to my sons, who are the bonafide sons of this family! The truth is that you have never loved us."

"Lillia, you should stop poisoning the minds of your sons against me. How else do you want me to show that I love your sons. I have not kept everything I own from them. They are responsible for my entire flock, but their greed and dishonesty has blinded them to the fact that their actions will ruin this family."

"I am surprised that you can even mention the word love. You have never, for once, loved me and my children. I was your baby producer while you showered your love on my friend and her spoilt children. Isn't it enough that you have treated me with disdain all these years? Now you want to cut my children out of your will. I swear to God that you will die a miserable lonely man if you dare disinherit my sons."

"I am not surprised that you will side with your children. Your envy has prevented you from seeing what is before you: your children's flawed character. All you ever cared about is position and power while you forget the hands that fed you."

"It's such a shame, you've bitten the hand that fed you. When my barren friend could not give you children, she begged me to help her and promised me heaven and earth. Is this how you will repay the favor? You are indeed a disappointment."

As the patriarch and matriarch of our family were at each other's throats, my brothers and I and the entire family watched in silence as they washed their dirty linen in public.

"Let's go, sons, you young men are the pillars in this family. He's only bluffing; no bastard can disinherit you." Lillia reaffirmed as she departed with her sons.

"Zeph, you won't be joining your brothers for grazing trips anymore. I want you to stay here with me. You can raise your flock here, I can teach you bookkeeping, and can even go on separate grazing trips with some servants if you wish." He ordered, out of concern for my safety.

I was disappointed at the turn of events and blamed myself for divulging their secrets. "I should have kept my mouth shut. This fiasco would not have happened."

"You and Bennnia need to stay clear of your stepmom and her children, they are dangerous ," Fathered order afraid of the escalating family crisis.

That afternoon marked a turning point in the relationship with my step siblings. During the following year, I worked with father on bookkeeping and business development activities as he explored potential investment opportunities in neighboring cities.

The discrimination, infighting, and dysfunction in our family escalate in the following months and years.

A few years later, our family suffered another tragedy. My stepsister, Leila, was sexually assaulted by her boyfriend who was from the most prominent family in Shalaptonia city. We were all shocked and incensed by his dastardly act. Senior officials from the neighboring cities and clan came to apologize to father on behalf of this young man and his family. But neither the young man nor his family even attempted to visit my family to apologize or make amends, Instead, words of his continued escapades with other ladies in town soon reached us. We were all incensed and waited on father to take a drastic action to defend Leila's honor, but he did nothing. He feared that such retaliation will damage economic relations with the neighboring communities, destroy my sister's reputation as a woman, and threaten the safety of our family in the Shalaptonia region. When my brothers pressed him further, he chose the easiest way out; he blamed Leila instead.

"If you have not dated an unserious young man from an influential family, we won't be in this mess."

This singular act of cowardice by my father further enraged my stepsiblings.

Rather than step up for my sister and rally the family together, father tried to distract himself from the issue by focusing on the family business and my brother and me, at the expense of everyone and everything else. My stepbrothers were incensed at his nonchalant attitude about Leila's situation.

"You are a coward, father! I cannot believe that you leave our sister to lick her wounds while you focus on business and your sons," Lamore retorted out of frustration.

Seeing that father was too afraid to stand up for his only daughter, my brothers took matters into their hands. A few months later, news reached my father that Leila's boyfriend and his entire family were murdered by unknown assailants overnight. When he heard of the news, he knew very well that my stepbrothers were responsible. The neighboring communities also knew that my family was responsible, but no one had any proof. Our family would go on to suffer disgrace among other neighboring communities, my sister's reputation was ruined, and most of our clients severed economic ties with us. Father was livid with rage at my brothers for the untold hardship and public embarrassment that their desire for revenge brought on the family. He decided to cut them off his will. When rumors of his decision reached my brothers, there was a public fiasco between my brothers and my father. Dangerous and negative words were exchanged in the heat of the moment. My brothers threatened to kill my brother and me if he goes ahead with his plan to disinherit them. Father, on the other hand, demanded that my brothers should move out of the family home with their families. With everyone reeling from betrayal, injustice, embarrassment, and disappointment, our family was never the same after this incident.

About a year later, my brothers left for Niminea valley to feed the family flock, but they did not return at the appointed time. Worried about their welfare, father sent Jamila, his aide, and me to check on them and to deliver food supplies to them. He also ordered us to return immediately after delivering the supplies. After a three-day trip, we got to Niminea in the hills of Mistra, but we learned that my brothers had traveled to the Astra region. Two days later, we arrived at my brothers' camp in Astra valley.

"Dear brothers, I hope you are all doing well. Father has been worried about you because it's over two months past the time you promised to return. He's asked us to bring you food supplies to make sure you don't run out of food."

None of them were interested neither did they receive us well, their whole demeanor was cold towards us.

"Why will father care about our absence now? Afterall he's got his golden sons to dote over" Dambi queried.

"That's not true, sir. Father cares about all of you and does not treat Bennia and me differently from all of you." I reaffirmed. This further incensed my brothers.

"Can you hear him? Do you mean that father loved us equally?" Saman asked.

"Ugh …huh…Yes, of course, sir."

"Where were you when your father maltreated our mother? Weren't you there when our sister was assaulted and father blamed her, instead of fighting for her? Wasn't he focused on protecting you and your brother at our expense?"

"No, sir. Of a truth, father, should have stood up for Leilla, but he was just concerned about the safety and the future of our family. My brother and I are not loved more than anyone of you."

At this point, Jamila interjected as he tried to douse the tension.

"Enough! You are right, sirs. Indeed, my Lord was unfair to you all. Of a truth, my Lord loved Zeph and Bennia more than all of you."

"The truth is that my brothers are jealous of the relationship I have with father and I won't allow them to continue their smear campaign against him!" I angrily yelled.

"Father's stupidity is the reason you have now walked into our trap." Charmoun replied.

"How do you mean?" Jamila asked.

"We do not need anything, we intentionally stayed longer, knowing fully well that he will send you to check on us. Pick him up!" Lamore ordered.

Meanwhile, five men with ropes stepped out of the nearby shrub and moved to encircle Jamila and me. Seeing that I was in trouble, I tried to excuse myself from there. "We need to head back home as soon as possible because father will be worried if he does not see us."

"Which father will be worried?" Zebdi said.

"You mean my father who never cared about us and our mother will be worried about our safety? Oh, I get it. He will be worried if his favorite son does not make it home on time."

"Take hold of this clown and his companion and tie them up near the provisions. I am not sure if we should eliminate him right here or sell him off. We'll decide what to do with him after dinner." Saman ordered. When it became crystal clear to me that they were determined to exact revenge, I changed my stance to a more conciliatory tone. After we were tied up, we begged for our dear lives, but my brothers would have none of our pleas. Instead, Jamila and I were beaten, kicked, and punched mercilessly. As I groaned in pain and with a bloody mouth, I alerted my brothers to the fact that I might have sustained a rib fracture.

"Hey, brothers, we cannot continuously hurt our little brother like this, we have to stop." Uwe pleaded.

"I know you are a chicken-hearted adult child. Are we not doing this to fight for your birthright?" Saman rebuked Uwe.

"The boy is just pretending so that we can let him go. He still thinks it's a game he can wiggle out of with tricks." Zebdi argued.

"Brothers, the roasted chopped lambs are now ready. I can see Astra girls coming down the slopes too. The party will soon begin!" Lamore hollered from distance.

"We should be there soon, Lamore!"

"We'll decide your fate after the party tonight."

Jamila and I overheard rowdy noises of about 50 people as they partied into the night. About an hour later, Uwe came by to check on me.

"Are you okay, Zeph? I am sorry you had to experience this. I am trying my best to get you and Jamila out of here."

He was worried about the situation while he checked my body for bruises.

"I am not alright, Uwe. I think I might have broken my left arm and my rib hurts. Why don't you order them to stop this madness? After all, you are the eldest and they will do what you tell them to do".

Uwe knew what he had to do but he did not have the courage to stand up to his brothers or tell them to stop. He only enjoys talking tough, but he has no spine at all.

"Well, I am the first born, but they don't always listen to me. Lamore, Charmoun, and Saman are difficult nuts to crack. Dambi and Zebdi are also rascals on their own." he explained out of an apparent introspection.

"But they all have mutual respect and admiration for Lamore, perhaps I can convince him to speak to the group."

"Uwe, do you mind letting Jamila go? Don't let him pay for my sins. He's the only child of his mama." I pleaded.

"No, my brothers will go crazy if they find out that he escaped."

After pleading for a while, he agreed to untie Jamila.

"I need to run before my brothers notice my absence. I will come back later at night to untie you too."

But he was not aware that the other brothers were watching his every step. Just as he was about to leave, my other brothers arrived with Jamila who they caught while trying to escape.

"We cannot believe that you are too afraid to do the needful. What a coward you are! It is too late to back out of this plan, Uwe. This kid is not getting out of here alive."

Charmoun chastised Uwe right in front of everyone.

To show how serious they were and to send a warning to Uwe and me, they executed Jamila right in my presence, despite my pleas.

"Now, we need to return to the party right away Uwe, the girls are waiting."

I was speechless for a while as I processed the monstrous brutality I had just experienced. I could feel their pent-up bitterness erupting like a volcano. Seeing that my chances of escape remain slim, I tried to appeal to the human side of my brothers but none of them would listen.

"Father must pay for all the pains he's caused us while growing up and till now." Dambi retorted. "Let's get rid of this clown as soon as possible; we can tell his father that he did not make it here." Charmoun demanded.

As the party continued well into the night, Uwe quietly came to check on me again. "I am sorry my brothers did this to you. I will get you out once they've all gone to sleep" he whispered.

"Thank you, brother. Please don't forget me here."

Tipsy Zebdi also stopped by to pee near the supplies where we were held. "We will avenge father's inhuman treatment of our mother and sister on you, spoilt brat!" He repeatedly belched as he staggered to find where to pee.

As the night wore on, I waited for Uwe, but he did not show up. Instead, the sounds of my brothers' snoring pierced the silence that night like sun rays percolating rain clouds.

I woke up the next day to find my brothers negotiating with a group of caravan traders nearby. When they noticed that I was awake, they approached the supply area where I was being held. I was shocked to realize that my brothers had already negotiated a price for my sale to a human trafficking ring. My voice thick with tears, I pleaded with my siblings to reconsider their decision, but my pleas fell on deaf ears.

"Where is Uwe? I want to see him before you sell me off." I asked after seeing that I could not change their minds.

"Don't bother, he is fast asleep with the girls he partied with last night. You will be long gone by the time he wakes up." They jeered while they sarcastically wave me goodbye.

Having no cards left and seeing that I could not convince them, I reminded them of the good times we had together, how I adored all of them as my heroes, and what each one of them taught me. In the end, I reminded them of how much father loved them even though he could not express it, but my words fell on deaf ears. I watched as they signed the bill of my sale and collected the coins before handing me over to the traffickers.

The traders continued other negotiations for more livestock with my brothers. Seeing that the discussion went a bit longer, I managed to quietly wiggle out of the ropes. I saw a nearby shrub and opined that I could make a run for the hill if I could sneak behind the shrub on time before anyone noticed. But I did not make it to the shrub before I was caught and brought back to the leader of the caravan. He was a stout, dark, pot-bellied man with a deep hoarse voice.

"Pick him up." He ordered.

I was helped to my feet by the two guards who had captured me and was face-to-face with the man. He was scantily dressed, one-eyed man with a plastered patch on his other eye and lots of partially healed bruises on his face and his body. He stared back at me with a stern and terrifying gaze that melted my confidence like cheese placed in the sun. I managed to utter a few words "You don't scare me, you fool! You'd better let me go or else I am going to make life difficult for you," I threatened.

"Next time, you try to escape or talk back to me, I will cut off that unruly tongue of yours." He sternly warned. I swallowed a lump in my throat as a wave of fear ran down my spine.

"Now, take him away and put him where he belongs." He ordered.

Immediately, I was stripped naked, put in chains, whipped, and dragged to the caravan.

At this point, Lamore was worried about my safety and how I was being manhandled.

"He is our brother. You cannot cut off his tongue or harm him in anyway. You people need to be gentle with him." He protested.

"You don't have any right to tell me how I should treat my property. I have his bill of sale. You should have thought things through before selling him to me." The man mocked as he waved the scroll in my brothers' faces.

"You are all traitors and not my blood brothers. You are monsters, cowards, and disgrace to our family!" I yelled as our caravan departed.

"My children, all we had in Libron was, at best, a

beautifully imperfect life which we had presented to your generation as very perfect. You might wonder what kind of men will sell off their little brother out of jealousy, I was not blameless either. I was an arrogant spoilt brat with a weird sense of entitlement. Father shunned his responsibilities to my stepsiblings, our mothers sowed the seeds of discord, and we all reaped family dysfunction, sorrow, regrets, and heartbreak. We were all victims of circumstances beyond our control, but we reconciled and forgave one another, leaving the past where it belonged – the past. During their lifetimes, my brothers and I nurtured our nostalgic "good old days" feelings of the good moments we had in Shalaptonia. We remembered how bad things got between us, the sadness, the regrets, the mistakes, and so on. However, we decided to spare you those negative feelings which we never wanted to pass onto your generation.

"My children, you all have good lives here in Nubia. The recently published national report has ranked our community as the wealthiest immigrant group in the country. We own several thriving businesses and various assets across Nubia. If you complain about unequal treatment, could you imagine what other less-privileged immigrant groups are going through? Rather than long for what you don't have, I advise you to rethink the vast opportunities you have in this land. As you fight and aspire for equality and inclusion, don't lose sight of the blessings and freedom you enjoy in this land. You have a bright and wonderful future ahead of you regardless of how you got here – by birth, as a refugee, or economic migrants." I repositioned Eran on my lap.

At this point in the discussion, I could sense that the younger children in the audience were growing bored and restless. I also realized I could use a bio-break and seize the opportunity to stretch my legs. "My children, I guess this is a comfortable spot to pause and take a break. There is still more food and drinks out there. Don't hesitate to ask my staff for whatever you need. We will reconvene in one hour." I announced.

CHAPTER 3

After the break, I was ready to continue my story, but not everyone had returned to their seats. "Where are the young ones - Philia and Eran and their group? I don't want to start without them." I asked.

"I am here grandpa; my elder brothers and cousins are still processing the story they have just heard. No one has ever explained our story this way, grandpa." Philia explained.

"I know Philia, and that is the reason I have decided to share it with you all while I can. I would like to continue with my story as soon as you are all here." I called to others as we waited until everyone arrived.

It was a humidly hot mid-summer afternoon when our caravan arrived in Nubia along with other slaves who were kidnapped on the way to Nubia. Having been tied to a horse cart, I had already passed out due to dehydration by the time we got to Buhen, the capital city of the Nubian kingdom. I became conscious of the raucous noise of the market square as people threw food scraps, crumbles, and other wastes at us. This was a welcome tradition for the so-called low lives and slaves in Nubia's most famous market. The caravan band to which I was sold was part of an international trafficking ring that scouted other lands for goods or men they can sell in Nubia. This trafficking ring had scouts and kidnappers who raided other countries, transporters who move the caravans to Nubia, and merchants who sell the goods and the people as laborers and aides all across Nubian cities.

I was enthralled by the glory of sun-drenched Buhen city. It was like nothing I have ever seen, it felt like I had just stepped into a different world. The magnificence of the edifices we went past literally blew my mind, talk of being fully being captivated. For a moment, I forgot about the chains that held me bound as my mind soared in the ecstasy of the moments. The natural landscape of city that included the sprawling urban settlement near the Nubia River and extended up into the nearby hills, the clashing sounds of grinding mills, the architectural wonders of the urban skylines and the religious temples, and the towering pyramids of the horizons were quite appealing and incomparable to the countryside environment where I was coming from. The caravan stopped at the slave shop where the band handed us over to Imram, a popular slave merchant in the market square. Back to the reality of the moment, I could feel myself ache all over, the blood from the wounds inflicted by my brother and the traffickers have dried up, leaving dark reddish stains. I was hungry, thirsty, sore, and tired. I would give anything to be back in my father's arm, just to hear him say to me that all will be well. I wondered what my brothers would say to him when they returned without me. My heart went out to him, knowing how much sorrow of heart he would be in when he realizes that his beloved son is nowhere to be found. Oh my dear father, I can only pray that the sorrow does not tip him over the edge. I said a quiet prayer for him, praying that God would give me the opportunity to see my father alive again.

"Welcome to Nubia, the land of magic and innovation.", Imram's announcement, in his hoarse voice, brought me back to my new reality.

"Pray that you find a good buyer who will pay me more money for you than what you were bought for, else I will make your life miserable."

Imram with a stone-cold face devoid of any emotions, his brows laden with sweat from the heat, outlined how his business works and our responsibilities as slaves. It was our jobs as slaves to market ourselves to Nubians who might need a domestic servant. Failure to find a buyer within a month might result in being shipped to brothels as slaves or to the desert to join the construction crew for the pyramids.

With no food and drinkable water, we all set out to volunteer our time in the marketplace and fend for ourselves. Every day, we would scavenge food scraps and water from shop owners in the marketplace who may need help with menial duties in the hope that someone might take pity on us and give us meals or pay a decent wage. Every day was hard and dangerous, it was definitely survival of the fittest. Shortly after we arrived, I was about to leave the shelter when

I heard a raucous commotion in the market square. While I wondered what was going on, someone mentioned that it is the gladiatorial Sunday when slaves are randomly selected to entertain marketgoers in a "fight-to-the-death" match. To be selected for this match automatically means a death sentence. Those who survive the fight are either stoned, knifed, beheaded, or beaten to death in a blindfold. As we watched these two young men fight each other to the death, I could not reconcile the level of barbarism on display in that market square with the beautiful landscape and the progressive civilization I had witnessed in the city. The gruesome death of these two men in the market square for entertainment was a picture that struck fear in my heart for months and traumatized me for years afterward.

The market square, during the day, became increasingly risky and hopeless as we searched for business owners to take us in, and the nights did not provide any relief either. About forty of us huddled together for warmth with scavenged items to help us keep warm at night. The memories of my life in Shalaptonia, my brothers' betrayal, my ordeal with the traffickers, and my current predicament regularly flooded my heart with great sorrow. I worried about my father's health, but I doubted if he would have survived the news of my death or sudden disappearance, depending on what my brother told him. When these thoughts come to mind, I quietly repeated that prayer I prayed on my first day in Buhen, that I may see him alive one day. One fateful night, I was so overwhelmed with emotions after observing our poor living conditions that I sobbed uncontrollably. An older lady interrupted my thoughts that night.

"You need to let go of your past if you are to survive in Nubia."

"You don't understand what I have gone through this year. So, you have no right to tell me to let go of my past. Please mind your business."

"Indeed, no one has the right to tell you what to do. Having been sold as a child slave in Mesta and Astra kingdoms and now as an adult slave in Nubia, I might have some perspective about what you are going through". She calmly explained.

"Really? You have been sold as a slave three times? Wow!" I muttered under my breath.

"So, do you want to share what brought you to Nubia"? She asked.

I went on to explain the family betrayal that brought me to Nubia. After learning about her past ordeals, I was inspired by her doggedness to survive adverse circumstances. She shared several tips that could help me survive and make the most of my time in Nubia. Her words, like a refreshing oasis in a desert, revived hope in me and the determination to survive. After reflecting on her advice, I approached several store owners to just volunteer my time, since no one was ready to take on new slaves. Two barley store owners were gracious to give me a chance. Even though none of them had money to buy me as a slave, working with them tentatively guaranteed me meagre breakfast and lunch.

About three weeks after my arrival in Nubia, I was busy

running errands for one of the shop owners when I saw a convoy of luxurious chariots slowly cruising through the market. The crowds made way and watched in admiration. I walked briskly to get near the convoy and managed to catch up with the last chariot in the convoy. I admired its pristine and well-crafted design up close for some time before the convoy came to an abrupt halt. Then one of the attending aides stepped out of the chariots and addressed the crowd in a loud voice:

"Dear citizens, settlers, and visitors of the great Nubian kingdom, I bring you greetings from his Excellency, General Aziz, a highly esteemed General in the service of His Royal Majesty. His excellency is represented here today by his amiable and competent chief aide, Master Banga."

"Pay obeisance in honor of the representative of his excellency", the attending aide announced.

Everyone in the market square bowed the knee in obeisance to the chief aide. Then a tall (about 6ft 7"), dark gentleman with a sophisticated look stepped out of the chariot. Dressed in a gold embroidered white attire with matching gold-laden white shoes, he waved his multicolored fan at the crowd and signaled for everyone to get up.

Turning to the audience, the aide announced: "Could anyone here point us in the direction of Imram's shop?"

There were lots of conflicting responses about the direction to Imram' shop.

"I can take you there." I blurted. The man turned around and wondered who volunteered. As his gaze settled on me, he realized that I was one of the lowly servants. Then he nodded in agreement.

"Thank you everyone. We have a young man here who can lead us there," the aide announced.

"Sir, I will lead you there, but on one condition". The crowd gasped in awe; shock written all over their faces followed by quiet mutterings. "A condition?" The aide answered in surprise, but then a gentle smile lined his face.

"I like your bravery, young man. Now let's hear your condition."

"Yes sir. I need to deliver these gallons of water for the barley shop owner who sent me on this errand first before I can lead you there."

A hush fell over the market crowd who marveled at my audacity to respond with such request to a representative of a member of the ruling class. Seeing the silence and the palpable fear on the faces of the crowd, I knew that I was in trouble.

"Do you know who you are talking to? That is Master Banga, General Aziz's household manager. You are in trouble!" Some bystanders whispered to me.

"What an effrontery! That is an offense against a member of the ruling class, punishable by death!" Someone in the crowd shouted.

The man stepped away from the chariot, surveyed the environment, and with a stern gaze, approached me. My heart leapt into my throat as I shakily held on to the two gallons of water on my shoulders. The terror I felt in my stomach, increased with every step he took towards me.

"I like your dedication to your work. Go and deliver to

your client and we will wait for you." he firmly ordered after patting me on the head.

I was much relieved having thought a few moments earlier that I was going to lose my life.

I walked as fast as I could through the crowd as everyone made way. By the time I arrived at the Barley shop, the shop owner had already shut his doors for fears of reprisal, having heard that I disrespected a revered General's chief aide. After dropping the water gallons, I paused to reflect on how my situation has been compounded by my impulsiveness. Even if this General's aide does not kill me, I would still be in trouble with the barley shop owners for putting their lives and businesses in danger. No shop owner will be willing to take me under their wings afterwards. Seeing that I had no other option, I rushed back to the market square to attend to general Aziz's aide.

Meanwhile, words soon reached Imram that general Aziz's entourage was heading to the slave shop. He mobilized all the slaves to be brought to the market square to meet him. By the time I arrived back at the market square, I met Imram appeasing General Aziz's chief aide. "My Lord, we are delighted that you have come to us to find servants worthy of service for his Excellency.

"Stop patronizing me, Imram, and tell us what type of servants you have for sale," the mean tersely replied. Imram paraded tall, good-looking servants kidnapped from Mesta and Berberian Kingdoms who might be more appealing, but the man was not impressed. Instead, he looked around the crowd wondering where I was.

"Where is that boy that promised to take us to the slave trade market?"

"He's here my Lord," the bystanders pointed in unison as they pushed me out to the open.

Then he beckoned me to approach. Trembling with fear, I stepped forward and paid obeisance as I bowed to the ground. The man stooped down and gently lifted my head while staring at me with a stern look.

"What's your name, slave? Where do you come from?"

"Huh…huh… I am Zeph, my Lord. I arrived…I came from…I was kidnapped from Shalaptonia, sir." I stuttered in fear.

"How old are you, Zeph?" he asked after staring at me from the head down with a disdainful gaze.

"I am seven…seventeen, sir."

Then the man stood up, looked around, and turned to Imram.

"I like this one." he said, to everyone's amazement. I was surprised myself.

Seeing that Master Banga's decision will not fetch him more coin, Imram sought to sway his decision by recommending other tall, well-built slaves. "My Lord, this boy does not have the needed physique to serve his Excellency."

"This 'weak' boy showed commitment to his duties even in the face of death. He might not be as physically strong as others, but he's mentally resilient and brave. With a strong character, he can fit in well into our system in the villa." "As you wish my Lord," Imram shrugged.

"Thank you, your Excellency, I promise not to ever let

you down."

Seeing that Imram was disappointed, Master Banga offered to buy two more slaves from the marketplace. After the negotiations were concluded, he paid for our Bills of Sale. The crowd at the marketplace was surprised that I was preferred above others but applauded that man's shrewdness and wisdom. We joined the entourage that accompanied the master and departed the market square.

The journey to General Aziz's villa was very long as we stopped at several other places in the lower and upper neighborhoods of Buhen before moving into the countryside where General Aziz's mansion was located. The three-hour trip gave me the opportunity to see more of the capital city, its high-rise towers, water dams, exquisite buildings, the affluent neighborhoods, the towering architectural wonders of the royal court, and an aerial view of the Nubia River. What a beautiful city, I mumbled to myself in admiration. I had thought I had seen all the beauties of Nubia, but when I got to General Aziz's villa, I knew this could not be farther from the truth. We arrived at the villa later that evening and alighted from the carriage right in front of the mountain-top ultra-modern sprawling villa with breath-taking view of the Nubia River and Buehen city. Several luxurious chariots were packed near the villa garden adjacent to the horse stable. We were welcomed by a group of well-dressed servants who were charged with unpacking the supplies and cleaning the chariots. Take them to the slave quarters and shave their heads." The master ordered.

At the slave quarters, the conditions were less pristine but better than the living conditions in the market square. The slave quarters, which was located behind the main villa had several buildings which included shared rooms, a common area, a large kitchen, and laundry area that borders the towering brick fence. The slave quarters hold about a hundred servants at a time, we were told. When we got there, everyone was going about their business while the assigned servants asked us to wait in the common area for the barber to arrive.

"I have never had to shave my head. Culturally, maintaining our long hair was part of our identity as Libronians. I wonder if I can leave my hair as it is." I asked the servant.

"You must think too highly of yourself that you are worth something. Have you seen any man with unshaved head in this villa? You are worth nothing. You are a lowly slave and a property of General Aziz. He can choose to discard you anytime he wants. So, get that into your skull." The servant sniped at me.

It was not long before a dark, stout man with thick grey brows approached us with barbing equipment.

"Here comes the barber!" The servant replied.

"Where are the newly recruited batch of villa servants who need hair cut?" The man gleefully asked.

"I am one of them, sir". I politely replied.

"Welcome to the villa of death where pleasure and wickedness thrive. You should consider this head shave your major initiation into the values and way of life in this villa."

The man enthusiastically explained.

"Villa of death? That description is a bit scary."

"Oh yes, everything happens here – your basic necessities of life are catered for, you get to enjoy all the parties, but you are always at risk of being a victim of seduction, greed, and politics."

"So, this is a dangerous place eh?"

"That's right. I believe you should be okay as long as you don't get carried away by the opulence that you see around."

"Thank you for that piece of advice. I will keep it in mind as long as I work here".

"No. I suppose you mean keep it in mind as long as you live. Well, if you are having any stupid idea of escaping from here, you should forget it now. You cannot escape these walls, because this estate has archers on stand-by with instructions to shoot down anyone who dares to escape". His explanation even struck more fear in me.

"Alright, thank you sir."

After my head was shaved, I felt a sense of emptiness and shame, but also felt a sense of newness and new beginning.

Since I was one of the youngest slaves, I was told that I had been assigned to share a room with another young boy. After I left the common area, I did not know where to go. So, I wandered around the slave quarters for a bit. I strolled by the servants as they worked on their assigned chores in the grind mill area, the slave officers' quarters and the bathrooms. Also, I checked out the area near the villa fence that overlooked a deep gorge. When I moved closer to the fence to observe the gorge, I looked up into the horizon and thought about my family in Shalaptonia. I wondered how my father would have fared after my disappearance.

"Hey son, don't even think about escaping from here; you will fall to your death." An older gentleman interrupted my thought.

"Thank you, sir." I replied with a fake grin.

"Suicide is not an option for you. You are too young to contemplate such a bad idea."

"Not at all, sir. I'm just trying to know my new environment." I replied with a dry smile.

"The only people who come here are those who have incurred the wrath of the General and are condemned to die; they are pushed off the cliff behind the fence."

This information sent shivers down my spine, I thanked him as I hurriedly walked back into the slave quarters where I had the opportunity to inspect the slaves' living conditions. I was glad to learn that the rooms were not overcrowded – a maximum of three people per room and that every servant has access to three-square meals daily. As I admired the living quarters, some of the slaves grew suspicious of my wandering around the slave quarters. I was accosted by a dangerous-looking hefty young man who quietly pointed a short knife to my rib cage, and speaking under his breath, ordered me to follow him into a nearby corner without making a scene. Seeing that I was in danger, I quietly complied until we got to the corner. I was met by two more threatening tall bare-breasted middle-aged men whose bodies were covered in tattoos. For some reasons, they thought I was spying on their covert operations.

"Who do you work for, young man? Who sent you here?" The men repeatedly asked while manhandling me.

"I am sorry. I don't work for anyone. I am new here. I just arrived in this villa a few hours ago." I stuttered as my mouth went dry and terror coursed through my veins.

"He must have been sent by Banga, the General's puppet. We should kill him now before anyone discovers our secret."

Luckily, a young slave, intervened at the nick of time. "Here you are. I have been looking for you," he casually stated, as though unaware of the situation he walked into.

"Onan, stay out of this. This young man has been spying on us all day. He must have been sent here by Banga."

"Gentlemen, this is the new kid that came today. Yes, I don't know much about him, but he seems harmless and if anything, naïve I would say. I am sure he means no harm."

"If he is the new kid, why is he wandering all over the place?" one of the men retorted.

"Well, this is his first day in the villa. It's normal for him to wander around for a while until he gets assigned his tasks."

I realized that this Onan is the young boy I am meant to share the room with.

"You have to stop covering for him. We want to hear from him." Another man asked.

Turning to me, he asked: "Where are you from?"

"I am from Shalaptonian region. I was kidnapped almost nine weeks ago. I arrived in Nubia last month and Master Banga purchased me from the market square today." I replied as my eyes darted from left to right.

"Oh, my family is from the Shalaptonian region too. I did not know you are a son of the soil too." One of the older men replied in excitement.

"That's great to hear, sir." I gave a timid smile.

"I lost an uncle and his family few years ago when a shepherd clan near Libron murdered them over night."

"You must have heard about that story a few years ago?"

"Yes sir, I remember learning about the incident as a kid." Having realized that the man was talking about my family, I bit my finger nails in anxiety wishing I could disappear into the ground at that moment.

"Lost in his own thoughts, he murmured loud enough for everyone around to hear. "I must avenge my uncle's death and track down this wicked family once I'm able to get out of here." At that point I was too frightened to even lift my head.

"Can I leave with him now?" Onan asked as he pulled me away from the men.

After we left the east wing of the slave quarters, we walked in silence towards the common area. I was lost in thought as I processed the man's threat to wipe out my family.

"You should have something to eat." the boy generously offered some sort of snacks while at the common area. Still feeling overwhelmed by my near-death experience and the words of the older man, I politely turned down his offer and walked towards the sleeping quarters.

Disappointed that I had refused his generous offer, Onan paused and thought about what else he could do.

"Alright, if you are still content keeping to yourself, why don't I show you to your room?" The boy suggested as he briskly walked after me.

I sheepishly agreed and followed him into the west wing of the slave quarters. "Welcome to our room, Zeph. You need to be careful out there, not everyone here is innocent."

The room was a grim stone box, with bare walls covered in a lot of inscriptions, and one small window that look out on the horse stable.

"Well, since you have refused to talk, let me tell you a bit about myself. I am Nubian by birth, but I was born and raised in Ethiopia. My parents died shortly after my birth; so, I did not grow up to know them. My aunt took me in and raised me with her children, but she was quite mean to me as a child. So, I ran away and spent the following three years as a homeless kid on the streets of Ethiopia. I was kidnapped by an international trafficking ring about six years ago and brought to Nubia."

"How old are you? You must have been less than 12 years when you were taken!" I asked as I stared at the walls and the window, avoiding direct eye contact.

"Yes, I was 8 when I ran away from my aunt and 11 when I arrived in Nubia. The boy narrated his life of hardship as a slave and how life had just been plainly unfair to him.

"Did your aunt and her family look for you?"

"No, they continued their lives as if nothing ever happened."

"Wow, you seem to have gone through a lot as a kid."

For the first time in my life, I realized I had lived a life of privilege and that my friction with my brothers was like a drop in the ocean of troubles that other kids have had to face elsewhere.

"So, how did you get to Nubia?" Onan tapped me on the shoulder seeing that I was lost in thought.

I got up, moved away, and stopped by the window opposite Onan.

"There is little or nothing to learn about me. I was sold by my brothers to the same trafficking ring that brought you to Nubia. My childhood was not as difficult as yours." I replied after a long silence. Later, I laid on the floor near the window.

After a while, Onan got up and came to lie next to me.

"You need a blanket for these cold floors. We could share this blanket if you don't mind."

I looked up at him and accepted his offer with a feigned smile. In my mind, I was grateful that he offered to share his blanket despite the silent treatment and unwelcoming demeanor towards him. I am not usually like this, but a lot had happened that's rocked my world in the last few weeks, and I sometimes fall into bouts of depression trying to process everything. I realized that I do, actually, have things to be grateful for, one of which is Onan. I really need to make it up to him in the following days, I fell asleep thinking about this, accompanied by the noise of cricket coming from outside our window.

I woke up the next morning with my face being bathed by light rays that pierced the dark room. I was thankful that I had a room and roof over my head and did not have to sleep in the cold. After reflecting on the events of the previous day, I realized my folly for being unnecessarily mean to a stranger who saved my life.

"Onan, I must thank you for coming to my aid yesterday. I am sorry I have been acting like a jerk."

He looked up with a big smile. "It's my pleasure. It's great to see another young person here." You need to stay away from the east wing if you can, a lot of bad things happen in those quarters."

"By the way, how old are you?" He asked with a mischievous smile.

"I am 17 years and 90 days old."

"Wow, I am 17 years and 91 days old." Onan quipped to the surprise of both of us. After staring at each other for a while in surprise, we both broke into a big laughter after realizing that we were born only a few hours apart.

That day marked the beginning of a life-long friendship. In those early days, Onan furnished me with information about everything and everyone in the villa and helped me with the language. Citing several instances, he painted the General as an ambitious but emotionally unstable man with top-notch business acumen. He's known to be overprotective of his wife, Mrs Aziz. In fact, he once ordered the execution of his previous aide for allegedly admiring his wife.

"This is a dangerous place, Zeph. Don't be deceived by the opulence you see around. Your handsome face might get you in trouble with Mrs. Aziz. Do your best to avoid the General's quarters at all cost." He sternly advised.

"Alright, thanks for sharing these. The barber also gave me a similar advice yesterday." Having been given the same information twice within my first 24 hours in the villa, I was worried about my survival there.

Two days after my arrival at the villa, Master Banga visited the staff quarters.

"Where is the new boy?" He asked in his typical loud Nubian voice.

"Zeph, the master is here asking for you. Hurry, you cannot be late. I can serve as your interpreter." Onan advised as we briskly walked to the assembly area. At the common area, I found all the slaves assembled as they listened to the household manager.

The man spoke pure Nubian language as he reiterated the villa's guiding philosophy and values by which servants are to live and serve. He also announced the pending arrival of the General that week and emphasized the need for everyone to be at their very best in welcoming him back. After addressing the group, he requested that I follow him to the main quarters. Onan accompanied me and served as the interpreter.

"The General will be home next week; we need to give him a royal welcome he deserves. You need to be well dressed and be ready to meet and serve him."

"I will be at my best sir." I replied.

Seeing that Onan was knowledgeable about the affairs in the villa, I asked him more about the General and his family. General Aziz is a retired military general who heads the Royal Guard, managing the security of the royal family. Although not a royal himself, the General enjoyed treating himself as royalty. He was mostly away on official duties for three consecutive months before returning home for 3 weeks, during which he rests and hosts parties with his socialite friends. Socialites and those who seek favors from the king and other royal cabinet officials often troop to the villa to network at his parties. Citing several instances, he again described the General as an emotionally unstable man whose utmost priority is to protect his public image.

"Zeph, this is a dangerous place, don't be carried away by the opulence you see around. You're handsome and that might be a problem if Mrs. Aziz takes interest in you. Do your best to avoid the General's quarters at all cost." He sternly advised again.

"You have said this countless times these past few days. Let me assure you that I can handle myself." I said with a feigned confident look.

The villa staff and servants spent the following week preparing and rehearsing our roles for the welcome ceremony. When the General final arrived, we welcomed him with much pomp and fanfare. He was a flamboyant, vivacious, and stout man who basked in the euphoria of the adoring audience. After stepping out of his chariot, he was met by the Master Banga who made obeisance before joining him to inspect the guard of honor and the musical band. Shortly after, a tall light-skinned woman in a flowing purple robe and a gold chain around her neck briskly walked up and embraced the General.

"That must be Mrs. Aziz, I guess." I quietly whispered to Onan, who nodded in agreement.

"Wow, she's a beautiful woman!" I unconsciously remarked.

"Don't entertain that thought, Zeph. She's as deadly as they come."

We watched as the General and his wife continued to publicly exchange romantic affection before they retreated into their mansion. "Oh, it's good to be back!" he shouted in excitement before entering the villa.

After settling in the house, General Aziz shared some updates about his work in the royal court and some official trips ahead of him. Master Banga then provided some high-level status updates about the villa and organizational details already in place for the welcome party that evening. The General and his wife later retreated into his chambers. Immediately, we switched gears to begin preparations for the welcome party which will be hosted on the one-acre garden adjacent to the main quarters. The guests began to trickle in about four hours later for the welcome party. The General and his wife arrived at the party later to much fanfare and dancing. They both wore flowing purple Nubian robes befitting royalty. As the musicians and comedians entertained the audience, the General and his wife greeted and exchanged pleasantries with their guests. As the celebration wore on into the night, Master Banga beckoned to me to join him for a formal introduction to the General. I quickly handed my food platter to someone else and approached, making obeisance as we got close to him.

"Who is the handsome brown boy?" Mrs. Aziz interjected as the household master made the formal introduction.

"He's the new personal aide I found for you, sir."

The General stared at me with disdain, wondering how

I could be his new aide. He inquired about my welfare and wondered why the master chose me for such a job knowing how frail I looked.

"Zeph is not physically strong, but he is mentally resilient and smart. He's a Shalaptonian sold to slavery at a young age."

"I am a quick learner; I promise I will add value to you and your business." I affirmed as I interrupted the conversation.

My response was met by complete surprise and hush by Master Banga and everyone in attendance. Judging by the expressions of those around and the complete pause of all music, I realized that I was in trouble already even though I could not understand what I had done wrong.

"Wow…this fool even has the guts to interrupt me with his terrible accent! Didn't you mention that he's smart? He is not well trained to stand before me. Either you train him or find me a better aide. Else, I will feed his body to the wild animals down in the gorge behind this villa" the General snarled at us.

I wanted to respond. However, a glance at the master suggested otherwise.

"My Lord, I am sorry for this embarrassment; he will be disciplined right away and will not appear in your presence any longer until he is fully trained. Once again, I am so sorry, sir."

"Well, my dear, you don't need to work yourself up. If he is not well trained, you can send him to my chamber to help with my oils and spices; he will be useful there." Mrs. Aziz teased as she drew her husband to the dance floor.

"Make sure the boy does not go near my wife's chambers."

the half-drunk General ordered.

Immediately, I was escorted by the guards out of the party and thrown into the villa cell.

I cried profusely that night, disappointed that I have, once again, squandered my only opportunity for a good life.

Later that night, I heard a knock on the cell bars; it was Onan; he felt sorry for me and stopped by to check on me.

"How are you, my friend? I managed to smuggle some flatbreads for you. Here, eat and have some strength."

"I blew it, Onan. I don't see any way out of this mess. I fear I would be sent back to the streets." Seeing I was too distraught, Onan encouraged me to hang on. He assured me that the household manager likes me and won't send me back to the market square.

The next day, Master Banga was still disappointed by the embarrassment the incident brought him and rebuked me openly before all the servants. "Royal etiquettes and protocols are essential qualities of the service we provide to all and sundry in this villa. You have let us down at the biggest possible stage; this is not acceptable at all. Although you are new to the Nubian society, this is not an excuse for your disgraceful actions and appalling break of villa protocol. As a punishment, you will spend the next month grinding mills day and night." He announced to the dismay of everyone, many of whom consider me too frail for such an arduous job.

Seeing the revolt from his audience, Master Banga angrily yelled at the entire assembly.

"Listen, Zeph's public gaffe is not only a disgrace to me, but a stain on all of us. So, you should be equally ashamed.

This villa is known for its excellence in service delivery. You all need to maintain that standard!"

I spent the following month grinding mills – one of the most tedious and stressful slave duties in the villa. For the entire month I worked grinding the mills, I replayed the incident at the party countless times in my mind. I was determined never to be embarrassed like that ever again. I took stock of all the undesirable qualities that the General mentioned – my accent, my physique, and lack of training in mannerisms and etiquettes of the Nubians. Also, I listed my strengths, which included my enthusiasm, aptitude for learning, handsome face, and knowledge of livestock agriculture. I resolved to work on my weaknesses as much as I could while leveraging my strengths to rise in the villa. Having learned that the previous aides of the general were all tall, well-built, brown skin men, it was clear that my physique was not a strength. I would need to compensate for those deficiencies in other areas if I were to stand any chance of freedom. So, I explored various ways I could add value to the villa through my critical thinking skills and aptitude for learning. My decision was informed by my understanding that the Nubians prioritize etiquettes, fashion, appearance, and knowledge. Like Ethiopian and Kush kingdoms of the time, Nubians were civilized, thanks to their advancement in engineering, architecture, and fashion. The only way I could prove myself to the General was to embrace learning and training as much as I could. By the time I finished the month-long punishment, I had formulated a plan to get myself out of the slave quarters and set a timeline for the target.

In the following months, I intentionally targeted five major areas of development, including physical development, language training, etiquettes, fashion, and business.

One, I must be physically fit. opined that I might not be as tall as people of the Berberian Kingdom, but I can improve my physical fitness and make myself more presentable to the General and his household. I resolved to spend more time willingly grinding mills every week to further strengthen my physique, build more muscles, and compensate for my perceived shortness. By the way, I was 5ft 10", but I was considered short by Nubian standards.

Two, my communication skills must improve. My mastery of the Nubian language was basic at best and laden with Shalaptonian accent. So, I planned to study native speakers to improve my oral communication skills. I intentionally made friends with fellow slaves who are of Nubian descent to consciously listen and watched how they converse. Also, I volunteered to assist the household master with copying and writing letters. My goal was to learn how to read and to improve my writing skills.

Three, I must master Nubian etiquettes to the best of my abilities. To achieve this, I would attend all royal etiquette and protocol training available in the villa and understudy the master, Mrs. Aziz, and her children, as they conduct themselves both in public and in the villa.

Four, I must develop an excellent sense of style and fashion. To the Nubians, being fashionable was everything. To be of value to the General, I would carefully study Mrs. Aziz's fashion sense and her recommendations for the General's wardrobe. Also, I planned to spend time with servants in charge of laundry to learn which types of clothes the General frequently wore and his color preferences. I would learn to dress and present myself before the General's family. Also, I decided to compile information on the fashion style of General's friends and other military members when they visit for parties.

Finally, I must be financially literate. Having realized that the Master Banga is the only staff that understood the General's businesses and investments, I planned to volunteer my time to assist him in whatever way he wanted. Although the General's investments were tightly guarded, I opined that the manager could use an extra pair of hands. Having learned book-keeping and business development skills while I assisted my father in Libron, I surmised that such skills will be useful if I can convince the manager.

As part of my plan, I approached Master Banga to formally apologize for my error and promised not to ever embarrass him again. Over the next few days, I frequently stopped by his office to ask how I could help him. During one of those visits, I met him sorting out a few scrolls which appear to be bills of sale and other accounting details.

"Sir, I learned bookkeeping from my father, and I am good with numbers. I am happy to assist anytime."

"Thanks for letting me know, Zeph; these are accounting stuff. It will take time to learn those." he replied.

In time, he appreciated my intention and would sometimes

invite me to assist with accounting and other administrative duties in peak seasons of administrative work. Having noted my aptitude for learning, he started me off with learning how to balance the books (i.e. accounting) the Nubian way, and, in time, taught me supply chain management. My aptitude for learning quickly endeared me to him and he was grateful that I could share his burden in managing the General's affairs and businesses.

In those days, I had to juggle my menial duties with the accounting work. I spent the day completing my chores and assisted Master Banga to sort out invoices and other accounting details at night. The chores were physically exhausting to the extent that I found it hard to stay awake to finish the accounting paperwork.

During one of those nights, I dozed off while completing the accounting ledger. By the time Master Banga arrived, he found me fast asleep with the scrolls uncompleted. Instead of chastising me, he helped pack up all the scrolls, and walked me into the spare room in the office quarters. I woke up the next morning to find myself in his quarters' spare room. I was confused and scared that I must have sleepwalked into the spare room without his permission. As I pondered on the events of the previous night, he walked in and asked whether I had a good night. I was startled and went down on my knees to apologize for passing the night in his spare room.

"Sir, I am so sorry for passing the night in your room. I was only working near your desk. I don't know how I ended up in your room. I must have sleepwalked here last night. I should not have done this."

Realizing that I had no clue what happened, he laughed hard for a while. Then he explained that he walked me into his spare room after he had found me asleep on the scrolls.

"You are hard-working and smart, and I appreciate that. You can spend your time in this room in case it's too late at night to go back to the slave quarters." he advised. It was such a relief to hear his approval and his support.

Over time, the master gradually reduced my workload by reducing the time I spend doing physical chores around the villa. This gave me more time to study and assist with his administrative duties without any distractions. By the end of my first year, I was exempted from all menial duties and tasked with more management and accounting duties. The more time I spent with him, the more he became impressed with my potentials and the more administrative responsibilities he assigned to me. One fateful night, after we finished reconciling the business accounts and other household affairs, we were both exhausted, but not ready to sleep. He brought out two cups and a bottle of Ethiopian wine. As we sipped the wine outside his quarters, I gazed into the night skies, thinking about my family in Shalaptonia.

"I think it is time for you to meet the General, again." he reasoned. But I was lost in thought and was oblivious to the reality of his statement.

He tapped me on my shoulder and repeated his point again after realizing I was lost in thought and did not understand his statement.

"What did you just say, sir?" I screamed in excitement.

"You heard me right, Zeph."

"Sir, do you mean I have a second chance to stand before the General? Are you sure he is not going to throw me down the cliff this time?" I asked after I remembered the general's comment the last time I was in his presence.

He laughed hard for a while before he got up and headed to his room.

"I think you will be successful. You should start preparing right away," he abruptly replied before bidding me good night.

I was too excited that night to sleep that night. Instead, I went back to my room in the slave quarters to share the news with Onan, but he was fast asleep.

"Wake up Onan, there is good news." I said with much excitement.

"What is it, Zeph? Have you gotten your freedom yet?" he drowsily replied.

"No, the master has given me a second chance to serve as General's aide pending a successful interview." I excitedly explained.

"Not surprised, Zeph. I told you that you have too much potential to be sent back to the streets." He responded as he rolled over and continued his sleep.

That night, I realized that Onan had so much belief in me than I have ever in myself.

Over the next two months, I rehearsed with the master and prepared on my own. Onan also prepped me for that interview by teaching me some of the Nubian folklore and history. The night before the interview, Master Banga and I again rehearsed the protocols, the greetings, and the possible questions the General might ask.

"You will be fine. Go to bed and get a good sleep. Tomorrow will be great."

When I arrived at the slave quarters, I could not sleep as I nervously rehearsed the protocol one more time. Onan could not sleep either because of my rehearsal. "You will be fine Zeph, as long as you avoid looking straight at Mrs. Aziz, who is the arch-devil in this villa."

He went on to narrate several stories about Mrs. Aziz, but soon realized that I had fallen asleep beside him.

I woke up the next morning to hear the steps of the villa guards who were sent to summon me.

"Oh, I am sorry sirs, you need to wait for me to dress up. Would you mind?"

"No, you are needed immediately."

"No, sirs, I cannot appear before the General this way. I have to be at my best." I argued.

"Don't worry about your bath, the household master has already arranged for that."

"Alright, can my friend, Onan, accompany me too?"

"Sure. Come on, boys, you are almost late." The guards replied.

We arrived at Master Banga's quarters and found him anxiously waiting for me. He had meticulously arranged for my attire, shoes, oil, soaps, and even the fragrances, and ordered his servants to bathe and dress me for the occasion while he paced up and down in the corridor. I was bathed, oiled, and dressed in typical Nubian attire. Afterwards, he meticulously inspected my appearance and ordered the fashion team to redo the makeup a couple of times until he was satisfied. After the preparation, the master and I, once again, rehearsed the protocols and the potential questions for the next hour before we headed to the main villa.

"Wow, you look like royalty." Onan exclaimed as he wished me the very best in the meeting. "I will be here waiting for you, brother!" He said with a big fat grin on his face. You could tell he was feeling both proud and excited for me.

We arrived early and had to wait for the General, who did not arrive until about an hour later.

When he eventually arrived with his wife, we bowed in obeisance as they took their seats. Then the master introduced me as his new aide and ordered that I pledge my allegiance to the General. After I pledged my allegiance, the General asked a series of questions and I responded appropriately as groomed by the master.

"You're such a well-polished young man with excellent command of the Nubian language," Mrs. Aziz exclaimed in admiration.

As the meeting went on, Master Banga gave his report on the current state of the General's chain of businesses. He then invited me to provide specific numbers on the return of investment in comparison to the previous years and to lead the discussion about the business projections for the next financial year. The General asked several questions related to new business opportunities. Rather than answer him, Master Banga asked me to answer his questions while providing input to clarify some of the points I raised. As the discussions went on, the General and his wife became impressed with my knowledge of the issues, my brilliance, and the insights I brought to the discussion.

"My dear, why don't you consider diversifying your investment portfolio into the fashion business too?" Mrs. Aziz suggested at some point, having listened to my projections about the global economy. As a fashionista herself, Mrs. Aziz's fashion interests date back to her youthful days. She has closely followed the industry trends over the years and identified several business opportunities that her husband did not.

The General was embarrassed and sought to dismiss his wife's idea. "Please don't mind my wife. Her fashion fantasies have no place in meaningful business discussions."

I politely interjected and asked the General to reconsider his wife's idea.

"Sir, I suggest you seriously consider her excellency's suggestion."

The General was taken aback by such a bold refutation of his point of view.

"Why will you ask me to consider such a flimsy idea?"

Seizing that window of opportunity, I provided some financial data about the current and projected profit margins for fashion and other female care products in Nubia to support her idea.

The General was not only shocked to learn about my knowledge of that industry, but he was also surprised at the incredible opportunities that the industry presents.

"Your excellency, her excellency has a great point. The industry is an untapped business opportunity that can present a huge return on investment." The master nodded in agreement.

"My dear, I know you don't believe in my "fantasies", but I am glad Zeph and Banga are helping you to see the business opportunities here. We have the opportunity to become the foremost fashion business tycoons in the kingdom." Mrs. Aziz concluded in elation.

"Listen, woman, business decisions are not made by emotions. You can keep your emotions in check for now."

After asking further questions, the General hesitantly agreed to invest 0.5% of his least performing investment portfolios in the fashion industry.

Mrs. Aziz was so elated that, for once, someone values the idea she's brought to the discussion.

The business meeting ended on a high note as the General confirmed my appointment as his next personal aide.

"Well, this young man here is the real deal. He's a thousand times better than the incompetent fool you brought before me few months back."

"Your excellency, Zeph is still that same man. We just retrained him." the master explained.

The General and his wife were surprised and impressed.

"That means our training program in this villa is still as effective as ever. Keep up the good work, Banga."

Then he ordered his servants to furnish a room for me in the main villa, just as we were about to end the meeting. I appreciated the offer, but politely requested that I'd be allowed to live with the master a bit more because I had a lot to learn from him.

"Very well then, that's thoughtful of you. Sure, you can stay with him until your training is complete."

As we exited the quarters, I turned to Master Banga for his assessment of my performance.

"Very well played. Stellar!" He tersely replied with a big grin.

Like a son who has just seen his father return after being away for a long time, I hugged him tightly and thanked him for his mentorship and help with this interview.

When we arrived at his quarters, we met Onan on the corridors nervously pacing across the quarters while biting his fingernails. He was glad to see us return.

"What took you so long? I was so worried that you flunked the interview and the General ordered for your execution. I had twice gone to the backyard, near the cliff, to check since you did not return on time." Onan anxiously stated.

"Do you think so lowly of me, Onan? I am not dying anytime soon. Besides, the master was there with me all the way."

"Anyways, I am glad to see you alive. How did it go my brother?" He nervously inquired as he repeatedly hugged me.

"It went well, Onan. You are looking at the newest General's aide!" I screamed in excitement.

Onan was ecstatic and we hugged each other as the master watched in admiration.

"You should thank the master for me. He graciously gave me a second chance and has mentored me during the past year."

"Thank you, master. Even though your stern look always sends some chills down my spine, I am glad that you helped my friend and brother." Onan gave a tongue-in-cheek reply.

The manager in turn smiled as he watched us savor the success.

"Zeph, you have an arduous task ahead of you, but I believe in you. Both of you should take the day off to celebrate. You both deserve it."

"Does that mean I am free of any chores today sir?" Onan asked.

"Of course, you have the next 24 hours off. You should book an appointment to see me next week. Let's see if we can find you other less strenuous chores in my quarters so that you can be close to your friend."

"I guess I am now a beneficiary of Zeph's successful appointment. Thank you so much for your generosity and kindness, your excellency." Onan and I bowed at the master's feet in acknowledgement of his kindness.

"As the newly appointed aide, you will be assigned the two-bedroom quarters opposite here, a daily food portion, and one domestic staff who will assist with your laundry and cleaning. New clothes will be ordered for you as well. The apartment quarters is being prepared as we speak. I expect it to be ready before the end of today. Of course, Onan is welcome to visit you anytime as long as he does not distract you from your work." He announced as he left, admiring the unique friendship Onan and I shared.

"Sir, you have been very kind to us. We are grateful. I

promise to give my very best to this role."

Later that evening, Onan and I had dinner in my newly furnished apartment to celebrate my promotion. As we discussed far into the night, we were grateful for the opportunity to have earned a bit more freedom. After Onan had dozed off, I reflected on my journey so far and the relative level of comfort I have achieved. I also felt a sense of loneliness as I thought about my family in Libron.

"How I wish father would know that I am okay and doing well even in a strange land." I thought to myself. That night, I resolved to do everything possible to earn my freedom and to return to Shalaptonia to find my family.

CHAPTER 4

My confirmation as the permanent personal aide to the General marked the beginning of my meteoric rise in status and responsibilities in the villa. Mentored by Master Banga, I learned more about the intricacies of running the General's household and businesses. It was not long before he released me to focus on managing some aspects of the General's business portfolios while he focused on running the household. My role as the personal aide involved spending much time with the General any time he was around. I was responsible for managing his personal affairs and business interactions. At the end of the first year, the General and Master Banga were effusive in their praise of my performance as they witnessed excellence in all my endeavors. Even Mrs. Aziz was impressed, having seen the significant successes of the investments in the fashion industry. In the following year, her business expanded into a clothing line and other women's products including perfumes, creams, and shoes which continued to exceed business expectations among the upper echelons of the Nubian society. Her clothing line was one of the high-performing business ventures among our investment portfolios that year. The more I succeeded, the busier I became. However, my time in General Aziz's service was not without its share of tragedies.

My successes in the villa were not without notable hardships and challenges that came my way. Other servants, especially those who had been there long before me, became envious and would gossip about me. I experienced unsolicited advances and harassment from many female servants in exchange for reduced work. Mrs. Aziz and her network of socialite women also got an eye for me; I was not immune to discrimination and harassments from her friends either, especially the caucus of the military wives, who often made passes at me during parties and social events. Seeing how frustrated I was with this situation, Master Banga appointed Onan as my personal aide to accompany me everywhere always and advised that I should endeavor not to be alone with the opposite sex.

Racial discrimination, on the other hand, was also unavoidable, especially since I was a non-black immigrant in a predominantly black society. Even though I had mastered the Nubian accent, education, and fashion, that did not stop the incessant racial discrimination and several microaggressions I experienced as I went about my work. Despite my accomplishments in leadership and business matters, I could not get the derogatory labels such as "immigrant dog" or "brown boy" label off my back. The popular racial slogan "You can dress, talk, and act like a Nubian, it does not make you a Nubian" was hurled at me countless times to diminish my accomplishments. But I refused to allow this label to affect my identity or my work. Instead of being resentful, I chose to view the aggressors in terms of their ignorance, lack of exposure, and superiority complex. I resolved not to allow the opinions of my aggressors or colleagues, who think so lowly of me and my work, to define me. I was determined to fully embrace my identity as a brown immigrant with a bright future. Armed with this strong sense of identity and my gifts of learning and leadership, no level of racial discrimination could break my spirit or make me feel inferior.

The more I grew into my position as the General's aide, the less daily contact I had with Master Banga even though I enjoyed every moment I get to work alongside him. One fateful afternoon, Onan and I had just returned from inspecting the farms when one of the aides mentioned that the master would like to see me. I left everything I was doing to go see him immediately in his office, but he was not there. "The master has not been feeling well for some time. He is in his chambers." One of his attending staff replied. I rushed into his chambers and was shocked to see he had grown frail, emaciated, and with breathing problems since I last saw him.

Master was not just my boss, he was my mentor, friend, and father figure in Nubia. He saw my potentials and gave me a chance when no one else would.

"How did things get this bad without my knowledge?" I asked his attending servant as I tried to make sense of the deterioration of his health.

When he heard my voice, he opened his eyes, looked around the room, and smiled at me as he attempted to get up by himself. His attending servant and I supported his back and neck until he was able to sit up against the wall.

"Master, what happened? When did the illness start? Should we send for the villa physicians?" I asked while choking back tears as I tried to make sense of this unexpected situation.

"Master Banga has been sick for a while. He has a problem with his heart and has consulted the villa physician several times. It appears his illness is terminal." his servant explained.

I was horrified by the news, but he seemed to have resigned to the fact that he might not survive this illness.

"Son, don't let my situation weigh you down at all. There is no cause for concern right now. I have lived a good and productive life. What more can I ask for?" He replied feebly with a hoarse voice.

I was angry and disappointed at the impending demise of the master.

"Why is it that I get to lose you just when I have come to know and admire you? Why now?" I furiously protested as tears ran down my face.

"Zeph, I have not sent for you to grieve over me. I wanted to give you some instructions about how to run the villa in my absence. So, wipe off your tears and be a man!"

"Alright, sir. I am fine." I replied while using the left hand to wipe away my tears.

"You need to buckle up, because there is a lot ahead of you."

Then he outlined instructions about his responsibilities in Aziz's house. He spoke about the day-to-day running of the villa - gardening, plumbing, food supply, maintenance, tailors, event planning, the chains of businesses, the investment portfolios, the finances, and other business relationships he made on behalf of the general. By the time he was done, I was shocked by how much weight of responsibilities he had shouldered for more than 40 years of working in the villa.

The news of my master's illness soon reached the General and his wife. They abandoned their engagements and rushed down to see him. To help the situation, the General summoned the royal physician to examine him. After the physical examination, the physician concluded that the master has terminal chronic heart failure and that he only had a maximum of three months to live. As much as the General and his wife were concerned for Master Banga's health, their major concern was about the welfare of their household and business enterprises after master's inevitable demise. Seeing the palpable anxiety on their faces, master sought to allay their fears.

"You don't need to be alarmed; I have made arrangements for Zeph to continue managing the villa in my absence. I have no doubt that you are in good hands." He assured in a feeble hoarse voice.

Devastated by the impending loss of master Bang, I spent more time by his bedside every day trying to maximize the remaining moments. He would tell me stories about his childhood in Ethiopia. During one of those visits with Onan, he managed to get up and discussed extensively with us. He narrated his life's story, especially his childhood in Ethiopia. He was captured as a teenager with his best friend near Nubia River delta on the Ethiopian border with the kingdom of Kush during the early days of the Nubian-Ethiopian war.

"As bounties of war, we were brought to Egypt and condemned to life o slavery. My friend and I were lucky to be assigned to General Raja and Aziz respectively. I was favored by General Aziz as I had a rare opportunity to earn my freedom because of my excellent contribution to the growth and prosperity his family. My friend was not so lucky. His boss returned to the war front and I did not hear from him anymore." The look in his eyes was distant, plagued with sorrow. He smiled sadly as he looked at Onan and me, "Any time I see both of you and the friendship you share, I am reminded of my childhood friend, Noba. The countless hours we spent fishing on the Nubia River delta, our hunting expeditions in the Kush-Ethiopian forest, and the serene moments we shared discussing our future dreams and aspirations. I encourage you to make the most of the precious relationship you boys share. You have a bright future ahead of you, but you need to keep looking out for each other."

"I am sorry to hear this master. Did you ever look for your friend?" Onan asked.

"Oh, yes, I have searched everywhere in the Nubian kingdom and even hired private investigators to help find him among the soldiers."

"It's sad to hear this, sir. I promise to continue the search until I find him."

"Don't bother, Zeph. The chances of finding him are slim. I hope you and Onan will cherish your friendship for a long time. You are both destined to do great things in the future," he said before dozing off that afternoon.

The impending loss of Master Banga filled me with much sadness and worry as I realized that his shoes will be too big for me to fill after his departure. Rather than comfort him, he was the one that encouraged me during my visits. "I know you will do greater things than I have done, Zeph," he would say in an assuring manner. He was strongly convinced that I had a greater destiny than the life in Aziz's villa. In his final moments, the master managed to warn me about Mrs. Aziz's advances and encouraged me to earn my freedom if possible.

Two months later, Master Banga died peacefully in my arms. It was a painful loss, I felt like my heart was literally ripped out of my chest. The General declared a forty-day mourning period in honor of the master after his burial. Two months later, the General confirmed my appointment as the new household manager although I had already started functioning in that role.

With time, I grew into the position of the household manager despite the crushing weight of responsibilities I endured during my first year. To improve my effectiveness in management, I trained some servants who demonstrated leadership potentials to share the leadership burden with me. Over the following three months, I ran evening classes on accounting, leadership, public speaking, fashion, supply chain management, and royal etiquettes for these men and women. In turn, I encouraged these leaders to also grow other leaders in their division. By the end of my first year in my role as the household manager, I had developed a team of leaders to whom I delegated some of my leadership responsibilities - catering, maintenance, event planning, laundry, and public relations. This eased the burden of responsibilities I shouldered, freed up my time, and made me more effective in running the villa. This leadership style earned me lots of acclaim and support among the hundreds of staff that worked in the villa. During my tenure, the General's businesses grew exponentially. My name got on the lips of everyone in and outside the villa, especially General Aziz's friends and other socialites who frequently visited the villa. This success came with more trust from him and more influence in the villa. Many of his military colleagues also sought me for advice on how to grow their investments.

The expansion of the fashion business into international territories required that Mrs. Aziz and I work and travel together more often to negotiate business deals with marketers, suppliers, transporters. Despite the growth we witnessed, the General imposed hiring restrictions which placed significant strain on the villa work force. However, the busier I got, the more vulnerable I became as I could not afford to always have Onan with me. the incessant sexual harassments from Mrs. Aziz's and other socialite women in her circle became unmanageable. While I could avoid the socialite women, I could not avoid Mrs. Aziz because we travelled together a lot. On one of those trips to the Kingdom of Berber, she began flirting with men after a few cups of wine at the motel where we lodged that evening after sealing a business deal. Her eyes became glossy and darted around the hall.

"There are fine young men in this motel," she observed.

"Unlike my stout, pot-bellied, good-for-nothing husband, those young men right there are the real deal. They are tall, handsome, and light skinned." She laughed hysterically, to the chagrin of the servants and everyone who sat at the table with her.

It was not long before she caught the attention of several men in the dining hall as she grew tipsy and staggered around that night.

"Come on here young men, you should join me at our table." She loudly invited the men.

By this time, bystanders and other men in the dining hall wondered how an honorable woman of her pedigree could behave in a shameful manner.

To stop the public embarrassment, her female aides and I quietly escorted her out of the hall into her chambers.

"Come, lie with me tonight. I will make it worth your while. No one needs to know. The General will not be back until the next two months," she seductively beckoned me to join her in bed.

"Your excellency, you are drunk. Such embarrassing display is not expected of such an honorable woman like you."

"You know I love you right? But you always find ways to turn me down despite all my advances," he lamented as she sucked her lower lips.

"Please make sure that her excellency does not leave her chambers any more tonight. The villa cannot afford any public drama." I ordered her two female servants as I bade her good night.

"You know I can destroy you at any time, right? So, make sure you get that into your skull!" She threatened as I left her chambers.

The next day, our delegation could not leave for Buhen as early because her excellency had bad hangover symptoms. We left about five hours later than we planned. After a few hours of traveling, Mrs. Aziz, turned to me and asked about what I remembered about her behavior the previous night.

"Your excellency, we should forget the past. Today is another new and bright day." I replied as I glanced into the horizon to avoid direct eye contact.

"My aides told me about how I embarrassed myself yesterday in the dining hall and how you saved the day. I was told that I said a lot of things which I did not really mean. I am sorry if I embarrassed you," she admitted.

"It's okay, your excellency. We can look towards the future."

"Thank you. But if the truth is to be told, I was conscious when I asked you to join me in bed. I know you have been doing your best to avoid me. The more you distance yourself from me, Zeph, the more I want you." She said as fixed her gaze on me.

A sudden chill swept through me and I stared in disbelief as I slowly processed her words. After regaining my composure, I turned to her and explained my stand.

"Your excellency, I appreciate your interest in me, but your husband is like a father to me and has graciously given me the freedom to run his affairs with complete trust in my abilities and respect for my opinions. At the very least, I should reciprocate this level of trust and confidence in me by being faithful to him, including staying away from his wife."

Mrs. Aziz felt insulted and disrespected and soon grew furious and belligerent. She also threatened to blackmail me to the General while raining several expletives on me for allegedly disrespecting her. Seeing that things were quickly turning ugly, I asked the chariot driver how close we were to the next town.

"We are about 20 miles away, sir. Do you want us to stay here for the night or should we proceed to the next town which is about 70 miles away?"

"We should stay at the next town for the evening. There is no point stressing madam any more today." Thankfully, the stop that night was a welcome distraction for her.

Several months after that incident, Mrs. Aziz's behavior, and attitude towards me changed. She became more antagonistic and sought every opportunity to discredit me in the presence of the General and their socialite friends. This surprised everyone, who had previously seen how she used to praise my diligence, brilliance, and great looks. But no one could understand her sudden change in attitude. She stopped communicating with me and requested that I train a handful of servants, handpicked by her, to work with her. At first, I was hesitant because of their limited knowledge of investment and business, but I later agreed to train these men to satisfy her demands. Mrs. Aziz resolved to run her business completely by herself and her team while excluding me from important business discussions. Although I was not comfortable with this decision at first, I was glad that her independence would minimize her incessant pestering.

One fateful afternoon, I had just arrived from the market square and was heading to my quarters for a meeting with the farm produce suppliers when Mrs. Aziz's personal aide arrived. They informed me that she requests my presence in the villa for a business discussion. I was upset at the impromptu meeting and wondered why she does not plan her day well, despite having several attending aides. Seeing that I might not return on time to meet with the suppliers, I sent Onan to meet with the suppliers instead. After giving him the instructions and the authority to negotiate the rising food prices and other materials used in the villa, I headed straight to the main quarters with her aides. While on my way, I wondered what could have gone wrong and why she would send for me after several months of not wanting me to be involved. I was unaware that she had ulterior motives for the invitation.

When I got into the villa, her aides led me to the waiting room in her quarters. After about an hour, Her Excellency emerged from her chambers all dressed up in a see-through flowing gown, fluttering her eyelashes and making seductive advances at me.

"Do you like what you see?" I thought to myself, the

devil could have as well dressed himself up so seductively and asked the same question and there would not be much difference between them. "A compliment from you won't be a bad idea," she purred with a coy smile.

I froze in my tracks, disappointed by what I had just seen while processing the conflict between what I was seeing and the urgency of the message I had received.

Zeph, you have just blindly walked into a lion's den, I thought in my mind while I managed to nod in agreement with a sly smile after regaining my composure.

"Have a seat, Zeph. My team and I have some little problem with our books, and you are the only one that can solve the problem for us."

Then she brought out the business ledgers and asked me to review them. My review of the accounting details even shocked me the more. There was gross mismanagement of business funds by her team that included incomplete entry of expenses, haphazard withdrawal of funds, excessive purchase of raw products, unpaid invoices submitted by suppliers, and many other questionable practices. After evaluating every line, I realized that the business had been running at loss for nearly eight months. I was disappointed by such level of mismanagement. When I asked for more details about her team and how she has engaged with them, she sidestepped my questions and seductively lobbied me to cook the books so that her business will appear profitable before the next annual business meeting.

"You need to do this for me, Zeph. If you do, you can have all these…", she gestured not so discreetly to her body, "and all of me to yourself as much as you want," she shamelessly entreated.

When I asked for her business staff, she admitted that they had all escaped with the funds after being sent to meet with the suppliers in the Kush kingdom. She later discovered that her staff had colluded with the suppliers and marketers to inflate the costs of raw materials and embezzle more funds. Many of her genuine suppliers have demanded to be reimbursed for unpaid invoices. I could not contain my anger and disdain for such incompetence any longer.

"You have been conned, your excellency." After pacing up and down for a while, I turned to her and asked.

"So, you believe you can seductively have me cook the books for you in exchange for sexual favors?

"Yes, Zeph. I will be indebted to you forever." She affirmed.

"I am sorry to disappoint you. I think your move is childish, unprofessional, and ill-advised. I would do no such thing. It is better you come clean with the General or else I would."

Then she got up from the couch in fury and yelled insults and several expletives at me.

"You fool! If you won't bail me out of this mess, then I make sure you take the fall for the entire mess." She threatened.

"Madam, that's fine as well. I have an impeccable record which will speak for me in front of everyone." I ignored her seething and turned on my heels.

As I was about departing, she briskly walked towards the door, blocked my passage, and went on her knees as she implored me to reconsider my decisions.

"Your Excellency. I cannot cook up the books for you. This secret will destroy your marriage, decimate the trust the General placed in me, and ruin the successful business enterprise you and your husband have built over the years. You need to come clean to him."

"If the General learns about this misappropriation, he's going to ban my involvement in his businesses - a decision I cannot live with. This business has given me purpose and vision. The last two years have been the happiest in my 25 years of being married to him. Banning my involvement in his business affairs is tantamount to destroying my purpose and sending me to an early grave. If you won't budge, I won't hesitate to destroy you completely."

"I am very sorry, your excellency. I have to include this new development in my business report to be presented to the General in two days." I concluded as I hurried out of her quarters after being incensed by her threat.

Then, I barged into her two female aides who seem to have been eavesdropping on our conversation near the door.

"Don't you ladies have anything to do other than gossip around? Where are all the male servants in this villa? Your incompetence has compromised the General and everything this villa stands for." I lashed out at the aides.

"They are not here. Her excellency sent them on errands to the market square before sunrise." They replied in unison.

When I got back to my quarters, I was met by Onan and a few other servant leaders who were waiting to share with me status updates and monthly reports in preparation for the business meeting with the General.

"You look upset, Zeph. What transpired between you and madam? It must have been a bad meeting, I guess." Onan asked as everyone else wondered.

"It's complicated. Let me just say that we had a heated debate over her choice of staff for the fashion business. They are mostly strangers and I don't see them around very much."

"You are not alone, Zeph. We also wondered why you were no longer in charge of her business affairs. Now we get it." Asnea, the chief cook replied.

As we settled to continue our meeting, one of Mrs. Aziz's personal aides arrived in panic.

"We need you all to come down to the villa. Madam collapsed a few minutes ago, and we are trying to resuscitate her. We had sent for the villa physician." She hurriedly announced while catching her breath before dashing out again. We all left immediately for the villa. When we got there, she had been revived by the villa physician, but she was too weak to speak. The physician diagnosed her as experiencing the aftershock of a traumatic event.

"In due course, we will need to investigate what type of traumatic event she experienced," the physician concluded.

Seeing that she was in good hands, I returned to the villa to continue my meeting with my team in preparation for the meeting with the General. Onan later arrived with an anxiously stern look on his face. "What's eating you up Onan?" I asked while focused on the report I was reviewing.

"Zeph, what really transpired between you and madam?"

I stopped everything and took a long pause before lifting

my gaze towards Onan and then looked around to see if anyone was around or nearby before saying anything else to him.

"Bolt the door behind you and proceed into my chambers. We need to talk." I ordered.

After we got into my chambers. I narrated my encounter with Mrs. Aziz, the discovery of her team's misappropriation of business funds, and her request that I should cook the books in exchange for sexual favors.

"Onan, I cannot agree to such a request. The General must know about it, but she threatened to destroy my reputation if I don't dance to her tune."

"Oh Zeph, you are in more trouble than you can imagine. Rumors have it that Mrs. Aziz has already set things in motion to really destroy you for good."

"How do you mean, Onan? What things are set in motion? What did you hear?" I asked as a raised brow graced my face.

"I learned she's instructed her aides to corroborate her story that you misappropriated her business funds and that you offered her sexual favors in exchange for her silence. You need to return to the villa to apologize to her."

"These are all concocted lies. She oversaw the recruitment of her staff and solely managed the business during the past year after she asked the General to relieve me of the responsibility of managing her fashion business. I have nothing to fear, and my records are there for all to see," I asserted after a pronounced sigh.

"Zeph, I believe you. But madam has a track record of

destroying people's future. I am worried that this is one of her attempts to destroy you. I hope i'm wrong."

It was not long until we heard a bang on the main door of my quarters.

"We have some visitors. Let's proceed to the common area." I advised.

When Onan opened the door, he was met by villa guards who had been sent to arrest me on the alleged charges of financial dishonesty and sexual assault.

"There is trouble, Zeph. You need to see this." Onan hollered.

When I got out of my chambers, I was met by the villa guards who had started ransacking my study and common area.

Then, I asked for details about who ordered my arrest and why I was being arrested.

"Sir, we received word from the General that you should be remanded in the villa cell until his return in two days' time. Unofficially, there are rumours that madam, has accused you of misappropriation of business funds and sexual assault, which by Nubian laws carries a death sentence, if you are proven guilty. We know how good you have been to us, but we are just here to do our jobs."

"It's alright, gentlemen. You should do your jobs. I am innocent of all the charges levelled against me. I have nothing to hide, and my impeccable record is there for all to see."

It was then I realized that I was in trouble. The guards put me in chains, ransacked my quarters and carted away several shelves of scrolls containing details about the

General's businesses and villa operations. As I was being led away, I kept on delegating responsibilities to Onan and my leadership team.

"Onan, you need to assume the mantle of leadership of the villa in my absence and coordinate our team. Make sure no one drops the ball on any tasks. The General will be back in 2 days. You need to give him a befitting welcome. I am sure he's going to vindicate me. So, I should be back in two days."

While in the cell, I pondered on what the outcome would be. A part of me was optimistic that I will be acquitted while the other part of me was not so positive, considering madam's threat and several stories Onan had previously told me about how vindictive she was. In those two days, Onan did not only stop by the cell several times to clarify a few instructions and ask for directions about some pertinent domestic issues that arose, but he also came to see how I was faring.

"I cannot wait to have you back tomorrow. This house manager role is not something for me. I don't have what it takes to run such a huge villa." He complained.

After a long loud laugh, I encouraged him not to give up on leadership.

"Those challenging situations are not fun to deal with, that's why they are called challenges. You have what it takes to lead the villa. These problems will strengthen and deepen your leadership capacity."

"Anyways, I cannot wait to have you back once you are acquitted of all charges." He repeated as he was about to depart.

"Onan, could you wait? I want to tell you one more

thing."

He stopped, and turned back, wondering if I have more instructions for him.

"If it happens that things go sideways at the hearing tomorrow, I need you to stay out of it. Don't try to defend or advocate for me. Remember that you once mentioned that Mrs. Aziz is very vindictive. I need you to keep your cool because I cannot afford to put you in harm's way."

Onan's eyes became misty as he lowered his head and pressed his lips together.

"I hope it does not get to that, Zeph. You need to stay positive," he encouraged. Yet, we both knew he had seen enough of Mrs. Aziz's to know that a bad outcome is most likely in these hearings. We stared at each in silence thinking about our friendship, the good moments, and that moment of sadness. Soon, we were interrupted by a servant who arrived to inform Onan that his attention was needed at the villa entrance.

When General Aziz eventually arrived, he was given a befitting welcome by the staff, but he was in no mood for pleasantries. Instead, he stormed out of his chariot and went straight into the villa. In the meantime, the atmosphere in the villa remained tense while the General discussed with his wife. "What would happen to the Zeph? Will the General support his wife or acquit Zeph? What will be the fate of Zeph if convicted?" The staff wondered as they quietly conversed with one another around the villa. Onan, on the other hand, frequently sent me word to me in the cell about the turn of events in the villa. Finally, I was brought to the proceedings which was held on the lawn beside the villa. There, I found the General and his wife, the military guards, and the villa staff, all seated to watch the proceedings.

The chief military guard read the accusations against me and asked if I plead guilty to the charges.

"Your excellency, General Aziz, invited guests, military guards, and honorable servants in this great villa. I was shocked to hear about these accusations. I hereby categorically deny these charges and cannot plead guilty because I am innocent."

"Are you saying we are liars?" Mrs Aziz yelled as she bellowed furiously.

"Now that the defendant has denied all charges, we will begin the proceeding by calling on the witnesses." The chief military guard announced.

It was then I realized that Mrs. Aziz had put more thought into framing me like an insect caught in a spider's web. The first witnesses were her two personal aides who eavesdropped while I discussed with her. "We overheard master Zeph threaten madam that he will force himself on her if she dares tell the General about misappropriated business funds," they claimed. Next, an external auditor was invited to review the business ledgers. After an hour of reviewing all the business reports, the auditor concluded that the accounts for the fashion business were forged after running at loss for more than 8 months. But he claimed he found all other businesses were extremely profitable and accurately reported.

"My conclusion is that the business under investigation had a separate accountant than the other investment portfolios.

It's hard to believe that only one person managed all the businesses. Consequently, I don't have sufficient evidence to conclude that the accused stole or misappropriated business funds from his excellency."

Mrs. Aziz flew into a rage, got up from her seat, and hurled expletives at the auditor for what she called incompetent expert witnessing.

The auditor's testimony was followed by testimonies from some suppliers I had not previously met who claimed that I paid them to overcharge the General and then share the profits with them.

Her male servants also testified that they had witnessed how I have flirted with her and have overheard from "reliable sources" that I desire her. Onan was devastated and wanted to speak up in my defense, but I forbade him from testifying for fear of reprisals against him after my departure.

She also found some of my trusted aides who corroborate her story and lied that I was a serial abuser. The General was enraged and disappointed by these accusations. He ordered my execution without any trial. Just before I was taken away, I asked for the opportunity to address the General and the entire audience.

"Your excellency, General Aziz, I have faithfully served you these past 10 years since Master Banga picked me up from the market square. Your businesses and household have witnessed unprecedented expansion and prosperity since I started managing your household. You have not suffered a single loss and none of your portfolios had been misappropriated till today. Apart from these paid liars, none of the servants and staff could ever claim that I have an inappropriate relationship with anyone. As a husband, you have every right to believe your wife's version of events. The only person who had spoken the truth here is the external auditor you have invited as the expert witness who concluded that the business account under question and other investment portfolios are managed by two separate people with different accounting styles. If I had forged the numbers in the fashion business accounts, why will I not cover my tracks by forging the other accounts to make all the business accounts look profitable?"

There was a complete silence as everyone meditated on my line of reasoning for a while. Seeing that the audience are beginning to process the veracity of the case against me, she wailed while reminding the audience at the trial that she was the victim here.

"Your excellency, God is my witness that I did not at any time, eye, harass, or assault your wife despite her incessant advances. I would not ask for mercy because I am innocent. I am only pleading that you carefully investigate the matter a bit more to uncover the truth, sir." I was punched and beaten by members of the military guard for publicly dishonoring madam Aziz's reputation. At the end, it was the word of a highly respected Nubian woman against a slave immigrant boy. At that point, the General was confused. He ordered that I should be stripped of my role, whipped, and sent to the royal prison pending the time he can decide what to do with me.

I cried profusely, disappointed at General Aziz's betrayal, despite my years of dedication to growing his household and businesses.

CHAPTER 5

The royal prison was a maximum-security underground jail that was home to several political prisoners, including Nobiin's enemies, cabinet members who had fallen out with the royals, political rebels, assassinators, co-conspirators, and defiant staff members. One wing of the prison housed the political prisoners, rebels, and errant cabinet members while the other wing was home to criminals and assassins.

Few months after my arrival at the prison, the director of the prison services, who was a friend of General Aziz, sent for me when he learned about my precarious situation.

"Oh my, you are a complete shadow of yourself, Zeph. You need to cheer up, or else you are going to become suicidal in few months. I believe you are innocent of the charges against you. I suspect that Aziz knows that too. Perhaps, that is the reason he did not execute you right on the spot, instead he chose to send you here."

I was happy that, for the first time, someone believed in my innocence. Seeing that he might be on my side, I begged him to help clear my name.

"You don't seem to get it, son. Aziz won't reverse this decision even though he probably knows that you are innocent. Commuting the charges against you is not good for his reputation." He explained.

"I think you should know that things have not been the same with him since he sent you here. His businesses have been hemorrhaging and the day-to-day running of the villa has been hampered since you left. With no known leader who can bring people together, his villa has lost its reputation for organization, excellence, and royal decorum. My friend has never been this irritable and angry in more than twenty-five years of our friendship.

It was not long before I understood why the director sent for me. He wanted me to assume the administration of the prison under his supervision. But I was not in a good place to even take on any role. I felt so empty and had nothing in me to give to any cause or anyone as I dealt with depression and the trauma of betrayal. I saw through the director's selfishness and concluded that he wants to use me to accomplish his goals, just like the General and his other associates used me to grow their businesses and discarded me. I turned down the offer right on the spot and requested to be excused from the meeting.

"You fool, don't you know that the director has the power to order for your freedom!?" One of his aides derided just as I was walking out of the meeting. I stopped and turned toward the aides,

"If he has any power, he would have prevented me from

getting here in the first place. I am more useful to him on the outside than in here."

As the guards escorted me back to my cell, a hostile group of inmates arrived with knives and clubs. Unknown to me, words had reached the inmates that I was the young man with the "golden touch" who helped the Nubian cabal build their businesses on the back of poor and the immigrants.

"Hey boy, your time is up. We know you are here to snitch for the cabal. We are here to send them a message." Their leaders announced as they surrounded me.

Their menacing demeanor sent fear down my spine causing my body to vibrate as my eyes darted around the mob. I stuttered for a while until I could find the right words. "Huh…Cabal? I don't know any cabal and have never worked with a group like that."

"There is no place for you to hide anymore "golden boy". Aren't you the personal assistant of General Aziz who helped him and the cabal cook their books and grow their wealth in the last few years?" one of the men asked.

"Of a truth sir, I was the General's former personal aide who managed his businesses and also helped a few of his friends, but I don't know any cabal which you mention." I explained as I was being kicked and punched. The mob roared in laughter at my response.

One of the men explained "Son, your boss, and his friends, are the cabal that owns more than 90% of Nubian wealth along with the royal family. This same cabal is behind the largest human trafficking ring that smuggles people from neighboring nations. We are here to send them a message by hacking you to death and sending your body parts to them."

"Sir, I have no clue that there is a cabal. I would not have worked for them if I had known, but I had no choice. I was kidnapped from Shalaptonia and brought here, sir. I don't know any cabal." I cried out as they continued to kick and beat me.

Then a loud baritone voice from a nearby cell ordered the men to stop and desist from hurting me.

"Stop hurting that boy, he is innocent."

"Not at all, old man. He's part of the cabal."

"Don't you know he is just a helpless young man like you all? He must have had no choice, but to obey his masters' orders." He reasoned before ordering them to stop.

"Lucky you, the old man came to your rescue today, but we will be keeping our eyes on you. If you make any stupid move, you are dead." Someone in the crowd warned as they all dispersed.

After the group's departure, I was shaken to my core and sobbed uncontrollably while lying there with sore ribs, bruised limbs, and bloody head. I reflected on my close brush with death, trying to get my head around what just transpired. Going by what the gang described, it dawned on me that the trafficking ring that brought me to Nubia belong to the cabal of which the General was a key member.

"What brought you here, son? Why are these men after your life?" The man with the baritone voice asked

"I was kidnapped and brought to Nubia by a trafficking ring and sold to General Aziz's household where I rose through the ranks to become his assistant. I helped manage his businesses and turned them into wealthy and profitable corporations. Also, I helped manage investments for some of his friends. But I did not know that the so-called cabal is involved in illegal business."

"Son, rumor has it that the cabal's wealth was built from human trafficking and prostitution. The money made from these dirty businesses are then re-invested in legitimate businesses which people like you manage for them." I was shell-shocked by this revelation for a while as I connected the dots. Finally, I resolved to destroy the cabal if I ever have any chance in the future to do so. "You are not alone, son. Most of those inmates are just like you, victims of life circumstances. Behind the physical toughness you see in these men, are stories of disappointment, betrayal, and hopelessness."

Over time, this man and I conversed regularly from our cells. He was friendly and inspiring. We got along well to the extent that we both looked forward to chatting with each other. Gradually, I started to feel lively again. Our conversation was always filled with laughter, life lessons, and general gossips about the prison. The man knew so much about everything and everyone, but I knew nothing about him. Memories of those conversations with him often brought smiles to my face when I was alone in my cell.

"You are no longer as moody as you used to be. What's going on with you?" My cellmate once commented.

After a few weeks of conversation with this man, I resolved to visit his cell. "It's amazing that I have been conversing with you for so long and we have not met face-to-face until now. I must stop by your cell to see you in person soon." I mentioned during one of our conversations.

"Don't bother, son. My cell is in the remote part of the dungeon." I inquired from other inmates about how to reach the ancient man. When I asked my cellmate about the direction to the old man's cell, he discouraged me from checking him out.

"You don't want to go there! He's been in isolation for so long and his cell is near the concentrated sewage area. People don't visit the old man because of the pungent odor around his cell."

But his explanations did not deter me from seeking out this man who saved my life a few weeks ago. Instead, I reached out to other inmates to find out about the direction to his cell.

Determined to meet the old man, I waded through layers of sewage to get to his cell. When I finally reached him, I found a dark-skinned man dressed in a flowing dirty robe with a long grey beard seated in a dirty cold room. The drainage flowed through the center of the cell

"Who is that? To what do I owe this visit?" He inquired in his characteristic baritone voice.

"It's me, sir. I am here to personally thank you for saving my life the other day and to put a face to the voice."

"Oh, my dear friend, it is great to finally meet you," he grinned as he gazed in my direction.

After exchanging pleasantries, he inquired about my welfare and we conversed for a while. As he continued, I surveyed the room and stared at the walls of his cell which were filled with seemingly familiar ancient writings.

"These writings appear familiar, but I cannot remember

where I first saw them." I interjected.

"Which of the walls my son?" he replied. It was then I realized that the man was blind.

"I am so sorry, sir, I was not aware of your condition."

"Never mind. This dungeon has, eventually, claimed my eyes, after living so long without sunlight."

"How long have you been here?"

"It's been nearly four decades in here, but it only felt like yesterday. As to those writings, they are ancient Ethiopian writings of my people. I wrote them before my eyes began to fail me." he proudly explained as he stroked his fingers over the walls.

"Yes, I remember now. I first saw these writings when I worked with my mentor." I exclaimed!

When he inquired further, I spoke glowingly of the role that Master Banga played in grooming and teaching me.

"My master was an Ethiopian brought to Nubia as a teenage prisoner of war about four decades ago."

I did not notice that the old man was shaking uncontrollably as I spoke glowingly about my mentor.

"What was his name?" he tearfully asked.

At this point, I stopped and wondered what was going on.

"We all called him Master Banga; he died two years ago."

The old man tore his robe and cried loudly and profusely as he rolled around in the dirt. I stood there confused, wondering what could have gone wrong. Despite all my attempts to console him or get him to explain what was going on, he remained inconsolable for a long time. He later managed to sit up against the wall and tearfully explained.

"I am Noba, Banga's friend." he replied. Immediately, I remembered my conversation with the master and his quest to find his childhood friend who was kidnapped together with him. I stared in disbelief and staggered a bit as I processed what I had just heard. Tears streamed down my face like a mountain dam that was let loose as I realized that I was standing before the man my mentor had spent decades searching for. After crying for a long time, I sat down next to him in the dirt exhausted and unable to utter any word of consolation.

"Banga and I grew up in the lower part of the Nubia River that flowed through the Ethiopian kingdom and the lands of the Kush. He's Ethiopian and I'm a Kushite, but we both speak Ethiopian language. Banga and I first met at the banks of one of the distributaries of Nubia River near the Ethiopian-Kush border one late afternoon. I had wandered from my village and found myself right on the border with Ethiopia when I noticed a boy about my age washing fishing nets near the banks. I approached and wanted to learn about fishing. We had a good time that day and promised each other to hang out every evening. We continued the tradition of hanging out every evening for a long time. Even though we were from different kingdoms, we loved each other as friends and would spend the evening telling each other stories, climbing trees, fishing, and sometimes swimming in the Nubia River distributary," he fondly recalled.

"Master Banga mentioned that you were both kidnapped and shipped to Nubia. Also, I learned that you have not seen each other since your master went to the battle front. My boss gained his freedom early on but chose to continue serving General Aziz in hope that he can find you someday."

"Yes, we were kidnapped by three young Nubian officers when they invaded Ethiopia. These three young officers were the crown prince of Nubia - now the current Nobiin, Raja, and Aziz. Since the crown prince had many servants, he allowed Aziz and Raja to keep Banga and me as slaves, respectively. After returning to heroes' welcome in Nubia, they were appointed to serve as part of the Royal Guard for Nobiin, the Great. Banga and I saw each other occasionally whenever our masters meet for drinks, but Raja was a restless soul who found royal routine boring and preferred to return to the battlefront. As his aide, I was trained in combat and accompanied him everywhere. When Raja returned to the frontlines, I did not have any chance to see Banga or exchange goodbyes before we left. Despite not seeing him, I took comfort in the fact that Banga was serving under Aziz and given his relationship with Raja, I hoped we would see more of him. Raja was a mighty warrior who conquered many lands. News of his exploits on the battlefront soon reached the palace. His Royal Highness considered Raja a legend and soon made him the commander of the Nubian army, the highest military position in the kingdom. The crown prince became envious and felt his future role as a king was being threatened by Raja's meteoric rise and fame. Few months after, Aziz and the crown prince visited Raja on the battlefront. We received them with pomp and pageantry befitting a royalty. During the visit, the three friends discussed strategy and the future of the kingdom. Raja held the belief that Nubia can become the most powerful kingdom and the seat of modern civilization. Since he was a battle-hardened warrior, he advocated for a sustained military invasion of neighboring nations to accomplish that vision. His mission was to conquer the known world for Nubia. But the crown prince and Aziz had a different vision for the kingdom. They favored a more diplomatic approach that focused on economic development and prosperity of Nubia. For days, they discussed and argued about their visions for the kingdom. Three days after their arrival, they were all in the tent drinking and discussing the future of the kingdom, but it was not long before their discussion escalated into a heated argument."

"We need more drinks here", Aziz hollered. I abandoned the cleaning of the General Raja's armor to get them more wine. When I returned, I overheard the crown prince and Aziz arguing staunchly about the crown prince's decision to stab General Raja.

"It's better we eliminate him once and for all to ensure that he does not rise against the kingdom in the future." The crown prince insisted. There was some rustling now and things were quiet for some time before one of them said "He is dying. Raja is struggling to breathe. What have you done?". When I peeped through the curtain, I saw my boss bleeding out on the leather rug. I froze in my tracks and unconsciously dropped the golden wine bowl. The crown prince and General Aziz were startled.

"Who is there? Show your face." They responded in unison. Then I rushed to the side of General Raja and tended to his wounds. As he struggled for breath, he tried to mutter some words. I tried to place my ear close to his mouth. "Run, Noba, run," he muttered as he died in my arms. It's too late to run, boss, I thought to myself. Then I got up to face the two murderers who by now were very nervous and confused about what they should do. Rather than excuse myself, I confronted them and took out my anger on them. "You men are murders and traitors. You killed a man who loved you and risked his life for you in cold blood. General Raja had nothing but love in his heart for you two and this kingdom. You have repaid his goodwill with this evil. Hence forth, evil will not depart from your homes. May you never find helpers any longer in your journey in life. I continued hurling insults and expletives at both men who watched in silence, with a look of terror on their face while I continued speaking through my tears, exhausted and full of anger.

"Noba, you killed your master, the commander of the Nubian army," the cold-hearted murderous crown prince declared to my utter surprise. He announced to the troops that I had killed the commander because I could not handle the continual raid of Ethiopia. At first, I denied the allegations, but admitted to the crime after endless torture by members of the royal military guard. The army demanded my immediate execution, but the crown prince and Aziz could not summon the courage to execute me. Instead, they repatriated me to the royal prison until a decision could be made. They have forgotten me here for the last four decades.".

After listening to Noba for a while, I was too overwhelmed with emotions and could not process these information as I should. So, I asked him to stop for a bit.

"I know this is too much for you to take in," he admitted.

"Are you saying both His Highness, King Nobiin, and General Aziz intentionally left you in this prison for the past four decades?" I gaped at the revelation.

"Yes, they knew I have been here that long. The king himself directly appointed one of his allies as the director of this prison to ensure that I am not released from here." he said.

"Why will General Aziz lie to Master Banga and even dedicate resources to help him find you when he was one of the people that put you here?" I asked as I stared at the ceiling of that dark small cell.

"Greed. Aziz knows too well that Banga won't agree to manage his household if he learns that I am here. Banga will go all out to secure my freedom and engineer our return to Kush. I know too much, and they would have killed me rather than release me to Banga." He explained.

I found this story unbelievable since I knew how General Aziz was supportive of Banga's search for his brother and even dedicated resources to help. The General needed Master Banga to keep managing their household while the King wanted this man silenced forever. Then my mind drifted into several alternative outcomes of this saga. What if my master had known that his friend was in this prison? Could he have lobbied for his release? How nice would it have been if Master Banga had the opportunity to visit his friend regularly? Several questions flooded my heart as I tearfully stared at the man again.

It was so hard to process everything so quickly. But I continued to ask questions.

"Did you know that Banga was still working for General Aziz?"

"I did not know that Banga earned his freedom. I had thought that they killed him to cover their evil, after they sent me here. Now everything makes sense. Aziz did not kill him but sent him on a goose chase even though he knows I am here."

"What happened to Banga? Did he live a good life?"

"He died of a congestive heart failure which had bothered him for some time, sir."

"He lived a good life, but all meant nothing to him because he could not find you. In his last moments, he had incredible joy as he reminisced about the time you both spent together. He ordered me to tell you, if I ever met you, that he died a free man and that he loved you and will continue to love you even in the next life."

The man further became even more inconsolable after hearing these words. "He was my best friend and brother too. Those good days near the Nubia delta brought me so much joy despite my ordeals in here."

After several hours of mourning with this man, I returned to my cell even more depressed. The events of the previous month weighed heavily on my mind. Learning that the man I worked for and trusted was a wicked murderer and human trafficker shook me to my core, as I wondered how I might have enabled such wickedness to thrive.

If I have my way, I will make him pay for all the atrocities he had committed, I murmured to myself. In the meantime, I sought for ways to fulfill the promise I made to Master Banga. I was determined to give Noba the best care I could afford for the remaining days of his life. To do this, I must accept the director's offer to lead the prison.

The next day, I requested an audience with the prison director who was excited to hear that I've had a change of heart when we finally met. "I would like to take up your offer, if it has not expired, but this is conditional on your acceptance of my two requests." I politely demanded.

The director was super excited when he heard that I was willing to reconsider my decision.

"Sure, the offer still stands. Tell me your conditions, Zeph. I know we can always work out something as long as those requests are reasonable." Then I requested two private and comfortable cells in the upper-class wing of the prison, closer to sunlight for myself and another, but similar room for Noba. After weighing the risk, the director approved both requests and I took on the leadership role in the prison. A few hours later, Noba and I were in one of the choicest cells in the prison. When I went to check on him, he was full of gratitude for looking out for him.

"Your mannerism and kindness remind me of Banga. Thank you for this good gesture, but I am not sure life is worth living without the hope of seeing Banga."

"Master Banga would want you to continue living and have a good life too."

"What good life can I have in a prison where I have spent almost 40 years? I am blind, having not seen the sun for years. Even if I am released today, what other enjoyment is out there without my eyes to see it?" I tried to keep his spirit alive with constant visits and engagements every day.

About a month after we moved into our new rooms, I woke up to the commotion among the inmates that Noba, the man with the golden baritone voice, took his own life. I was devastated that my efforts to revive his spirit had been in vain. I had been successful in rehabilitating his physical condition and environment, but he remained despondent since learning about his friend's demise.

After mourning him for days, I turned my attention to understand the situation of the prison. Several senior and criminal elements in the prison wanted nothing to do with me, yet I chose to reach out and offered a more inclusive leadership which they refused. Instead, they sought to assassinate me because of my perceived relationship with the cabal. I was fortunate that the guards were there to foil several attempts to assassinate me. Disappointed by the repudiation of my offer of friendship, I sought others way to engage the inmates. While I was still grieving the sudden loss of Noba, I realized that hopelessness and lack of purpose were the major reasons for the increased violence in the prison. So, I devised a strategy to make my vision more about giving hope to the inmates. I started meeting with a few inmates, who are receptive to my ideas, to share our stories and encourage one another. During the first meeting, I shared about my journey to Nubia, the highs and the lows of my time here, and how Noba helped to rekindle the dying fire of hope in me. It was a good time of reflection on my mistakes, regrets, successes, and future plans. For subsequent meetings, different inmates shared their stories with the group. Everyone was reluctant at first, but, with time, participants opened up and learned from one another. Those that shared in the group soon realized the power of storytelling in healing wounds, clarifying purpose, and restoring hopes in them. Within months, the group continued to grow, and many of the inmates embraced the message of hope. After most inmates bought into my vision, it was easy to help the inmates find a purpose for their lives.

Later, we embarked on the second phase of my vision which was to equip every inmate with something to live for. To do this, we reached out to inmates with specialized skills - cooks, farmers, accountants, carpenters, stone cutters, military folks - and documented the skills inventory in the prison. Then we offered skills training workshops. I mobilized the inmates to start making products - furniture, low-cost jewelry, and clothes - and enlisted the help of the prison guards and the director to market our products to the community. To further motivate the inmates, we arranged to send proceeds from each inmate's work to their families and/or friends. Many inmates felt a renewed sense of purpose and a sense of kinship with other inmates. The news of the transformational leadership I brought to the prison soon reached the upper echelons of the Nubian kingdom. As the face of the transformational program, the director received countless accolades and awards for his transformational leadership. The news of the transformation even reached the royal court where the king organized a reception in recognition of the director's excellent work.

Hours after the director met with his highness, he sent for me. I had just finished a meeting with my leadership team when the guards arrived.

"You need to come with us quickly. The director wants to see you."

When I got to his office, I found him nervously pacing up and down.

"Sit down, Zeph."

"Sir, what's going on? You seem unsettled. How can I help?" I asked as I took my seat.

"The news of the great work you are doing here has reached every part of Nubia. I am just coming from a meeting with His Royal Highness who hosted a reception to recognize the transformational leadership we have brought to the nation's prison services. However, he did not know that I was not the brain behind this laudable transformation. I worry that the king will suddenly turn on me if I ever tell him the truth."

"Why will he do that to you sir? Afterall, it was your idea to appoint me to lead the prison."

"Huh…let's just say that His Highness is a brilliant, eccentric individual with a short fuse and erratic tendencies. He might be happy in one hour and then flare up in fits of rage the next hour."

He then continued "while at the palace today, His Highness was so excited about our work that he ordered a toast. But as we were about to dine, the royal chef accidentally spilled some wine from the cup on the royal dining table. He got irritated and that started to ruin the evening. By the time we got to feast with him, he lost his appetite and took out his anger on the royal chef and his dietician claiming he found the food to be tasteless, even though everyone at the table thought the food was delicious. He ordered them to be whipped and hung in 24 hours. Fortunately, the queen was there, she appealed to his better judgment and tried to calm him down. After much persuasion from the queen, he commuted the death sentences to life imprisonment here in the maximum-security prison".

Worried that a similar punishment might befall him if the king uncovers the truth, the director swore me to an oath of secrecy that I will not put him in danger by coming forward with the truth. I reassured him that I would not do anything that will put him in danger. Personally, I was content with flying under the radar, as long as that ensured my survival.

"So, when are these chef and dietician arriving at the prison?"

"They will be here tomorrow if His Highness doesn't change his mind before morning."

CHAPTER 6

The next day, both officials arrived in the prison and became inmates just like everyone else. At first, they kept to themselves and felt participation in group activities was below their status, but with time, they participated in our Hope Reignition programs. We also leveraged on their expertise and leadership experience to train inmates in wine mixing and catering. These officials were impressed with the impeccable organizational and management systems we have developed in the prison.

"I am impressed with what I am seeing here. I even feel a sense of belonging despite having arrived here with a bleak future," one of them responded.

"We can see that you are the real architect of the famed transformational leadership in our prison system. Why do you allow the director to take all the credit?"

"Well, I don't care about credits. The director hired me to lead this initiative. It was his vision; I would not take anything from him." I politely explained, hoping to quell the chances of this discussion being repeated.

"You will be a great asset to His Highness if you can get out of here," the other official interjected.

I gently smiled and refused to let anyone get my hopes up in vain, plus I don't think I am quite ready to face General Aziz's cabal again.

During one of the Hope Re-ignition sessions with these two officials, I asked them about their lives working for His Highness. They went on to describe the king as an enigmatic figure who is difficult to please. As they were describing their royal responsibilities to me, it occurred to me that working in the corridors of power is not all glamourous as I previously thought, indeed not all that glitters is gold as the saying goes. They had similar problems like we had in the villa, but at a much-intensified scale.

Nobiin's daily routine involves getting up at 6:00 am for meditation followed by an hour of personal care before he begins the business of the day at 8:00 am. During these two hours, the royal musical band plays for him as he prepares for the day. On a fateful day, the musical aides played for an hour, before realizing that His Highness was not yet up. At 7:00 am, the care aides arrived as usual, and they soon noticed he was still asleep. What worried the care aides the most was that His Highness was sleep-talking. When he still wasn't up at 9:30 am, the royal chief aide and his team were worried about the unusual turn of events.

"In my twenty-five years of serving his Highness, I have never seen him sleep in this late," the chief aide stated.

"He must be tired. Keep on playing the music. I will cancel all engagements for this morning." But shortly after the chief aide left for the Judgement Hall, His Highness screamed out of his sleep. His aides rushed into his chambers and found him covered in sweat and crying profusely while still asleep. Confused about what to do, they continued to play soft music while they sent again for the chief-aide who later arrived with the royal physician to check on him. The royal physician tapped him on the shoulder until he opened his eyes.

"Easy...easy...it's a nightmare, your Highness. What happened?" the royal physician cooed, but the king could not mutter a word. Instead, he was weeping and shaking uncontrollably for the next hour.

"His Highness is in shock. He must have had a very terrifying dream. You need to keep on playing the soft music to calm him down. Also, I will order some herbal tea to calm his nerves."

As the day wore on, words soon reached the queen mother and the queen, and they rushed down to his chambers. After almost five hours o f uncontrollable shaking, the king calmed a bit and uttered his first few words.

"The kingdom is in trouble."

Unfortunately, no one could make sense of these words. When asked to elaborate on his sentence, he resumed crying again.

"His Highness must be in shock. Isn't it time for the royal council to appoint someone else to fulfill the royal duties until he gets better?"The queen mother wondered to the utter surprise of everyone, including His Highness, but the queen did not waste time to shut down the idea.

"We don't need any interim ruler in his place. His Highness is not having a meltdown. He will explain what's going on soon."

After 24 hours, the king's condition did not improve. His aides and physicians became increasingly worried about his mental health status.

"He is suffering from an unexplained traumatic nightmare and panic attacks. He has only uttered a few words since yesterday," the physician explained to the royal family. As the royal physicians contemplated the appropriate treatment strategy, His Highness spoke up and assured everyone that he's fine.

"You are not well, Your Highness. You've been sobbing all day and unable to sleep in the last twenty-four hours," his chief aide retorted.

"I am fine, I am just shocked by the dream I had. Our nation is in perilous times. We need all the help we can get. We need to act quickly to avert the danger that lies ahead," he explained while fighting back tears.

Confused by his words and teary plea, the royal physician responded "Your Highness, we don't understand what you mean by trouble. Could you elaborate further?"

"There is a pending danger that has been determined against this kingdom. We will be in trouble if we don't act as fast as possible. I need you to send word to all royal officials and members of my family. I need to address them this evening."

"Your Excellency, what danger has been determined against our people? Who are the people behind this danger?" the royal physician asked as he sought to assess the king's mental state.

"I will speak when we have everyone here. We need to do something to avert this pending crisis, else, this kingdom won't survive the next twenty years," he explained with a sense of urgency to the dismay of those around him.

The chief physician and his team dissuaded His Highness from holding any meeting in his current state to avert the risk of any public embarrassment if the incident of the last 24 hours was anything to go by. They reasoned that if the meeting with the royal officials goes sideways and he appears incoherent, it could trigger a major power tussle within the royal family. Despite their disapproval, his aides convened an emergency royal cabinet meeting which was to be held in his home that same evening. The senior officials wondered what could have been going on with His Highness to have ordered for a meeting in his personal quarters.

At 7:00 pm, the royal o f f i ci a l s convened as requested. But the king did not arrive until one hour later. In his chambers, the royal physician and the queen tried to persuade him, one more time, to postpone the meeting, but he would not listen to any of them.

"He is in no shape to give any coherent speech to anyone tonight. Your excellency, you can as well kiss your husband's reign goodbye after tonight if there is a public meltdown before the cabinet," his chief aide explained to the queen. When he finally joined the meeting, he was in his sleepwear, with unshaved stubble, and without any make-up. The entire cabinet was surprised at the appearance of His Highness.

"My people, we are in a perilous time in our nation's history. If we don't do something, our nation will be non-existent in the next twenty years," he tearfully announced while shaking uncontrollably. But his words made no sense to the royal officials and military generals.

"What danger are we in? What's going on, Your Highness? Is there some high-level information you have that we are not privy to? The officials asked. But the king confused and unable to answer any of the questions from the officials. With a known history of erratic behaviors, the cabinet officials discussed among themselves whether the king was having another emotional breakdown. It was not long before some in the cabinet began to suggest that the king should be replaced.

"Enough!!!" the king snarled at the audience. "I am well and not insane as many of you might have thought. Two nights ago, I had a vision of what is to become of this kingdom in the next twenty years. I know most of you think that I am emotionally unstable and sick, but I tell you that the Nubian Kingdom will go into extinction if we don't do something." he warned. Then he went on to describe his dream.

"It was a sunny afternoon as I walked barefooted along the banks of the Nubia River. As I looked inland, I saw the entire Nubian landscape full of dense green vegetation supported by a rich, black earth. I have never seen any land so rich and prosperous like that before. The Nubia River also overflowed its banks with lots of fishes and other aquatic animals. I was proud and elated about the prosperity of this kingdom. While I was still processing this beautiful sight, I saw a desert storm move in from the north and rolled through the lands. Instantly, the Nubia River was filled with floating dead aquatic lives that brought a strong stench along the banks. The stench was so bad that I had to walk away from the riverbank and turn inland where I had an aerial view of the destruction and death brought about by the storm as it moved over all the lands of Nubia. I wailed as I watched the horror of the devastation of the dense vegetation while hunger and disease ravaged the land leaving destruction and hopelessness in their wake. As I looked further, I saw men and women wailing in anguish as they accused me of doing nothing until the destruction claimed their loved ones. I saw many malnourished Nubians gather on the steps of the royal court to protest the destruction that is ravaging the land. They continued to protest vigorously shouting "Death to the royals!" while raining curses on me and other officials for several days. While they protested, they threw stones and mobilized others to destroy the royal court and all aristocrats in the land. It was not long before the protesters overpowered the royal guards and rushed into the court grounds. Some ran into the royal kitchen to scavenge available food, some ran into the throne hall to desecrate the throne, while others looted royal treasures and artifacts. Unable to locate the members of the royal family and other royal officials, more protesters arrived with rock boulder catapults as they built a hedge around the royal court. I cringed in horror as I watched the catapulted boulders destroy the royal edifices in the royal court. The most agonizing part was watching the entire structure collapse on members of my family and many of you and your families who had taken refuge in the underground royal vault. I kept screaming until I woke up only to realize it was a dream. My people, this may sound alarmist to you, but the horror and the destruction I witnessed may come to pass if we don't do something about it."

An abrupt silence enveloped the room for a while as the officials and service chiefs realized that the king is not insane as they initially thought. Aksah, who was the head of the Nubian Treasury got up and politely questioned His Highness's rationale and plea.

"Your Highness, I don't doubt your dream at all, but I don't understand what you want us to do differently that we have not done. You would remember that our economists have forecasted that we are due for another economic correction within the next decade. I wonder if your dream is only buttressing these recent economic forecasts."

"Not at all, Aksah. I believe that the forecasted recession is only a tip of the iceberg of impending trouble. We need a more comprehensive action strategy on how to avert this danger."

"What kind of action plan do you want us to come up with?" Another cabinet member asked.

His highness stuttered and rambled on for a while: "Uh... uh... we need to come up with a strategy to save the nation. Erm... erm, perhaps we can start the "Operation Save

Nubia" campaign. We need to start tonight, right now."

The cabinet officials were flustered and at loss for words on what action plan the king wanted.

"Your highness, we know that this is a matter of national security, but we are not equipped to start work right away. Besides, we are in your home. We don't have any of our permanent secretaries and aides to brainstorm with us. Can we reconvene tomorrow to deliberate on this matter?" Akhousta, the minister of agriculture, asked.

"No. No. No. We are starting tonight. This council consists of some of the brightest and the smartest experts in intelligence, wisdom, and power in this land. Are you saying that all of you cannot come up with a single idea that will save my kingdom from extinction in two decades? You men should get to it because no one is leaving here until we come up with a plan.".

Seeing that His Highness refused to be reasonable, the officials resigned to the fact that they were going to spend the night in his Chambers.

After about 6 hours of back-and-forth deliberation about the dream, its meaning, and the strategy to save the nation, the king became frustrated by the lack of progress. He flew into a fit of rage cursing all his cabinet officials, calling them names while breaking royal artifacts in frustration.

"Since you cannot think without your aides, I think I should just sack all of you right away and replace you all with your aides who think for you!" he railed against his cabinet as they watched in silence. While His Highness continued to nervously pace up and down while mulling his next decision, the queen mother entered the meeting chamber and scolded her son.

"Son, you've put your officials through a lot in the last 7 hours. They have been deprived of sleep, food, and an intellectually stimulating environment to work. Despite these deprivations, you have tortured these brilliant minds to produce innovative ideas in this cramped small chamber of yours. Come on, I taught you hospitality better than this." After thinking this through for a while, he ordered the postponement of the meeting.

"Alright, you are all free to return to your homes this morning. I give you all thirty days to find me a concrete strategy to save this kingdom. Otherwise, you will all be executed and hanged at the steps of the royal court. You will be replaced by those personal aides who have been doing your jobs for you these years." The king announced as the royal officials stood shell shocked. This new decree threw the officials into a frenzy as they sought to find a solution to the problem.

Weeks after, we noticed the prolonged absence of the director from the prison, but no one odared ask what was going on. When I finally asked the chief security guard, he admitted not to have all the details. He admitted to hearing a rumor that there is commotion in the corridors of power. We later learned that His Highness had scheduled the public execution of all royal officials if they do not come up with an idea that can save the nation in less than four weeks. We all wondered what could have warranted such a drastic decision from His Highness. During those four weeks, the royal officials brought in different experts, including scientists, mediums, astrologers, and anyone who had any viable idea that can save the nation and, most importantly, their lives. Of the several ideas they came up with, only four were presented to His Highness. However, he rejected the four proposals on the basis that they were not comprehensive enough.

During the final week before the deadline, the director stopped by the office to pack his belongings as the officials made one final push to request for me time to find a solution. When I learned he was around, I rushed to his office to check on him.

"Good afternoon sir, it's been a while you were here. I learned about the trouble you and other royal officials have been facing for the past few weeks. Is there any way I can be of help, sir?"

"Zeph, I have no time to attend to anything you want me to deal with now," he dismissively replied with his face buried in the piles of paperwork and boxes.

"Sir, I am not asking for anything. I just want to know how I can be of help."

"You should stop disturbing me. You can be of help by managing the prison instead of belaboring me with stupid questions," he roared as he hurriedly left for another cabinet meeting.

Disappointed that he won't even give me an audience, I trudged back to my cell.

"Zeph, you don't have to blame the man, you know. There is nobody that will behave rationally after learning they have barely a week to live. I know you mean well." the security chief called out as I walked away. After a second thought, I turned back and decided to ask the security chief what he knew.

"My chief, thanks for the encouragement. I was just thinking about how to help the director, but I can see that he does not need my help. I am wondering if you know the problem the cabinet officials are trying to solve." I asked.

"Zeph, it's way above your clearance level. Only the most powerful people in the kingdom are privy to the information." he replied brusquely.

"Try me, sir. You know I enjoy problem-solving. You've seen me in action these last few years here. If there is anything, you know full well that this prison is a microcosm of life above this dungeon." I insisted.

After thinking about my request and checking to see if there were others around who might eavesdrop on our conversation, he agreed.

"Alright, why don't you stop by my office in the next hour and I can share the problem with you." About an hour later, I peeped into his office and found him waiting for me.

"Welcome Zeph, please come in and bolt the door behind you."

"Thank you, sir. I appreciate this."

"The secret I want to share with you today is only known by a few powerful people in the kingdom. Please keep this to yourself alone." Then, he narrated the saga about the king's dream, his frustration with the royal officials, the royal decree, and the officials' desperate efforts to present a sustainable and acceptable proposal to the king.

"They will be executed in a few days if they don't come up with a solution."

"My chief, I want to thank you for explaining the situation to me. This is not in any way a small matter at all. I have just been thinking about how I can help the officials. Now that I know the whole story, I will think about it and see if I can come up with a solution." I affirmed.

"Forget about it, Zeph! Even our best scientists and astrologers could not come up with an acceptable proposal, let alone you."

"Well, you never know. God may give a solution that trumps any of those previously developed ideas." I replied as I returned to my cell.

Later that night, I had a strange feeling that this might be my season of freedom, but I was too scared to hope for my emancipation. Instead, I prayed about the king's dream and meditated on what it might mean. Few hours after praying and meditating on the dream, I understood the king's dream. The dense green vegetation, black earth and the booming aquatic life in the Nubia River signifies the season of abundant economic prosperity in Nubia while the wave of destruction represents the season of global economic collapse that will completely wipe out the gains of the economic boom and lead to the collapse of several kingdoms. Then I realized that His Highness was not insane as many people had thought. He understood that the pending economic disaster would lead to the collapse of his kingdom. Hence, the reason people around him could not comprehend his sense of urgency about this.

I spent the night thinking and praying about this pending interpretation and the best way to avert this danger.

The next morning, I facilitated the Hope Re-ignition sessions and later had a discussion with the procurement officers and security guards about the low inventory of food supplies for the prison. When I inquired about how soon we should expect the supplies, I was told that it might take more than a month because of the recent flooding of the farms and the supplier's lack of a storehouse to store excess grain. Shortly after I left the meeting, it dawned on me that investments in agriculture and harvest management might be our only way out. Throughout that day, I mulled over the idea, penned my thoughts on a scroll, and critiqued the idea repeatedly for a while. As the days passed, I became convinced that this idea was the winning formula, but I had no courage to declare that I had the solution. About two days before the scheduled execution of the royal officials, the security chief met me on the corridor and asked about my plan to find a solution.

"Zeph, didn't you claim you could help by coming up with an idea? The director will be executed in two days, and I feel so powerless," he sighed in exasperation.

"Yes sir, I came up with an idea which I am sure will be a solution to the problem, but I just don't know if the director will believe me enough to put his life in my hands."

"Well, what choice does he have, knowing that he has only 2 days left? Why don't you let me reach out to him and see if he can hear your idea?"

"Alright sir, it will be great if you can convince him."

Later that evening, the guards came to inform me that the director was waiting for me in his office. When I got there, he appeared distressed and hopeless, with unkempt hair and a shabby appearance. It was obvious that he had been sleep-deprived for days.

"Zeph, I learned you have a solution for us. I want to hear it," he desperately asked.

"Sir, I have an idea that I cannot share with you or other cabinet officials now. I must see the king before I share this idea. I believe only he can understand the idea and I am sure he will be convinced."

Surprised by my demand, he resisted at first, but later changed his mind after realizing that he had nothing else to lose.

"Sit tight, I will let other officials know and we will arrange an audience with His Highness."

I could not sleep that night; I nervously paced up and down my cell rehearsing my speech to His Highness and praying for a favor. I knew this was my only shot at freedom and I must maximize this opportunity.

Around 6:00 am the next day, the royal guards arrived as I was facilitating one of the early Hope Re-ignition sessions.

"Zeph, your presence is needed in the royal court," they announced. The inmates were all afraid and could not understand why the king would send for me, but I assured everyone that all will be well. I was escorted out of the prison by the royal guards into a waiting royal chariot. On our way to the royal court, the escorting royal guard gave me a piece of advice.

"When you get to the palace, I suggest that you just come out clean to the officials if you don't have a concrete solution. Don't lie before his Royal Highness; he is a god who discerns falsehood very easily. He's really on edge these days and you don't want to join the royal officials on the gallows tomorrow."

I thanked the man for his advice and assured him that I am confident in my ideas and that everyone will come to appreciate my proposed solutions.

It was clear to me that this is my only shot at freedom and that I must take it well. I thought about every royal court protocol Master Banga ever taught me in the General's villa. "Appearances and substance are everything in Nubia," he would say. Also, I rehearsed my introductory speech and presentation of my proposed solutions.

When we arrived at the royal court, I was met by the royal officials who were eager to meet with me. "Zeph, thank you for volunteering to come up with an idea, but we want you to tell us about your proposal to the king. The director mentioned that you had insisted that only His Highness can hear and understand your proposal. However, we want to be assured that your idea is good enough." While they explained, my gaze fell on General Aziz and many of his friends for whom I had previously worked begging for my help.

"Your excellencies, indeed, I have a proposed solution for his Highness, but I cannot share my idea before meeting him. You will hear the solutions when I stand before him and you can judge whether it is enough or not."

I have worked too well with these aristocrats to ever share any idea with any of them. If I do, they will take credit and I'll lose my only shot at freedom. Having seen that I was not ready to shift grounds, they agreed to the plan because they were desperate to save their lives.

After my brief interaction with the officials, I requested for some time to prepare. I was taken to the royal quarters where I requested for new Nubian clothes, worthy of Nobiin's presence. Instead of being prepped for Nobiin's presence by royal servants, I demanded to personally dress myself for the occasion. I bathed, shaved my head and beards, chose the right clothes for the occasion, and supervised my makeup. The royal guards were surprised that I knew the royal protocols and etiquettes; even my outfit wowed the royal fashion experts. When I was ready, I was escorted into the waiting room near the throne room. While there, I tried to rehearse in my mind, the royal protocols Master Banga taught me. The royal officials also stopped by to check on me. After waiting for an hour, I heard the trumpets and music being played to herald the arrival of His Highness to the throne hall.

Shortly after, I was informed that His Highness demands my presence. I was escorted into the throne hall where I found the royal officials and the noble men of Nubia ready to hear from me. As I entered, I paid obeisance seven times as customary of Nubian citizens. My eyes darted around the hall where almost all the powerful people in Nubia stood eager to hear my idea. The king was a tall, dark stout man adorned with a golden crown, a purple robe, and a chain made from several precious stones. He stared sternly at me before turning to the royal officials with a stare that questioned their choice of an immigrant for the job.

"Young man, I was told that you have a solution that can save my kingdom."

"Of course, your Highness. I am confident that we can find a workable solution for the issues that bother you," I replied as I made obeisance again. His Highness not only doubted my ability to proffer a lasting solution to the problems, but he was also disappointed that his trusted officials could not find a solution within the 30-day period.

"Royal officials, I hope you are all aware that this is your fifth and last time to present your ideas before your execution tomorrow. Let's hope this young man can save your lives and, perhaps, save the kingdom." He jeered.

"My Lord, you would not need to execute any of your officials tomorrow after you have listened to me. By the way, I am not sure if you have thought through the consequences of executing all your officials including military generals, experts, and leaders who have helped your kingdom run smoothly. Your kingdom will collapse even before your doomsday prophecy comes to pass." I shot back in an attempt to get his attention. The king and the noble men standing there were shocked by the insightful, but stern critique of the king's decree from a young immigrant. Everyone expected His Highness to fly into another fit of rage, but they were surprised by his silence and perceived calmness as he thought about my response. Seeing that I had everyone's attention, I seized the moment to begin my speech.

"Your Highness, I learned about your dream recently. I believe that your dream is a prophecy about the future of this kingdom. I can relate to your sense of urgency and your desperation to save this beautiful kingdom. The green dense vegetation and the booming aquatic lives that you saw in your dream signify a coming season of unprecedented economic prosperity, but this season will not last forever. It will be succeeded by a terrible season of global famine and economic collapse that will destroy several kingdoms, including yours. Many lives will be lost during this economic destruction and many people will rise against the royal family out of frustration, hopelessness, and hunger if you don't act now. You are right that these events might happen within the next two decades, but there is a way out."

After I paused for a while, His Highness and I locked gazes with each other for what seemed like forever, but was just a couple of minutes.

"You should continue. What's the way out of this crisis?" He tersely replied with a stern stare at me.

"Your Highness, we cannot punch our way through this crisis. We need to return to the basics - agriculture. The Nubian kingdom used to be the breadbasket of this region, thanks to the fertile coastal regions of the Nubia River and the savannah vegetation to the northwest, and the rain forest to the southwest. In recent decades. We have abandoned our core strengths in exchange for civilization and other technological advances. May I suggest to your Highness and noble men in this hall that you need to appoint a wise and experienced administrator who will spearhead an agricultural campaign across this beautiful kingdom? Such a person should have unlimited powers to collect grains produced during the economic boom and stockpile them across all the cities in this Kingdom. The stored grain will sustain the kingdom through the famine. In this way, the kingdom won't be devastated by the famine." I politely advised as I once again made obeisance.

The king and the noble were stunned by my assessment of the problem, my recommended solutions, and knowledge of Nubia.

"Young man, who are you? Where did you say you come from?" His Highness asked as he processed what he had just heard.

"My Lord, I am an immigrant slave kidnapped and trafficked to Nubia as a teenager. General Aziz paid for my Bill of Sale and I was his aide for years before I was sentenced to prison for misappropriation of funds - a crime I did not commit."

" For the very first time, I see someone who truly shares the same sense of urgency about this dream. I am impressed by your articulate understanding of this land and the idea you have laid out." He replied after meditating for a while.

"How long did you say you have been in my kingdom?"

"Thirteen years, my Lord; I arrived as a 17-year-old in the slave market."

His Highness was silent for a while as he continued to process my ideas. There was palpable tension in the hall, and everyone wondered what his conclusion would be. Having studied his body language, I was confident that the king was seriously considering my idea as a viable solution.

I seized the moment to survey noble men there and take in the magnificence of the throne hall. When I turned briefly towards General Aziz's direction, I could see that he was very uncomfortable with my explanation of the situation and his expression was quite apologetic, but I could care less now. After what seemed like a half-hour-long silence, His Highness announced that he had decided to cancel the execution of his cabinet officials. There was a huge sigh of relief as the officials congratulated themselves in excitement.

Then he ordered everyone to leave the hall, except me. The royal officials departed from the hall congratulating each other and excited that their execution had been cancelled.

When I was left alone with His Highness, he stared at me for a long time.

"Why did you truly end up in prison?"

Then I explained my role in General Aziz's villa and my contributions to his success before describing the unfortunate encounter with Mrs. Aziz. I seized the moment to declare my innocence as a man of integrity citing my accomplishments and successes as an administrator in the General's villa and the prison.

"Rumilat, could you send out the team to confirm this young man's story?" His Highness ordered his personal aide.

"Alright, sir. We will confirm right away." Rumilat nodded in agreement.

"I have known Aziz and his wife for more than three decades," he interjected as his gestures seem to question the veracity of my claim.

His Highness then asked for details about my proposed solution. After sharing my big picture idea, we brainstormed on how to prepare for the coming prosperity and challenges bound to arise because of the impending famine.

"Your Highness, every challenge presents a unique opportunity. If we can adequately prepare for this pending disaster, Nubia can become the most powerful nation on earth." Over the following three hours, His Highness and I discussed a wide range of matters including politics, the economy, agriculture, science, and international relations.

"I like you, Zeph! Your impeccable eloquence and command of our language, vast knowledge of our history and national issues, keen insight about existing and emerging opportunities, and your humility are quite remarkable for a young man of your age. I cannot believe that you have been in a dungeon for this long."

Then he revealed his intention to appoint me as the administrator to lead the kingdom through the pending economic boom and bust.

"I have pondered on your idea and it appears it is the best idea I have heard so far, but I cannot think of anyone else well-equipped and prepared to lead the kingdom through this challenging time in our history. You will be my second-in-command and will have unilateral powers constitutionally to make sweeping changes in our nation. Is that something you will be interested in taking on?"

Astonished by such a decision, I fell to my knees in tears for a while and then paid obeisance to the king before accepting his offer.

"Come on Zeph, you have so much work to do. You can process your emotions later. You are now a free man." His Highness declared as he invited me to sit next to him. I got up from my knees and looked around the throne room to appreciate the opulence and exquisiteness of the throne hall before taking my seat next to him.

Then we discussed the next steps following my appointment. His Highness outlined some of the political implications of his decisions for the kingdom.

"Zeph, you need to know that this seat has never existed until now. So, you are going to face unprecedented challenges with my people, my family, and even internationally. They will resent your appointment and might even take up arms to protest what they consider a national insult. This decision will upset the balance of power and royal succession. I am saying all these to prepare you for what is to come," he pensively explained.

"Here are the next steps for us. First, I will invite the royal officials and the entire General Council back to the throne hall to formally announce your appointment. Second, you will ride with me in my royal chariot to the public square where I will officially announce your appointment after which, we will ride together across the city. Third, I will introduce you to the key members of my family. I am sure that they will seethe in anger about my decision which I will need to explain to them as calmly as I can. You will need to be patient with them because it will take them some time to warm up to you. Finally, we'll need to arrange a marriage for you with either one of the aristocratic families or the religious order." As he outlined these steps, Rumilat took notes and wrote decrees which were to be signed by His Highness.

In the meantime, the king invited me into his office where we continued our discussion while Rumilat assembled the general council for the formal announcement. His office was the most beautiful chamber I have ever seen. After the council had assembled, Rumilat came in to inform us that the council was ready for us.

"By the way sir, the team has just sent me word that they have confirmed his excellency's story. Indeed, he was framed by madam Aziz and her goons to take the fall for her misappropriation of business funds. He is innocent of the charges leveled against him. His excellency is known in the upper echelons of the kingdom to be industrious, productive, and a proven leader. His story checks out."

"Thank you, Rumilat. That will be all for now."

I was surprised but also happy that "the Team" was able to corroborate my story and exonerate me as I quietly wondered who "the Team" was and how they could have confirmed my story so quickly.

Then, the trumpeters and the musicians played to herald our arrival into the throne hall. As His Highness made his grand entrance, everyone in the hall made obeisance until he took his seat on the throne. After acknowledging the council, His Highness asked me to step forward. Then he looked around the hall and expressed his disappointment at his royal officials and the general council who, despite their brilliance and impeccable qualifications, could not proffer solutions to an urgent problem that could threaten the survival of the kingdom. Then he called out General Aziz and the prison director"

"I am shocked to learn today that there is a man in my kingdom that could solve problems, and I never knew about him. Even more shocking is the fact that you also went as far as to unjustly incarcerate him and used him to your own advantage."

The prison director went on his knees and apologized: "Your Highness, I am very sorry sir. I did not have any clue that he was unjustly incarcerated, but I took very good care of him in the prison. He oversaw the famous Hope Re-ignition program and ran the affairs of the prison under my supervision. I was the one who recommended him to you, sir.

"What do you have to say Aziz?" His Highness asked.

"My Lord, it is true that I wrongly accused Zeph and unjustly incarcerated him because I was misled by my wife and the witnesses. My household and businesses have not been the same since I sentenced him to prison. I apologize for this error in judgement." General Aziz confessed.

"Zeph, could you please forgive me?" General Aziz confessed.

"This same man whom you have maltreated, tortured, and unjustly incarcerated saved your lives today and holds the key to future of our kingdom. I believe this is the man we need for the hour to lead us through the most perilous time in our kingdom," he announced.

The officials reluctantly applauded his decision unaware

of what His Highness was about to do. Then, he turned to me and formally announced my appointment as his prime minister and second-in-command, giving me unilateral powers to run the kingdom. The general council members were stunned and murmured against the royal decision. Seeing the reluctance in the audience, the king got up and asked:

"Is there someone else that feels more qualified or suited for this job description than Zeph? If you know anyone, kindly let me know right now."

As the hush fell on the council, His highness removed his signet ring and slipped it into my finger. He ordered that I should be dressed in royal purple apparel and adorned with an exquisite chain made out of precious stones. Then, hee gave me the royal scroll that confirms my appointment as the second-most powerful man in the kingdom. All the members of the general council made obeisance to me and each one of them, including General Aziz, came forward to kiss my signet ring, a sign of acknowledgment of my superiority and leadership.

The news of my appointment rocked Buhen and spread like forest inferno across the kingdom of Nubia. The news of my appointment also rocked the royal family, leading to an emergency royal family meeting where they sought to convince Nobiin to change his mind. The family meeting had many senior royals in attendance, including the queen mother, his twin brother and other siblings, the queen, and his older children.

"His Highness must have been bewitched by a strange deity to have appointed an inmate as his second-in-command," they reasoned.

However, the royal messengers arrived to announce that the king had postponed the meeting with his family.

"He will meet with you later today, with Zeph in attendance." The messenger announced.

"There we go again. Did I not mention this early on? You see, my son is bewitched," the queen mother retorted, dismayed by the king's violation of royal protocol.

That same day, His Highness and I rode together in his chariot to the public square where I was accorded full military and royal honors that included music and military parade. His Highness addressed the citizens about his vision to revive the economy and build a lasting Nubian empire based on his administration's commitment to agriculture, innovation, and technology. Then he introduced me to the people as the technocrat to lead the nation through this change after which he invited me to give a short speech. In my speech, I emphasized the unprecedented challenges that faced Nubia and the need to pull together to plan for the period of prosperity and the times of challenges. Using my improbable "grass-to-grace" story, I preached hope and gave inspiration to the audience while extolling the patriotic values of the Nubian kingdom. We later rode through the city as the entire capital city celebrated by appointment.

Shortly after we returned to the royal court, His Highness and I had a tense meeting with members of his family who were already aggrieved for being blind-sided by such a decision. His Highness explained my role as a technocrat tasked with growing the Nubian economy and reassured them that his succession plan would not be hindered by my appointment, but all of them were dismissive of his ideas.

" Welcome, Zeph. His Highness mentioned that you are a technocrat. Could you let me know which institution and under which philosophers you trained?" the queen mother asked to the embarrassment of the king.

"Your excellency, I did not have formal training in any of the royal business schools neither did I train under any famous philosopher, but I was the personal aide of General Aziz and I was trained by Master Banga who was his chief aide. I worked with the General for nearly a decade and was responsible for managing his businesses, which I grew into multiple chains of industry-leading businesses. You must have heard about Mrs. Aziz, the fashion mogul, who owns several chains of businesses across Nubia. I helped start and grow her businesses. As a technocrat, I bring cross-industry expertise in business development, strategy, investment banking, project management, and consulting." I politely explained to the surprise of the royal family members.

"A technocrat or an ex-convict? You are nothing but a fraud and gold-digger who has bewitched our husband." the queen quipped. The king was enraged as members of his family cast aspersions on my character and hurled insults at me in his presence. After he motioned for silence, I asked for the opportunity to respond to the queen and other hecklers.

"Your excellencies, you are right! I am an ex-convict

because I was an innocent man sent to jail for a crime I knew nothing about. I was sent to jail without any trial, because I was an immigrant with no wherewithal to hire an advocate, but I am not a fraud. You must have learned about the famous Hope Re-ignition transformational program in many correctional services across Nubia. The program was my brainchild and I led the design and implementation of that program under the leadership of the prison director. Through the program, we reduced the national recidivism rate by more than 60%, inmate violence by 75%, suicide rate by 50%, and improved inmate productivity by 50%. You can check the records. So, I have been super productive as a slave and even more inspiring as a convict. I believe I have what it takes to grow Nubia's economy into the most powerful nation in the world. I have no interest or desire to be a royal, I serve at His Royal Majesty's pleasure."

Members of the royal family were stunned by my eloquence, professional experience, and insight into economic issues and were speechless to ask any further questions.

"Well, that is enough for today's introductory meeting. Zeph will be available to answer more questions later." His Highness announced as he rose from the throne. Words soon reached the crown prince, who was away on international duties. Enraged and disappointed, he headed back to Nubia intending to fight what he considered an attempted coup to rob him of his inheritance.

My grass-to-grace story became an inspiration for several slaves, foreigners, and less privileged people in Nubia. There was a week-long celebration of my appointment in the royal prison and there were jubilations among the household staff of General Aziz. However, many of the mainstream Nubians felt that the eccentric king had lost his mind to "surrender" power to a slave and a foreigner to Nubian traditions and culture.

CHAPTER 7

The day of my appointment as the prime minister of the Nubia kingdom marked the first day of the rest of my life. After a long day of meetings, I was left alone with the most powerful, eccentric, and most dangerous man in the kingdom.

"Zeph, it's been a long day. My servants have prepared one of the international guest houses for you pending the time they will build a new villa befitting of a prime minister for you. If you are not satisfied with it, Rumilat will arrange for a better villa for you." His Highness explained before he departed.

When I finally entered that furnished guest house, I could not believe that such a huge, well-furnished house befitting of kings would be my home. All the staff and aides in that guest house paid obeisance while I watched and struggled to curtail my emotions.

"My Lord, welcome to your temporary apartment while your official residence is being built. I am Amram, your newly appointed domestic chief aide. With me are forty domestic servants with specialized skills and several years of experience providing total care for elite members of the royal family. We are here at your service."

Seeing that I needed time to process the events of the previous twenty-four hours, I dismissed the household staff for the night. When I was alone, I walked around the house as I reflected on my sudden change in fortune. The previous night I slept in the dungeon as a prisoner and 24 hours later, I was the second most powerful man in the Nubia kingdom. I sat one one of the luxurious sofas overcome with emotion and not knowing what to do next. So, I cried, sang, danced, and jumped for joy around that villa for hours to soak in my new reality. After thoroughly reflecting on the events of that day, the reality of the enormous task of leading a nation through prosperity and famine began to dawn on me. Yet, I found strength and hope through the challenges I had faced during the last 13 years in Nubia.

I woke up the next day to the sound of melodious music near the doors of my chamber. When I stepped out of my chambers, I found the music band playing near the door. After asking what was going on, they all made obeisance and politely explained the culture of the palace in which royalties must wake up to the sound of soft music of their choice. I did not learn about this in General Aziz's villa. This is just excessive, I thought to myself. I dismissed the servants citing the need for my privacy while I returned to my room to plan for the day. Confused and dismayed by my repudiation of the music, Amram returned with another set of musicians and made obeisance while apologizing for the poor music played by the previous cohort of servants.

"Sir, we are here to provide a satisfying service of whatever kind you desire. I understand that you did not appreciate the services rendered by the previous cohort of musicians. I have brought even more experienced musicians to replace them. Also, the maidens who will clean your room and prepare you for the day are here, sir." he politely requested. Even though I was trained in royal etiquettes and services, I could not come to terms with receiving these services for myself. I dismissed all the services offered, requested to be left alone, and ordered Amram to get my food ready. Rather than being bathed, I preferred to take care of my personal grooming. When I finally stepped out of my chambers all dressed and ready for the day, my household staff and the servants were shell shocked. Amram approached and bowed at my feet to plead for the lives of the household staff, but I could not understand what was going on.

"We are sorry, your excellency! Please have mercy."

"You have not offended me in any way. What's going on?"

"Your excellency, dressing up by yourself is a violation of royal protocol and dereliction of duty on our part. We want you to know that this gaffe will not repeat itself."

"You do not need to worry about me dressing up by myself. In fact I prefer to do this myself."

"Your excellency it's not that simple, sir. Dressing up by yourself is tantamount to gross negligence of our duties. The punishment is a death sentence according to the royal constitution."

"Oh, now I get it. Get up, everyone. You have all behaved excellently well, but it will take me some time to get used to all of these. Besides, I don't need these excessive royal vanities right now, considering that I have got quite a lot of administrative work before me in this new role."

"Alright, sir. We'll do as your excellency pleases."

"By the way, you all have strategic roles in helping fulfill my mission. You need to return to your duties while I get ready for the meeting with His Highness," I added.

"Thank you, your excellency," they chorused in unison as they trudged back to their posts.

I spent that morning in a meeting with His Highness where I outlined my plans to prepare the nation for the coming economic prosperity. On top of my agenda was the need to travel across Nubia with royal town planners and agriculture experts to survey the arable land of Nubia, and other information that can inform capacity building that will optimize the anticipated economic gains.

"Zeph, you have the sweeping powers to accomplish your goals. You don't need to check in with me every day. I trust your ideas completely."

I sent for the chief town planner and the minister of agriculture, shortly after meeting with Nobiin. In my meeting with them, I shared my vision for Nubia and the important roles they will play in the plan. About a month later we embarked on a two-month tour of the Nubian cities along the Nubia River, the desert lands in the northern region of Nubia, and the forests to the south west near the borders with the people of Ethiopia and Kush.

While I was away from the royal court, the crown prince returned from the battlefront, having learned about my appointment. After throwing tantrums publicly by breaking sculptures in the royal gardens, he stormed into the queen's chambers to discuss with his mother after which he demanded an audience with the king. His Highness was excited to welcome his son, but he was surprised at how quickly he returned from the battlefront. After welcoming his dear and favorite son, His Highness asked for progress on the battlefront, but the crown prince was not in the mood for details.

"Your Highness, I heard rumors while away that you recently appointed a stranger to be a prime minister of Nubia, but I immediately dismissed the rumor as one of your enemies' attempts to paint you as incompetent, misguided, and foolish." he sarcastically explained.

His Highness, in turn, smiled and confirmed the news was not a rumor. At this point, Prince Nublin exploded in a fit of rage as he claimed my appointment has robbed him of his birthright as his father's successor.

"Son, I am disappointed by your continued demonstration of foolishness through your lack of self-control and short-sightedness. The appointment of Zeph was not to usurp the balance of power or the succession plan I drafted. He is here to strengthen the kingdom."

Despite all reassurances from the king, the crown prince remained unconvinced.

"You need to meet Zeph. He's a man filled with wisdom and solutions from the gods. I am sure you will get along with him when he arrives."

"Father, I can never work with that ex-convict. I will make sure that he won't last long here." He spat as he stormed out of the palace in anger. Frustrated by the prince's failure to accept his decision, the king added a secret security detail to keep an eye on me.

While away on the trip, I learned a lot from Akhousta, the director of Agriculture, and Ajala, the Chief Officer of City Planning, about the national resources available for our program. Akhousta outlined the cutting-edge agricultural expertise and various innovative and top-level agricultural innovations our nation has under wraps and are only made available to the royal farm alone. These include crop breeding technology, prototypes of insecticides, and new agricultural technologies under development. It was clear to the three of us that we would need to make the expertise and the techniques available to small-scale and subsistence farmers for us to reap the gains of the season of economic prosperity. I also turned to Ajala, to ask about the best places to situate the store towers, but he was ambivalent with his responses.

"My professional opinion is that we should strategically build the towers in strategic cities across the kingdom to ensure even distribution. However, this might not be a welcome idea by members of the royal family who might feel otherwise." he explained. When I probed further, he explained that situating the store towers near the capital will lead to traffic congestion which might put the royal family at risk during the famine. Even our enemies might seek to attack the store towers.

On the other hand, he thought that the royal family might consider our plan to build the towers across Nubia as a power play aimed at decentralizing their political power.

Akhousta also agreed with this perspective that any attempt to share the royal farming expertise with the subsistence farmer will be considered as a political move by the royal family. While we all agreed that those two ideas will anchor our plan to prepare and optimize the anticipated economic boom, we concluded that we would need to sell these ideas to Nobiin and other senior royal officials in Nubia to get their buy-in. We spent most of the travel time brainstorming on how best to prepare. By the end of the tour, our next line of action was clear. We needed to develop a national agricultural policy for all the cities along the Nubian River. This policy would mandate royal scientists, soil scientists, engineers, plant scientists, botanists, and economists in the employ of His Highness, to work with farmers on seed management and soil management to enhance crop yield all year round. With Ajala's help, we identified strategic cities and towns where we would build the food storage towers. As we headed back to Nubia, an entourage of royal guards arrived to join us and accompany us back to Nubia. When I asked why the king would send us additional troops for our journey, "your security is of utmost importance to His Royal Majesty," they said. We arrived in Nubia two days later at night.

When I woke up the next morning, I spent some time thinking about my villa's staff. For over three months since I was appointed, there had not been any clarity from me about my wants and what kind of services they need to provide. As a former servant myself, I knew that Amram had no clue on how best to mobilize his team to serve me. While I did not want to let him go, I knew that the status quo won't change until I had time to meet with them. Unfortunately, I had little or no time to even meet with them. After giving this some thought, I decided to address them just before heading out that morning. As I stepped out of my chambers, I overheard two servants conversing in the corridor. They expressed their concern about my "erratic behavior" and how this might spell their doom if the king finds out that I'm not being served according to royal protocols.

"I cannot understand our master in any way. He does not eat well and barely sleeps. Sometimes, he's moody and sometimes he is excited. All he cares and thinks about is his work," one servant said.

"In spite of his hard work, the royal family is still scheming on how to get rid of him. I hope he does not run himself to the ground because of these royal monsters who don't need any saving. I just worry that we don't find our heads on the gallows soon if His Highness finds out that we are not serving him well," the other servant sighed in exasperation.

After hearing this conversation, I realized that I need to treat these servants right and protect them as I should.

"Nothing will happen to you. I will protect you if you promise to do your jobs and stop gossiping." I interjected as I came out of my chambers. They were shocked and started pleading for their lives for gossiping about me and saying bad words about the royal family.

"You are forgiven, but you must know, I don't tolerate

gossip of any kind around me. I need to speak with Amram and every servant in this villa right now."

After they all gathered in the reception hall, I spoke to them from my heart. Sharing my life's journey and experience in Nubia, I sought to inspire them to be better versions of themselves while working in my house. I took the moment to share my vision for Nubia and pointed out the strategic roles that they play in helping achieve that vision of saving Nubia and saving millions of lives.

"Working in this house might involve waiting till late in the night, getting up very early in the morning, or even not being able to go home to your loved ones for days. I want you to know that all the unconventional services you offer are unique contributions to my vision of saving lives. In turn, I promise to protect you and your families as much as it is in my power. And when all is said and done you can look back and confidently say that you helped change the course of history by saving lives." Inspired and encouraged, they all bowed their knees and swore their allegiance to serve me faithfully.

Later that day, I reflected on the complex politics in the royal court and the potential challenges I could face in securing unanimous support for our programs. I mulled over ways to accomplish my goals despite the political impediments. I decided to hire a chief aide who knew the politics of the royal court, adept at handling information, and is an excellent communicator. Onan was the name that readily came to my mind. "Why don't you send for Onan who was your aide in Aziz's villa? After all, he knows and understands you more than many. By the way, he's also a Nubian." So, I sent a message to General Aziz requesting the immediate release of Onan who was my aide when I was his household master. I ordered my servants to treat Onan as my special guest upon his arrival and furnish a chamber for him.

Later that day, I had a meeting with all the wise men of Nubia who were knowledgeable about agriculture, engineering, town planning, and construction. I shared my vision with them and outlined the important roles that their expertise and experience would play in implementing our ideas. Specifically, I started the meeting by sharing Nobiin's dream, its interpretation, and political opportunities to save lives and turn Nubia into the most powerful nation on earth. Then I shared my plan which was to build several storehouses across Nubian cities where harvested grains will be stored and to discuss how we can develop a national policy that will mandate all farmers to grow crops, not only for their families, but also for the nation. Most of them found the ideas to be ambitiously brilliant, but untested and not feasible. It would take me few more hours to convince them that we could do it. While they were hesitant to support the idea, they proposed that we begin with a pilot program for all the phases of the project. After agreeing to their recommendation, I ordered the initiation of a pilot program that involved matching crop production experts from the royal farms with a few subsistence farmers across Nubia on improving soil management and crop yield. In the meantime, through inputs from the construction engineers, architects, and stone cutters, we developed a plan for the type of structures that will be used to preserve the grains. They would go on to research how best to build the structures that will allow for sufficient aeration for the stored grains to ensure long-lasting preservation.

Also, I commissioned a team of scientists who would research preservatives that can ensure the preservation of the harvested grains for at least a decade. This was a tall task for the scientists, many of whom thought that this could not be done. I reminded them that Nubia already has the science to embalm a body for three months, but no one was buying that analogy. Instead, these wise men debated among themselves. After listening to the scientific debates for a while, I decided to address them.

"Gentlemen and women, a few years ago, my mentor, who was the household manager for General Aziz's villa passed away. I remember that he was embalmed in the house for more than forty days before being buried. That tells me that Nubia has the science to preserve a dead body for at least 40 days. Can we just leverage this science to develop a preservative that can last for a decade?" I asked the scientists as they debated each other. There was silence in the room for a while and then their eyes brightened up after they saw the possibilities. After bringing everyone together, we commissioned these wise men and women to study how to develop preservatives for our grains. After almost a whole day of meeting and brainstorming, I ordered the writers to draft a communique documenting the conclusions from this meeting, the action points, and the responsibilities of the three commissioned teams - agriculture pilot program, storehouse construction, preservatives discovery. The three teams would update me on their progress every month or as at when due.

Just as we were about to wrap up the day-long meeting, the door of the conference hall swung open, and many royal guards rushed and took position with their weapons drawn. The crown prince entered the hall clapping his hands as he approached the high table where I was seated. He was a dark, about 6 feet 7 inches tall, with broad shoulders, oblong face, and thick stubble. He was dressed in his night robe and reeked of wine.

"Well... well... well... Zeph the slave, the ex-convict now the prime minister. What a world! You've played your game well, bewitching my father so much that he cannot even think on his own except to sing your praises all day." he barked.

Looking at my hand, he sneered derisively. "I can see that you are wearing my father's signet ring. I will end things for you before you begin. I am going to be your worst nightmare." he vituperated while standing right in my face. Every wise men and women in that hall stood up shocked at the crown prince's disregard for protocol and his shameful display. Unfazed by what anyone says, he proceeded to mess up some of the scrolls on the table after which he poured wine on the faces of some of the wise scientists around the table.

The royal guards with me were between the rock and hard place; their mandate was to protect me, but they also revere the crown prince. As he continued to denigrate the wise men and women in that hall, I stood up and lashed out at the crown prince in a harsh loud voice.

"Stop! What a shameless display of foolishness! A crown prince dressed in his night robe and reeking of wine at noon? What a disgraceful sight. Royalty is known to count for something - honor, respect, and class. You continue to drag royalty in the mud the way you throw tantrums, threaten innocent people, and even dishonor these noble men and women on whose wisdom your father has relied on for years to build this kingdom you call your inheritance. I would have asked the guards to throw you out if not for the honor and reverence I have for His Highness!"

As he tried to respond again, I shut down his babbling. "Your father, the wise (wo)men here, and I are busy brainstorming how to sustain Nubia through the coming famine and to grow the empire into the most powerful nation on earth so that you can inherit a stronger kingdom to govern, but you are here threatening to kill me. You can as well kiss the kingdom goodbye if you ever attempt to get rid of me. Now, if you don't have anything to contribute to this discussion, please get out of here right now, or else I will ask the royal guards to throw you out." I announced as I watched to see what his response would be.

Prince Nublin was shell-shocked to see someone stand up to him for the very first time.

"I promise I will still deal with you," he blabbed as he stormed out after realizing that he had embarrassed himself.

As his royal guards withdrew from the hall, the scientists and the other officials were surprised that I could stand up to the crown prince. I apologized to them on behalf of the royal family and ended the meeting as normally as I could. At the end of the meeting, I informed them that I will schedule a meeting with His Highness in which all of them will be in attendance.

I was still shaken by the confrontation with the prince and could not explain where the confidence to stand up to the bully came from. As I reflected on the confrontation, it was evident that I had underestimated the complex politics and power-mongering in the royal court. It became clear to me that my appointment fanned the flame of dissent, power-mongering, and infighting among several political camps. However, just before I left for my next meeting, one of the aides brought the message from my chief aide that Onan was no longer serving in Aziz's villa. He had been shipped to work as a slave in one of the construction sites and no one knew his whereabouts. The General sent a message that he was very sorry and that he would schedule an appointment with me to discuss. My heart sank as I wondered what could have happened to Onan. I was infuriated that Onan would be treated in such a manner. I sent back a message to General Aziz demanding that Onan should be produced alive and well within the next 72 hours and that I would not meet him until I have seen Onan first. For the rest of my meetings that day, the thought of Onan's whereabouts filled my mind.

When I got back home that night, my chief aide filled me in on the search. "My Lord, it does not appear that your friend is in Nubia at all. The servants reported that they could not find him with the stone cutters. It appears they have shipped him off to the deserts through the lower Nubia River." He nervously explained not knowing what my reaction would be. I was devastated when I heard this. Memories of Master Banga's failure to find Noba, his childhood friend, haunted me throughout that night. Later that night, I sent for the royal guards and ordered them to go search the stone cutters' market for Onan and to find him even if he's been shipped to the end of the earth. Unable to sleep and overwhelmed with emotion that night, it dawned on me that I have been juggling many balls more than I could handle. The weight of running the nation was crushing, the threats from the royal family were frightening, and the fear of failing again consumed me all day. I was not sleeping well, and I could not hold things together anymore. For the second time in about thirteen years, I felt afraid and alone. I wish my father was around to console me. I spent the rest of that night fasting and praying in my chambers for the safe return of Onan, patience to deal with the royal family, and wisdom to be effective in running Nubia as an administrator.

As we waited for good news about Onan, none came. It was such a distressing time, but I had to remain strong and professional. About a week later, the royal messengers arrived with the message that the king requested my presence at a strategy meeting with the military leaders. I arrived at the meeting, which had His Highness, the crown prince, distinguished military generals, and military analysts in attendance. My arrival was met with disdain among many generals who questioned Nobiin's decision to invite me to the meeting.

"I am glad you are here, Zeph. We've been in a deadlock about the Ethiopian war which has lasted for the past 25 years and had cost us many lives and resources. I am inclined to just cut my losses and move on, but Prince Nublin and some generals there thought otherwise. What would you advise?" the king admirably asked.

As I looked around the room, I asked the prince to elaborate on his argument.

"Father, you don't expect me to explain our war strategies to this fool!"

"Zeph is brilliant and having the idea of such a "novice" isn't bad after all. So, go ahead and explain as he has requested."

Prince Nublin reluctantly explained the initial war strategy; face-to-face combat and undercover missions which involved sending Nubians as undercover rich Axumisians visiting Ethiopia (both kingdoms had a peace agreement in place). By his account, the undercover mission initially worked as they learned about Ethiopia's armory, walled cities, and governing structure, but the spies were caught and hanged. As the prince explained, I realized that his insistence on continuing with the war was borne out of his desire to prove to everyone that he was an accomplished warrior, but in reality, he had no real strategy. As I stared at him, I saw someone who was craving validation and success, but did not know how to ask for help.

"Your Highness, if I may speak, I would recommend that we persist because the crown prince can win this war, albeit with a different strategy," I politely suggested.

"I'm surprised that you would side with the crown prince. Could you elaborate on your thoughts about this war"?

I had learnt about the region while under the tutelage of Master Banga who had grown up near the intersections of the borders of Nubia, Kush, Ethiopia, and Axumise kingdoms. My strategy for winning the war was based on that knowledge of the region. To make my point, I requested for a map of the region to be put up. As everyone watched, I explained my idea which was to attack Ethiopia's main water supply which is from one of the distributaries of the Nubia River, and pointed to the strategic locations for the attack.

"If you will pretend to build a dam on that distributary here, the Ethiopians will surrender to you within six months. When they, eventually, come to the negotiating table, don't demand their surrender. Instead, put the Ethiopians under tribute to Nobiin. That tribute will further strengthen Nubia's economic prosperity."

Most of the audience considered the idea to be brilliant, but some of the battle-hardened Generals thought that my call for diplomacy was naïve and uninformed. His Highness was reluctant to go along with the idea, but decided to try out my suggestion. "Alright, you have until next year to pull out our national forces from Ethiopia." Prince Nublin was gobsmacked that I would first support his idea and even go as far as to give him a winning formula.

"You see! I told you all that Zeph would provide a solution to the problem. He is a man filled with wisdom from the gods." King Nobiin proudly announced as he wrapped up the military council meeting.

After the meeting ended, Prince Nublin walked up to me and asked why I chose to support him.

"Because you need me; and I need you. As I promised you the last time, my job is to make sure you inherit the strongest empire possible when it is your time. Stick to the plan and you will thank me again in six months," I replied as I walked away to join King Nobiin's entourage.

He was confused, but he reluctantly accepted the idea.

As we walked out of the military council meeting, one of my royal guards whispered to me that Onan has been found, but he was barely alive. "We are not sure he would make it. He's being transported to the villa as we speak, sir." The guard whispered. My heart leapt within me when I learned he is alive. "Good, get the royal physician and his team to give Onan the best round-the-clock care as soon as possible. I will see him once I'm done with my meetings for today." I spent the rest of the day advising the king on matters of national security, economy, and day-to-day running of the kingdom, but Onan's welfare was very much on my mind for most of that day.

I rushed back to my villa later in the night to see Onan. When I arrived and checked with the doctors, I could hardly recognize him. He was in a coma and his ragged bare-bone body was covered with lots of bruises and sores. My heart sank as tears welled up in my eyes.

"How did Onan end up like this? Is he dead?" I angrily inquired from the physicians and the team that found him.

"According to the story we were told, he was a slave to one of the stone cutters working on the construction site near the Nubia River, but he was too weak and could not hold down his place as a slave. He had been punished endlessly until his master decided to sell him to another trafficking ri ng e r cr ui ting slaves for the Nubian pyramids being built in the desert. We found him abandoned near the ship deck unresponsive," the aides explained. When I asked how quickly he can make a good recovery, the doctors assured me that he can make a good recovery in six months. So, I gave the order for the doctors to nurse him back to health and give him a refresher training in royal etiquettes and history once he recovers. As I left his side that night, I thought to myself about how much I need Onan and the skill set he can bring to my administration. For the following weeks, I would spend every night sitting by his side, hoping for a miracle that he would come to life.

During the following six months, the wise men and I continued our plans to prepare Nubia for the coming prosperity. The three pilot projects led to important breakthroughs that catalyzed our mission. The construction team confirmed that the architects and construction engineers could build such well-aerated towers, but they needed projected estimates of the volume of the grain to be stored. The preservation team reported their breakthrough in developing a preservative for grains that could last more than sixty days, but they have not been able to confirm its safety in human lives. The agriculture team revealed bumper harvest of barley by farmers in the pilot program when supported by royal crop scientists. All the reported results reassured us that we are on a path to success. However, I was worried that we were running behind on our scheduled timelines.

To help the team, we invited Nubian mathematicians, cost estimators, and accountants to assist with cost calculations, and projections about construction calculations, capacity building, and forecast of crop yield. While I enjoyed brainstorming with these most brilliant minds in Nubia, they struggled to understand the big picture of what we were doing. I found the scientists to be mostly eccentric nerds who focused on the little details in their area of expertise. I was more of a big picture person in the room with little appreciation for the minute details. Akhousta and Ajala helped to bring both perspectives into focus to achieve our goal.

As our team grew, we could not efficiently accommodate the growing staff in the royal court any longer. So, I commissioned the construction of a dedicated research park that included furnished apartments for our resident scientists, research labs, botanical gardens, meeting halls, entertainment areas, and so on. The park consisted of a massive sprawl of high-rise buildings that was fast-tracked and completed in record time as we built momentum for our work. Concerned about our project timelines, I ordered a mandatory two-year residency for all staff members who lived outside the capital city to ensure their undivided attention while all their needs and families were taken care of by Nobiin. We assisted the scientists and staff with families who reside outside the capital city to move to the capital city by offering them all-expense paid relocation to minimize distractions. To better engage with the scientists, I spent time learning the rudiments of mathematics, civil engineering, biochemistry, and crop production.

Back at the royal court, my decision to move our entire program to the research park was interpreted as a power play by the power mongers and political vultures. The queen and her camp promoted the narrative that I was seeking to hijack the throne even though all my executive decisions were made after consulting His Highness. In contrast, Nobiin's twin brother, queen mother and their camp pushed the narrative that I was hired by the queen's camp to divide the kingdom. The rumors continued to swirl across Nubia and the upper class of the kingdom that I had eyes on the throne. But His Highness himself came to my defense and ensured that our work continued unhindered. He also ordered a 24-hr high-level security detail to ensure my safety. When the research park was completed, we held a celebratory launch of the research park which was commissioned by Nobiin himself, and an open house for the attendees. We used the open house to further promote our program.

Shortly after our team moved into the research park, I traveled to the upper regions of Nubia to inspect the building of sample store towers with Akhousta and Ajala. Having been impressed with the structures, I commissioned the full construction of the stores to begin in the upper region of Nubia known for its rich arable lands. During that trip, I had the opportunity to meet with the farmers of that land and shared our vision with them. "The King's goal is to make your region the food basket of not only this kingdom, but also for the whole world." However, these farmers were hesitant to embrace any kind gesture from a king who has never visited their region since his ascension to the throne. "I have heard you. I will take your message to His Highness. I am sure he has you all in mind." As part of our initiative, the agriculture minister left two crop scientists to train these farmers in state-of-the-art crop production practices that would enhance their yield.

When we returned to the capital, we learned that His Highness was hosting a royal dinner for the king of Berber Kingdom who was visiting Nubia. It was clear that I had to join that state dinner as Nubia's prime minister, even though I was too tired to even remove my shoelace. By the time I arrived at my villa, my servants had already prepared my attire for the state function. Seeing I was exhausted, Amram brought in the massage therapist to help as I was being prepared for the royal dinner. My domestic aides then swooped into action to prepare me for this state dinner. The preparation would continue for the following four hours and it included lots of beauty regimens, including an hour-long bath in aromatic solutions, manicure and pedicure, and other makeup routines.

"Raji, what should I expect at the dinner and who will be there?" I asked my chief political aide while I was being dressed. He filled me in on the protocols, the seating arrangement, the speeches, and possible discussion that happened at the state dinner.

"The royal dinner is the biggest honor a sitting king can give to anyone. It's an opportunity for a king to show all the glory, wealth, and strengths of his kingdom. As you know, His Highness is a reticent and conservative king; he had only hosted four royal state dinners during the last fifteen years of his reign, three of which are for the king of Berber Kingdom who is a known ally of our kingdom and his brother-in-law. The royal dinner allows both kings to strengthen their alliance, forge new ones, and map out plans to grow their kingdoms. Sometimes, these dinners serve as the platform for marriage alliances between royal families." He explained.

"Wow, then this is a big deal for everyone," I surmised.

Just before I departed for the state dinner, Amram came into my chambers, frightened as he bowed the knee.

"What's going on, Amram? You seem frightened."

"My Lord, one of your domestic staff has just informed me that there is an order for your assassination tonight."

Raji and I froze completely for a moment thinking that the king had ordered my execution.

"Bring in the servant," I ordered as I nervously paced up and down in my chambers. When the female servant came in, she knelt and explained that her son, who works as an attendant at the downtown pub overheard some foreigners, possibly of Berberian descent, and members of our royal guard discussing a plot to assassinate the crown prince and me that same evening.

"They planned to attack your convoy on the way to the royal dinner and to assassinate Prince Nublin, who regularly visits the pub. If they don't succeed in killing you both, the survivor will be blamed as the architect of the assassination." She further claimed that the royal guards at the pub were attending staffs of the king's twin brother.

"My Lord, you have been good to all of us and our families, the least I could do is to alert you to dangers against your life. I beg you, my Lord, to avoid going to the state dinner, our lives and future and that of our families depend on your safety," she pleaded.

"What could I have done to deserve being murdered

when all I have done is to watch out for the interest of the royal family? How true can this information be?" I thought aloud. Unaware that the servants heard me, Raji assured me that it is most likely that the information is true.

"My Lord, if I may speak, it appears your good heart has prevented you from seeing the royals for who they are. They are all a bunch of power mongers who would stop at nothing to kill anyone in the way of their ambition or glory. The information is most likely true sir. There are several caucuses in the royal court, but they can be summarized into two major camps. All your plans and decisions are being watched closely and interpreted cautiously by these two camps who saw you as the outsider and threat to their power tussle, since your appointment. Let me suggest that they won't even mind working together to get rid of you, sir. The two camps belong to the queen mother and the queen. By the way, the animosity between these two women dated back to the early days of Noobin's courtship with the latter. Also, it's no secret that she was not the favorite daughter-in-law for the queen mother who believes that the king should be succeeded by his twin brother rather than the crown prince." Raji explained to my utter amazement.

"I wonder why the king's brother would seek for my assassination even though he's always championed my ideas and supported my initiatives above everyone else in the royal family?" I asked the servants.

"Sir, the royal court is a cesspool of political sharks who view you as food in their treacherous competition for the throne. None of the camps really cares about your vision for the kingdom. Nobiin's brother would support your ideas

as long as it hurts the crown prince and the queen," he continued. As he explained, all the experiences began to come together for me. I could not believe how much my servants knew about the politics of the palace, but I was grateful because they chose to save my life.

"None of you should ever mention this to anyone else.

You have saved me, and we will need to save the crown prince

too tonight and, by the way, I am still going to attend the dinner," I announced while the royal guards deliberated on an alternate route. My security detail then decided to change my traveling route between my villa and the royal court. I also sent word to the queen about the information received.

"Make sure your son does not go out drinking tonight. There is a bounty on his head for tonight."

At the state dinner, the visiting king introduced members of his official entourage. King Nobiin, in turn, rose to introduce his cabinet.

"Please meet Zeph who is helping us shape our economic prosperity. You will find him to be an intelligent and a well-groomed young man." He gushed about my impeccable qualities to the amazement of everyone at the dinner. I later learned that he had violated the royal protocols for state functions in introducing his cabinet. According to royal etiquettes, he should have started his introduction with the queen, queen mother, crown prince, and other members of the royal family before introducing any appointed official.

Since I sat next to the queen, I felt her disdain and rage for being overlooked and insulted in such a public manner. After introducing his entire cabinet and family, the king ordered an exhibition of Nubia's wealth, glory, and riches. I watched the military salutes and the exhibition of Nubia's cultural heritage, scientific innovation, agricultural produce, natural resources, fashion, and people. This brought me a greater sense of appreciation of the greatness of this Kingdom. As we exchanged formal pleasantries and sat at the table, I listened carefully to conversations between Nobiin and his friend, the Berberian king.

"What information do you have to order my son not to go out tonight?" the queen whispered as she questioned the source of the information I had sent to her.

"He is going to die tonight if he goes out drinking. Some Nubian and Berberian assassins have been paid to assassinate the crown prince and me, but I have ordered the royal guards to investigate." I whispered as the king called for a toast to the Nubia-Berber Alliance.

"You charmed my husband and now claim that my son's life is in danger. Where are you from? Why are you interested in my son's birthright?" she asked, confused by my kind offer.

"Your excellency, I am not interested in ascending the throne. I am just a servant of Nobiin, sent here to save lives and to make sure your son inherits the most powerful Nubian empire in modern history. That is my mission." I declared.

"Not interested in ascending the throne? Working to help my son inherit the strongest Nubian empire?" The queen repeated these words to herself, confused at how I could be working to help her son when I was the second most powerful person in Nubia. I left her meditating on those words as I exchanged banter with the visiting royal entourage. I deliberately sought to engage officials on the visiting entourage as I wanted to know if they are privy to the assassination attempt on the crown prince.

"You are Zeph, the most powerful slave immigrant in Nubia," one drunk official announced as others roared in laughter. As we drank and partied that night, I became wary of the visiting entourage because they all asked the same set of questions from our attendees. I knew that this was not a friendly visit, but a visit to know the strengths and weaknesses of our kingdom.

As the night rolled on, the queen ordered her guards to apprehend the crown prince, who by now was already drunk, and to take him to her chambers. After the dinner, I waited for a word in my office with my security detail all night until the royal guards returned and confirmed that they had found the assassins dead in the alley.

"My Lord, we found them dead. Someone beats us to it. There is another player we have not identified," my chief guard reported. Confused by the turn of events, I sent word to the queen about the assassins but left out detailed information about the alleged sponsors.

"I know that this is the handiwork of the queen mother and her camp. Thank you, Zeph, I am now sure that you are on our side."

"I am neither on your side nor on the side of the queen mother. I serve at the pleasure of His Highness and I would request that you don't bring this assassination attempt up with the king." The queen was relieved that I was not an enemy but could not understand why I refused to join forces with her. As I pondered on my mission to serve the King, it became evident that I could no longer be on the fence as the royal politics and power tussle raged on.

The next day, I waited in my royal office to speak to the king, but he was not awake until around noon, having held meetings till the early hours of the morning. When I, finally, had an audience with him alone, I wanted to inform him of the developments of the previous night, but the Berberian king walked in and interrupted the discussion with His Highness.

"What is going on, Zeph? The King is my brother, there is no secret between us. Spill the bean." Instead, I greeted him and excused myself from His Highness to allow them to discuss. As I headed back to my villa, I was enraged that His Highness was oblivious of attempts to destroy his legacy and kingdom, but I kept those things in my heart. When I arrived at my villa, I thanked my domestic staff and security team again for having my back. Considering the situation, I demanded the royal guards train all my domestic staff in basic self-defense combat skills and extended covert security detail to them and their families.

"They should be able to defend themselves and my household, should there be any other assassination attempt."

Also, I ordered my chief aide to give everyone a lump sum of money to cover for the extra days they had worked in the past few months.

As I was about to dismiss my staff, I saw that there was an expression of surprise on their faces as if they had seen a ghost. Wondering what was going on, I saw Onan standing at a distance with tears rolling down his face; he did not know that I was the one that ordered his rescue.

"Onan, my brother." I ran into his embrace and we cried on each other's neck for quite a while. "Oh Onan, I thank God that you are alive, brother. It's so good to see you."

"Is this you, Zeph? I have always known that you are going to be a big man someday," he joked as we hugged each other again. He was so full of gratitude for saving his life.

"I'm glad you are in a better shape than when you arrived. We have so much to catch up on." I canceled all my non-essential appointments for the next day to spend time with Onan.

Onan narrated his journey from Aziz's villa and his suffering at the construction sites. Tears pooled in my eyes when I thought about the hardships he had faced since childhood. I also discussed my experience in prison, the circumstances that led to my royal appointment, and the enormous task of leading the nation that I shoulder. Onan was a genius at reading people and picking information between lines. Like a machine that can process millions of information, Onan could read people, find patterns in data, synthesize information, organize teams, and simply communicate complex information.

"How are you doing, Mr. Prime minister?" Onan asked after listening to me for a while.

"Hmm, let's just say that not all that glitters is gold."

"Well, you are the prime minister now. I just want to plead for a role as one of your domestic servants. I cannot afford to be sent back to the streets, please. Your servants have taught me royal etiquettes for the past two months. He sincerely pleaded for his life, unaware of the plans I had for him."

"Hey Onan, you are my friend and brother. Do you remember the first day we met in the General's villa and how you extended your hands of friendship when I had no one?"

"Of course, I do. You were quite naughty though...you snubbed me for a while," he added.

"Do you remember the bond we shared? Let me assure you again that as long as I live, you are not going back to the streets. You are now a free man."

Wondering what type of job I would give him, I asked him to patiently listen to a brief description of my vision for the nation.

After listening to me for about ten minutes, Onan interjected:

"Your vision is to save the world from global famine by saving the Nubian economy. In the process, you plan to strengthen your role and become indispensable to the Nubian royal family. However, you have found yourself in a shark tank, constrained by your office, and caught in between several warring factions. Your fear of failure haunts you, seeing that you have little or no control over all the players in this dangerous game. Did I get you right?"

"Onan, you are too good. Genius stuff. Perfect." I replied as I marveled at his sheer brilliance.

"Don't praise me yet, Zeph. You've got so much in front of you."

"Okay, go on my friend."

"You need to restructure your team, but we can chat about that later," he quipped as he changed the subject to pleading for a domestic servant position in my villa.

"Onan, how can you be so brilliant and not see what is before you?" I asked. "You are going to serve as the communications director and project manager for my team, Onan! Stop asking for a domestic role on my staff ." He dropped to the floor, speechless, as he bowed in gratitude.

"I cannot believe this! Is this why you asked them to train me in royal etiquettes? Thank you…thank you…thank you. You are not only my savior, but you are also my mentor." Onan was effusive in his appreciation for my belief in him even at the point of death.

"No need to thank me, Onan, you are my brother. You start the position immediately, but you will live with me. I cannot afford to lose you again. However, you need to bring your A-game." I warned as I raised him from the floor.

Onan and I spent the next two days catching up on time, showing him around my villa, and even riding in Nobiin's chariot with me to the countryside where we had a picnic. The joy of having Onan back in my life was indescribable. With him, I no longer felt lonely. I was ready and more confident to take the challenges of running Nubia.

CHAPTER 8

The arrival of Onan catalyzed our preparation for the expected economic boom because I had already boasted to our team about his smartness and outstanding qualities. Onan's first day in our research park went well as I introduced him to our staff scientists, engineers, policymakers, and cost estimators. Everyone was excited to see what magic he would bring. During the following two weeks, Onan was brought to speed about our programs, but he could not hit the ground running. It was like Onan had a brain freeze. He listened and absorbed all the information about our activities and our plans, but he could not offer any significant input on our programs. Unfortunately, it did not take long before our staff members and scientists began to feel that Onan was overrated. Everyone, including myself, was disappointed that he could not live up to the famed expectations during his first month with my team.

One fateful night, I sent for Onan to join me for dinner. As we wined and dined, I inquired about his welfare both in the villa and at the research park. After realizing my reason for the dinner, he got upset

"Oh! Is this the reason you treated me to a lavish dinner? To get into my head? Is this why you've been nice to me? Maybe I should just leave." Onan angrily questioned my motive as he walked away from the dinner table.

"Please come back, Onan. Have a seat. You are still my brother and a free man, even if you decide not to work with our team anymore. It's just that I miss the insight you used to bring to my leadership team while we were in General Aziz's villa. We were such a tag team."

"Of course, we accomplished so much as a team. From investment to fashion, to party planning, to managing the staff." Onan nodded in agreement as his tight-drawn lips succumbed to a smile.

"By the way, do you remember when two friends of General Aziz got so drunk to the extent that they puked on you while you served them?"

"Oh Zeph, haven't I warned you not to tease me with such a disgusting tale again?" Onan replied with a big fat grin.

"Touche. It's great to see you smile finally. Frowning your face isn't good for your health."

"Stop it, Zeph!"

"Now that you are smiling, why don't you tell me what's eating you up?"

"Well, I am afraid that you are going to fail and that we might end up back where we started - as slaves," he explained. I realized that the fear of failing again has already paralyzed Onan mentally. I stood up and walked over to his seat.

"We would not be enslaved anymore. We are now free men," I assured him.

"Had I not been in Aziz's villa, I would not have learned all the royal palace etiquettes, finances, business, accounting, management, and many other skills which have so far served me well in this palace. If Mrs. Aziz had not lied against me, I would not have been to the prison where the director recommended me to His Highness."

"Well, that's right."

"Onan, God has prepared us for such a time like this. It is okay to be worried and fearful, but I have learned to turn my fear into strength by bringing my best to every challenge I face. Saving the Nubian kingdom is scary enough for me. Sometimes I also doubt whether there will even be any season of prosperity and famine. I also fear that many opponents in the royal court will call for my head if none of my predictions come to pass. The assassination attempts on my life, the opposition by the royal family, the racial discrimination, and the hatred from the religious cabal of Nubia who saw me as the devil, are examples of ever-present dangers I face running this kingdom. But I am confident in the fact that I am favored by God and I am working under His light."

After listening to me for close to an hour, Onan was relieved to hear that I also get afraid sometimes and that he is not alone. He also realized that he could live beyond being in a survival mode while turning his fear into motivation.

"Come on, brother, I am super-pumped with your inspirational speech. Let's get on with our food."

That night marked a turning point for Onan. The pep

talk I gave over the dinner inspired him.

I woke up the next day to find out that Onan never went to bed. He had analyzed all the information he'd accumulated during the previous month. His attending servants, who thought he had gone insane, rushed to inform me that something was wrong. When I entered his room, he had scrolls pasted against the walls where he had scribbled several ideas, decision points, and many other scrolls on his bed and reading table.

Then I turned to my staff to assure them that Onan is not insane.

"Young men, the real Onan is back. You can relax." I smiled. As I read through the scrolls, I realized that Onan had discovered my big-picture vision and had broken it down into smaller projects with different actionable decision points. Also, he drafted an implementation protocol and conducted a gap analysis to examine how our current implementation plan compares. His work also included an impact analysis of our programs on several aspects of the Nubian economy, including national security, financial services, and immigration, areas I have not thought about until then.

"Zeph, you are such a brilliant mind. How did you conceive such a big revolutionary idea?" he hurriedly bowed in reverence.

"I have broken your project into small bits. My gap analysis revealed some weaknesses in your current project management plan. I need to quickly dress up and ride with you to the research park to share this with your leadership team. I need some input from the engineers and botanists to complete my modeling," he concluded as he started packing up his bag.

" Onan, I can see that you are turning your fear into strength." I said in admiration. Seeing that the ideas he presented are sensitive information about our project, I ordered his servants to pack up all the scrolls and lock them up in my chambers.

"Get him ready for bed; he needs uninterrupted sleep."
"Zeph, I don't need to sleep right; I need to go with you," he insisted.

"I need you in your best self; calm, refreshed, and ready for a meeting with His Highness."

"You want me to meet King Nobiin? Wow, that is something!"

"Yes, you need to present these ideas to him, but not today, and certainly not in this state. Come on, brother. Go get some rest, you need lots of it."

The next day, I convened a leadership team meeting where Onan presented his ideas. They were all amazed at his outstanding insight and suggestions. His presentation revealed several weaknesses of our project plan. More specifically, our project plan did not make provision for the hiring and management of manual labourers, public relations officers, and project managers. His impact analysis also revealed the potential impact of the anticipated economic boom and famine on national security, education, immigration, and international trade – sectors of the kingdom we had not previously considered. We revamped our cost analysis and project timelines, drafted new protocols, and expanded our pilot programs, based on his recommendations.

About a month later, I arranged a clandestine meeting with His Highness and the crown prince to discuss the potential impact of the pending economic boom and global famine on the national security. Having learned that I saved his life from an assassination plot, the animosity between the crown prince and I subsided. We warmed up to each other even though he still harbored some suspicion that I was a competition. However, he was more receptive to ideas from my team than ever before. At this meeting, Onan's presentation of the findings of his impact analysis of the anticipated economic boom and bust on several national sectors sparked a broader discussion among the four of us about actionable plans we needed to make to avert these problems. At the end of the discussion, we identified the need to invest in national security as the most urgent priority for the Kingdom. His Highness charged Prince Nublin to oversee significant investment in military training and equipment. With approval from His Highness, the shared ideas were kept in the royal vault and only known to us.

During the following two years, we made significant progress on several fronts including seed management, soil management, harvesting, and crop management. Our geneticists and biologists discovered novel ways to enhance crop yield for several grains like barley, corn, and wheat. Our mathematicians came up with new forecasting models to determine how much harvest we could expect during the boom. They also developed models to estimate the expected volume of grain Nubia would need throughout the years of economic recession (after adjusting for inflation, birth and death rates, and immigration net flows) and the number of storehouses we would need to build. Our engineers and hydrologists built drainage and irrigation systems across Nubia and harvesting machines that would facilitate large-scale harvests. The construction engineers also swooped into action as they began building many storehouses.

As recommended by Onan, we started a public relations campaign that alerted Nubians to the impending economic boom and the need to save for the rainy day. We also launched "Operation Grow Nubia" to encourage Nubians to embrace agriculture. Since my public approval continued to be dismal among mainstream Nubians, I could not be the face of this campaign. Instead, I implored the crown prince and the queen to be the face of this campaign. While we continued to make progress with our program, Onan also grew into his role as the communications manager for our program. He mastered all the communication etiquettes, along with other royal norms, with the help of the royal staff. He was funny, witty, and a people-person who answered all questions about our program. The Nubian public, royal critics, and the royal family loved Onan and how he presented complex ideas in simple, easy-to-understand ways. Popularly known as "Mr. Nubia", Onan earned the confidence of everyone and later became the face of the campaign. Having seen Onan thrive as the communications director, I appointed him as my chief of staff to oversee all our staff and managers, serve as public relations liaison, and report directly to me. His appointment was very much welcomed by everyone on our team and the royal family because of the spark he had brought to our national affairs and our agenda. Onan held the forte for me for months while I was traveling across Nubia to inspect the farms and construction works in those days.

Onan and I got so busy for months that we rarely had time to discuss, especially after he moved into his official residence. When I returned to the capital city, Onan and I compared notes on project activities. He gave me a detailed account of the progress made and emerging bottlenecks that cropped up in my absence. Also, I shared with him my takeaways from inspecting several ongoing projects across the nation.

"I am impressed, Onan! You have handled things well in my absence."

"Thank you, boss. You should get some rest for a few days before we start pressuring the modelers for more forecasts."

"I am not sure I have sufficient time to rest, brother. I have a high-level meeting with His Highness immediately after this meeting and then the general council meeting, followed by a meeting with the military commanders. I might be here till evening."

"Well, that's why you are the prime minister. Not everyone has the strength to juggle multiple responsibilities as you have always done."

"Anyways, we should catch up soon. How about dinner tomorrow?" I suggested.

"Hmm, not sure I am available. My week is all booked with meetings and dinners with different immigrant groups to discuss stakeholder engagement for the campaign. How about next week?"

"Next week is too tight for me with meetings as well, except you want to have dinner at midnight." I replied after checking my diary.

"No, I don't do clandestine meetings. I love my bed too much." he quipped.

"Since we cannot find a time that works, why don't we ask our aides to compare our calendars and find us a mutually convenient time?"

"Great idea, Zeph. I have got to leave too. I love you, brother."

We hugged each other before he left my office for his next media interview. After he left, I reflected on how much change Onan and I have experienced. Two teenage boys who were once victims of human trafficking and slavery have both grown to be successful men. We now need our chief-aides to find us a mutually convenient time for them to meet. My heart was filled with gratitude and pride, having seen how far we've come.

Onan and I finally had that planned dinner about 3 months later. We spent the first half of our time discussing our work.

"Everything is the same, Zeph! We are ready for the economic boom, although I don't think we have prepared enough for the famine," Onan opined while we wined and dined far into the night. As we discussed, I observed his pensive mood.

"Spill it, Onan, I know something is eating you up." I demanded.

"Zeph, I have been concerned about your dismal approval ratings in Nubia, despite all your hard work. I worry that others will be taking credit for your successes."

"It does not matter as long as the job is done." I got up and moved onto the reclining sofa with my dessert unfazed by Onan's concerns.

"No, you need to take credit for what you've done. History needs to be properly recorded or else no one would remember you."

"I don't care, Onan. I just want to save the kingdom."

"Zeph, visibility and how people perceive you matters a lot in leadership."

"Alright. You are the communications director. So, how do you plan to have Nubians like me when most of them see me as a fraud and usurper?"

"Now, you are asking the right questions, brother! I think that you should marry from the ruling class to improve your favorability rating in Nubians," he suggested while avoiding eye contact with me.

"You have spoken well, Onan. His Highness first raised this issue with me on the first day of my appointment. He suggested a marriage alliance with one of the noble families in Nubia or from the religious order."

"Wow, long live the genius king who foresaw the likely reaction of Nubians to a single immigrant prime minister with no attachment to Nubia. Marrying into one of the noble families or the religious order, which hold sway over more than 60% of the Nubian conservative society, will deliver that approval to your laps instantly. I think we should remind His Highness of this," he pressed further.

"How can I marry someone I have never met? What happens if we don't have a similar vision or perspective about life? What if I don't love her? What if she does not like me? What if we don't share similar religious beliefs?"

Onan tried to calm me down as I bombarded him with a flurry of questions that night about the evil of a forced political marriage.

"Take it easy, Zeph. I can see that my questions have touched a nerve in you. Allow me to investigate this matter a bit further. I will bring you a report as soon as possible." Onan suggested as we ended the night.

Weeks later, Onan traveled to Aniba to investigate the noble families of the religious order. He specifically investigated the Grandmaster of Aniba and his family. The Grandmaster is the leader of the foremost religious sect in Nubia and is quite influential with the public. He is a spiritual adviser to the royal family, but he does not consider the King Nobiin a true devotee. He believes my appointment as the second most powerful man in Nubia was an abomination. As one of the prominent families in Nubia, his family and his religious sect thrived on political and economic alliances with the royal family and aristocrats across Nubia. His Holiness, as he is often addressed, had five highly educated daughters -three were married to other aristocratic families. Upon his return, Onan visited me and filled me in on his findings. After giving a long overview of the religious sect and the influence they hold over the Nubian public, he got into the nitty-gritty of His Holiness' family life.

"I found the grandmaster's eldest daughter who is known to be non-religious to be suitable for you. Her name is Asenath; she is a beautiful, intelligent, educated, and independent Nubian woman who believes immigrants have a lot to offer the Nubian society."

"Why will you suggest an obstinate woman no Nubian wants to marry as an ideal wife for me? If she does not listen to her father, how will she listen to me? What if Nobiin has another family in mind?"

"Wait Zeph, are you threatened that she won't make a good wife because she is independent and can think for herself?

"Not at all. I like independent women, but marriage is more about interdependence, you know." I tried to reason with him.

"I see! The idea of women's independence bothers you, Zeph. By the way, she supports immigrants and considers your policies brilliant. Why don't I arrange for you both to meet and then you can decide?"

"I am heading to the royal court to give His Highness an update on our project. Would you like to join me?" Having observed that I was not interested, Onan decided to give up on the discussion and joined me as we headed to the royal court. On our way there, we met the royal messengers on their way to my villa.

"His Highness would like to see you right now. He's in the royal throne hall," the chief guard explained.

"I can wait here while you meet with Nobiin." Onan responded, disappointed that he won't be able to visit the throne hall for the first time.

"Come on, Onan. We are still going together. You will need to give a presentation to Nobiin," I beckoned as we briskly walked past the guards. Just before we entered the throne hall, I asked Onan to wait in the reception while I approached the king. As I entered, I made obeisance to the King, he got up and in excitement asked me to come near.

"Have you heard the good news, Zeph?" His Highness asked. As I was still wondering what news could have gotten the king so excited, I looked around the hall to see adoration and happiness on the faces of the members of the general council.

"The Ra priesthood and the royal watchers just released the forecast report confirming that there will be abundant prosperity in Nubia for the next few years. Thus, you were right with your prediction of the events in the next few years. Many of our people believed I was crazy when I appointed you into this role, but now they can see the wisdom of Nobiin." He proudly announced. I could only respond in humility while propping up Nobiin's ego.

Then His Highness invited me to give an update on the preparation for the pending economic boom. After reporting on our preparations for the pending economic boom, I spent much of the time outlining our aim of getting the public to embrace agriculture in this time of economic prosperity. As I presented, I ask the guards to bring in Onan to pay obeisance to the King. I introduced Onan as the brain behind most of our initiatives and gave him the floor to present the second part of the presentation. After paying his respects, Onan went on to outline the importance of saving and leveraging the economic boom to build Nubia into a world superpower. From national security to economy, agriculture, immigration, fashion, education, and international relations. He explained our plan to turn the pending economic boom to build Nubia as the next world super-power. His Highness and the royal officials were impressed by our progress and our ideas to strengthen the kingdom. I also seized the opportunity to acknowledge the fantastic leadership of Akhousta and Ajala who were part of the executive leadership team. Excited by the progress made, His Highness announced his visit to Aniba temple to worship Ra the following month. This announcement was well received by the royal officials who had not witnessed Nobiin's visit to Aniba in years. It was customary for Nubian Kings to visit Aniba twice a year to worship, but His Highness was not as religious as his predecessors.

As Onan and I headed back to my villa, Onan inquired whether he had performed up to expectation, but I was not in any mood for compliments. I was bothered by the King's planned visit to Aniba. I knew that the planned visit is not just to worship at the temple, but to arrange a political marriage for me.

"Oh, I know what is eating you up. The visit to Aniba… the political marriage," Onan mischievously teased. Not in any mood for any chit-chat, I went home tired and depressed. I spent the night in bed praying and reminiscing about my family back in Libron. I wondered if my father was even alive and well. The next day, I asked my aides to cancel all my engagements for the day. As I mulled over this decision, I was worried that I might make the same mistake my father made.

My father never enjoyed his marriage; he lived a miserable life for most of his life. How am I sure this arrangement won't condemn me to another miserable life like my father? I thought to myself.

Later in the afternoon, my chief aide informed me that Onan had arrived and wanted to see me for a matter related to our national project.

"Let him in. Onan is a friend. It must be a very urgent matter." I ordered while I tried to rearrange my chambers.

"My Lord, I hope you are well. I learned that you canceled all your engagement today because you were not feeling well."

"Well… uh…sort of, but I am not sick," I tried to clarify. "I am glad to know that you are not sick. So, I need you to tell me what upsets you?"

"Hmm… Onan, I was told you came because of an urgent matter about the national project. What's going on?" I asked as I sought to change the subject of our discussion.

"Hahaha…your well-being is the urgent matter for the national project. I know you will not want to see me if I had told your chief aide the main reason for my visit. It's only work-related reasons that could get your attention."

When I realized his true reason for his visit, I ignored him and just kept to myself, hoping that he would leave eventually.

After sitting there with me in silence for a while, he began to just talk to me. "I can see that this marriage thing makes you so uncomfortable. It's only a trip. If you don't want to marry, let the king know. He will find a way to delay things."

"I am not afraid of marriage, but I feel marriage is not the next thing on my priorities. I have been too busy running the country that I don't even have the time to search for my father, my brothers, and my family. What kind of man have I turned out to be? I am not even sure if this position is changing me. You know very well that I can forgo all the glories and glamour of this position to just find my family, but I am not even sure if my father and my brothers are still alive. If they have, they should have heard about my glory in Nubia. To go ahead with celebrity marriage and live happily ever after while I have not located my family does not sit right with me." I listened as tears pooled in my eyes.

Onan understood what I was going through.

"It is called survivor guilt, brother!" Onan interjected.

"Survivor guilt?"

"Yes, it is the kind of feeling that prevents you from living your life to the fullest just because you feel guilty to be experiencing happiness and success when others are suffering. You cannot blame yourself for surviving or for being happy. If your father and your family are alive, they are also probably living in guilt for getting rid of you. Perhaps, it is why they could not search you out."

"Come on Onan, you did not tell me you are an avid reader of materials on the philosophy of psychology."

"I am serious here, Zeph. For years, I blamed myself for

the death of my parents. I was consumed by survivor guilt so much that when you promoted me in General Aziz's villa, I was only effective when you were there. I could not move a needle forward when you left; survivor guilt kept me in the past, robbed me of the present joy, and left me with no hope for the future. I was ineffective as the chief aide to the General after you were sent to prison, and I ended up being sold as a slave. You cannot allow that to happen to you brother."

After mulling over Onan's words for a while, I heaved a sigh.

"Alright, I hear you. This feeling has always been with me since I got to Nubia. I am not sure I can get rid of it now." I thought aloud to myself.

"Well, if you have been this successful while living with this guilt, can you imagine what you could have accomplished without this burden? Have you had any personal joy lately? No love, no marriage, no children!" Onan explained as he encouraged me not to allow worries about my family to stop me from growing in Nubia.

He reasoned that my family would visit Nubia during the famine if they are alive. Even though I did not like the way he teased me, I appreciated the moral and emotional support that Onan gave me.

"Not sure I could have done anything well without you. You are not just a brother, you are my counselor, confidant, and therapist."

Then I turned the discussion around to tease Onan about marriage and relationships.

"When are you going to marry Mr. Counsellor? I can see

that one of the princesses has caught your eyes."

"Oh no, don't you dare change the topic, Zeph. We are still discussing your situation."

"What's her name again? Nubilinia? No, it's Astalinia!" I teased as I tried to remember the girl's name.

"She is Minaeka, the daughter of His Highness's second wife. She has just returned from Northern Nubia where she completed her 3-year fashion training." Onan smiled as he explained.

"There you go, brother. You're in love with her."

"How do you know that? I am not in love with anyone." "Come on brother, I see her coming to your office every day to have a chat. Or are you teaching her communications skills too, Mr. Nubia?"

"Well, I like her. Indeed, we've been talking for a while, but I don't think that relationship is going anywhere. I don't have what it takes to be a royal son-in-law."

"Come on man, you just gave me a lecture on survivor guilt. If it's money or class, you should not let that intimidate you."

"Oh, not at all. It's more than that" Onan replied as he exhaled. "Zeph, you just touched a sensitive topic. I don't think you should bother yourself with this. You've got a lot on your plate already." he quietly mentioned.

"Spill it, brother, you know Nubia's Prime Minister has got your back." I teased Onan.

"It is no secret that I love princess Minaeka, but I don't have a future with her. I have an ailment I have been dealing with since General Aziz shipped me off to the construction sites. I was always at the receiving end of brutal punishment for being frail. I was flogged so mercilessly that one of my reproductive organs was damaged. I did not know until your servants found me and started treating me in your house. You see, even if I become a royal son-in-law, I may never bear children in this life," he tearfully explained.

"No way, brother. You can achieve your dreams. I am so sorry you had to go through this. Let's plan to meet with the royal physicians again to discuss treatment options for you."

After wiping his face and controlling his emotions, he looked up at me and smiled.

"You don't have to worry about me right now, brother. I just wanted to check on you tonight. This is a matter of the heart and I want you treat it with utmost importance. I urge you to consider things when we visit Aniba in the next few days. It's okay if you are not interested, but just keep an open mind when you are there. The God of your ancestors will favor you and give you happiness."

"Amen. You have such a way with words to make me commit to things I don't want to do. What will I do without you, brother?" We hugged each other and called it a night.

CHAPTER 9

King Nobiin's visit to Aniba dominated the national headlines for weeks. Since His Highness had not visited the Aniban temple for almost 8 years, rumor mills continued to swirl in the royal courts with several speculations about the purpose of the royal visit. Some suggested that the purpose of his visit was to take a third wife, a rumor that distressed the queen, others believe that the king wanted to visit the temple to mend the relationship with the religious class to boost his public image, while Onan and I believe that his intention was to find me a wife among the families of the religious order, but no one really knows what the king has up his sleeves. We will have to wait until we get to Aniba to find out. On the day of our departure, Onan and seven of my aides also joined the royal entourage for the trip. As customary on such trips, none of the royal queens or princesses accompanied the king on this trip. Instead, the crown prince and I were the most senior officials to join him on his trip. After bidding farewell to the royal court, we headed out for a two-day journey to Aniba.

After traveling for about 100 miles outside the city walls, we stopped for lunch in the countryside. Given the incredible amount of time required to set up camp, we decided to spend the night there. The Prince Nublin, Onan, and I along with some officials dined with His Highness that afternoon. During that lunch break, I learned that the king stops at that exact spot every time he travels out of Buhen. Out of curiosity, I asked him why he prefers to stop at that area.

"Zeph, no one has ever asked me about this, but I will tell you the reason today," he smiled, excited to recount his happy memories.

"Thank you, your Highness. I love learning about history."

My best friends and I used to camp in this area back in the day. As young men, Aziz, Raja, and I abhorred the hustle and buzzle of the capital city and would camp here for days. We would go hunting and fishing, or sometimes just sit down to soak in the beautiful natural scenery here." Hit by a wave of nostalgia, he radiantly stared into the horizon as he reminisced about the happy times they had. Having learned about the historic friendship of His Highness with Aziz and Raja while in the prison, I was not surprised with his explanation but curious to check whether the story panned out.

"Who is Raja my Lord?" I politely asked, my question jolting him back into reality. His Highness lowered his head as tears welled up in his eyes and the broad smiles on his face was replaced by a gloom that heralded an abrupt but palpable silence in the tent. After seeing that my questions had rubbed

His Highness the wrong way, I bowed the knee and tendered my apologies for upsetting him. The crown prince and other officials also bowed as we all waited on him to say something.

"Out! I want to be left alone," he shouted as rage coursed through his veins. Shocked by his sudden change in mood, we left his presence while wondering what could have triggered his emotional outburst. Prince Nublin pulled me aside to explain that His Highness was not upset with me, but he had always been sensitive about Raja. his close friend who died on the battlefield.

"General Aziz and Raja are my father's closest friends. His Highness has not gotten over the loss of Raja who died on the battlefield till today. Please avoid raising matters like this with him in the future," he warned. After being alone for an hour, His Highness sent for Prince Nublin and me. When we entered, he was still in tears and on the floor. We both rushed to his side and offered to help him up. "I am fine. I was just overcome with sorrow about Raja," he admitted as he got up by himself back to his seat.

"I want to truthfully answer your question, Zeph, but I was overcome with emotion. I'm sorry for lashing out at you boys." After wiping his face, he looked up and asked:

"Do you boys really want the truth about Raja?" His Highness asked after wiping his face with his white handkerchief.

"Yes, my Lord," the prince and I hesitantly answered in unison after staring at each other for a while.

"Raja and Aziz were my best friends since childhood. Raja was special, loving, and an outstanding individual who became a renowned warrior despite his humble beginnings in the slums of Buhen. His meteoric rise through the military ranks was unparalleled having attained the rank of General and commander of the armed forces in his late twenties. He was beloved by all and sundry, especially my father, and gained more respect from everyone than me. I became jealous of his fame and felt threatened that he might gun for the throne later. I secretly conspired with Aziz to kill him when we visited the battlefront with the Ethiopians. We blamed his death on his servant who was an Ethiopian and locked him up in prison for years." he explained.

Nublin and I were shocked and could not mutter a word for a while. Nublin could not believe that his could father stoop so low to murder someone out of jealousy. On the other hand, I was shocked that His Highness would come clean to me, unknown to him that I knew the entire story.

Turning to Nublin, the king continued, "I have decided to share with you my deepest secret which I have borne alone for the past 40 years because I don't want you to make the same mistake for egotistical reasons. Could you imagine how soon the Ethiopian war could have been won had Raja been alive. We only brought this war to an end barely a year ago, thanks to the brilliant idea Zeph gave us. I killed my friend and helper 40 years ago and the people of Nubia and I paid the price for years. When the almighty Ra miraculously sent us Zeph, I realized our god is giving me a second chance." His Highness explained as he sought to turn his moment of grief into a teachable moment.

"Father, I am speechless."

"Of course, it's okay to be speechless. You would not expect something like this from me."

"Zeph is your helper sent by the gods to help you inherit the strongest empire the world has ever known. I have tested him several times and he is true. He is not interested in the throne. Instead of hating each other, you boys should be allies. By telling you my secret, I want to bring you both together as allies."

"Indeed, he is God sent," Prince Nublin admitted.

"What can I say, your Highness? I'm glad the prince and I now get along just fine," I admitted as I processed the king's confession.

"Zeph, let me formally apologize for publicly embarrassing you especially shortly after your appointment. I acknowledge that I made life difficult for you, but you are a mature man and rightly dealt with my immaturity."

"It's okay, we are friends now. We can forget about the past now."

Then His Highness swore the prince and me to an oath of friendship all the days of our lives and for generations to come. We departed from the presence of his Highness laughing at our past frictions.

Outside the tent, the officials and royal guards wondered what could have transpired. However, when they saw Prince Nublin and I were all smiles as we stepped out of the tent, they were relieved that all must be okay. Finally, His Highness emerged from the tent and announced the newly formed covenant friendship between Nublin and me and ordered a feast for all members of the royal entourage that evening, to celebrate our covenant friendship. When I returned to my tent later that night, Onan wondered how I was able to get the crown prince to become my friend.

"Let's just say that His Highness works wonders sometimes," I answered as I trudged towards my bed.

"Come on Zeph. How did that happen? Tell me more?" Onan curiously asked, but he was disappointed to find out that I was already fast asleep.

As we continued our journey the next day, His Highness invited me to ride in his chariot alongside the Nublin. It was clear that something was bothering him.

"Zeph, I am concerned about the public's underappreciation of the important work you are leading in this kingdom."

"It is okay my Lord. I don't expect our people to warm up to me initially. It will take time to convince them. I am patient enough to earn their trust whenever they are ready to give it." But the king would have none of that because he was concerned about the public perception of his administration.

"This is the reason I have decided to visit Aniba to arrange a marriage for you."

"I had thought that the purpose of your visit is to spend some time in the temple, sir." I asked, after a long pause while pretending that I was not aware of his intentions.

"Haha, you want me to take you down the memory lane, don't you?" King Nobiin smiled wryly at my perceived naivety about the intersection of religion and politics in the upper echelons of Nubia.

"You're naïve about what goes on behind the walls of the

royal court, son."

"Even though the Nubians regard me as a god, I hold a liberal view on religion. The senior religious order are aware of my nonchalant attitude about the worship of Ra and the expected role of Nubian kings and they continue to use this against me. They initially supported my twin brother as the next king even before my father passed away. But my father, Nooblin the Great, saw through my brother's gimmicks and knew that consolidation of powers was all he ever cared about. I, on the other hand, was not religious, but father knew my heart lies in the welfare of every Nubian. His decision to appoint me as his successor did not sit well with the religious cabal in our kingdom."

After listening to His Highness for a while, Prince Nublin and I glanced at each other, wondering whether it was the right decision to keep the latest assassination attempt on us from him. Finally, Prince Nublin opened up and narrated the attempted assassination on both of us by the visiting entourage of the King of Berberian kingdom and spoke glowingly of how I saved his life that night.

"Your highness, I believe that the Berberians have some sinister agendas to destabilize your administration." I added. Appearing unperturbed by the information shared, His Highness expressed his disappointment that we did not bring the information about the attempted assassination to him, but also appeared to understand the dilemma I was facing.

"Father you don't seem to appreciate what Zeph just explained. The Berberians attempted to assassinate me so that you don't have an heir to your throne," he repeated.

"Alright, but you fail to mention the Queen mother and my brother are part of the plot too!" We were shocked to learn that King Nobiin knew about the coup plot all along and that members of the royal family were involved.

"Come on boys, you don't believe that I was not aware of the assassination attempt on your lives, right?" he laughed at our naivety.

"I intentionally invited them and organized a state dinner for them to know more about their intentions. I will quietly deal with my brother in my way, perhaps, when Queen mother is out of the picture," he sternly stated.

Nublin and I were dumbfounded. "You are a genius, your Highness. You are truly the ruler of the land, four seas, and the planetary bodies." The three of us bonded for the rest of the trip as we discussed a wide range of topics including, national security, economy, Nobiin's succession plan, and his health.

We arrived in Aniba later that evening to a warm royal welcome from the city officials and the religious leaders. After exchanging pleasantries, the royal schedule for the week was discussed after which His Highness proceeded into his chambers. While the crown prince was lodged in the same quarters as the king, I was lodged near one of the mid-level military guards, to the chagrin of the royal entourage. Onan stepped up to demand a lodge that is consistent with my status as Nubia's Prime Minister, but I stopped him. I knew that it was an intentional act of discrimination and provocation, but I chose not to dignify the hosts with any reaction. Instead, I spent the night working at the lobby of the royal guest house until the next day. His Highness was not aware of this until the next day when Onan raised the situation with Prince Nublin. Enraged by such humiliation, the prince openly rebuked the city officials who pleaded and confessed that the grandmaster insisted on this lodging arrangement. While the city officials scrambled to arrange for a new lodge, he invited me to share his quarters until a befitting accommodation can be arranged for me.

That morning, His Highness invited me to join him for worship at the Ra temple, but I politely declined, citing my religious beliefs as an excuse.

"Zeph, I know that you are of a different faith. I just want you to accompany me to the temple and watch our mode and ways of worship."

"Alright sir, I will join the worship." I hesitantly agreed.

So, we joined the royal procession to the Ra temple briefly. As I watched the proceedings of the worship, I was thankful that religious freedom and tolerance were enshrined into the fabric of the Nubian kingdom. But I ponder on how people could worship the deity that represented the sun. I wish they would learn about the almighty God that made the heavens and the earth. The worship lasted about three hours, after which His Highness was left alone to commune with Ra. On our way back to our lodge, I was accosted by a middle-aged man, about 6 feet tall, dressed in a white religious regalia, his shaved head revealed tattooed images of Ra. I assumed he was one of the Ra priests.

"Hello Zeph, the throne usurper, it is great to meet you."

Taken aback by such an effrontery, I greeted him politely, despite his rude introduction and then asked for his name.

"I am His Holiness, the humble servant of Ra, and the grand supreme master and head of the Ra Religious Order."

How can a man be so full of himself and be this aggressive? Such a combination of attributes does not bode well for any man's character, I thought to myself as I stared at him with a feigned smile.

"I am surprised that the "prime minister" of this kingdom did not worship with his boss and other senior cabinet officials."

"Your Holiness, my faith does not permit me to worship other gods, but I was able to –"

Like a bucket of hot oil poured into a raging inferno, the man couldn't wait for me to complete the sentence before he exploded in rage.

"Do you even have any idea that Ra is the national god of Nubia? You are not part of us, regardless of your accomplishments, power, or fame if you are not a worshiper of Ra."

Unmoved by his racial overtones, I smiled and politely replied that a person's patriotism has nothing to do with who they worship or the color of their skin.

"Your Holiness, I am not sure if you are aware that more than 40% of Nubians don't worship Ra and no one could doubt their patriotism, except the Ra religious order. I wonder why you doubt my patriotism and call me names." I shot back.

"I am not calling you names; it is just what you are. A

charlatan who is bent on leading Nobiin away from the path of righteousness," he argued.

"Sir, it seems you have made up your mind about me, even though you know nothing about me. I think it is useless trying to convince you otherwise. You are free to think anything you want about me, but that would not lessen my devotion to this beautiful kingdom." I answered, frustrated by his incessant heckling and interruption.

It was not long before our heated conversation caught the attention of members of the royal entourage and priests who had just exited the temple.

"Ideally, Nobiin should not have even appointed you, an ordinary slave and ex-convict, to be the prime minister in Nubia! He's been misguided by a strange deity because he has abandoned his devotion to Ra," the grandmaster yelled, to the dismay of many onlookers.

"Wow, you are something, your Holiness. I cannot believe that you, as a religious leader, would publicly denigrate his Highness and question his mental health!"

"I am not disrespecting his Highness, but he knows the truth that he's wrong to appoint you to this role."

Seeing the crowd of worshippers had gathered on the steps of the temple to listen to our intense conversation, I tried to douse the tension as I jokingly reminded him that it was lunch time for us Nubians who are not on a week-long fast like the religious leaders and His Highness. The audience broke into laughter as they dispersed, but the grandmaster was even more incensed and embarrassed that I consider myself a Nubian. "We will have to continue this discussion at a later date," he affirmed while disappointed that he could not ruffle my feathers as much as he thought he would. "Sure, I will be looking forward to it," I asserted, just as Onan and my chief aide arrived to escort me into the royal chariot, to his utter indignation.

Later that afternoon, Onan, Prince Nublin, and I explored the city while we awaited King Nobiin's return from the temple. It was a buzzing beautiful city, albeit with many temples and remarkable architectural structures. We visited the city museums and the temples to learn more about the religious history of Nubia. As we approached the steps of Menhit temple, we saw a lady descending the temple steps. She was tall, dark, and beautiful, with dark eyes that were specially contrasted against her white sclera. Her oblong face was supported elegantly by her graceful long neck, like the pillars that supported the beams of the Menhit temple from where she emerged. She was dressed in a sleeveless long purple gown that fully revealed her towering, long arms while concealing her curvy frame as she walked down the stairs. She held a few scrolls and carried a small leather bag that matched her casual leather sandal. As I watched her descend the temple steps, it was like the entire planetary bodies froze at that moment while I stood there, awestruck by her striking beauty. I continued staring at her back side and beautiful frame like someone who had just seen a goddess. "Oh my, I cannot believe that there are still living goddesses among humans. What a privilege to see one this afternoon, I mumbled to myself. As she walked away, an idea popped into my head.

"Excuse me, my lady. Good day. We are new to Aniba

and are just exploring this city. We wonder if you can tell us more about this temple and the goddess worshipped here." I called out as I briskly descended the steps to catch up with her.

The lady stopped abruptly, looked back, and smiled as she glanced at us before hesitantly nodding in agreement. She gave a brief introduction about the Menhitt goddess and before she continued to walk away.

"Thank you for that introduction, but we would like to know more about the worship practices in that temple with us?"

Prince Nublin asked.

"I had thought that the crown prince and the Nubia prime minister would be men who pay attention to details and not rush to conclusions based on appearances, seeing that the future of Nubia is in your hands."

We were surprised by her rhetoric reply and the fact that she could recognize us in the crowd.

"I am not a worshipper but a student of history. I enjoy learning about goddesses of our lands and the important roles they played in shaping societal values." She tersely replied as she walked away.

"Where are you from and whose daughter are you?" Prince Nublin asked, surprised by her sassiness. At this point, Onan beckoned to us for a tete a tete, but I was too enamored by her beauty and intelligence to listen.

"She is the sassy, ultra-liberal daughter of the grandmaster that I told you about." Onan loudly whispered in my ears.

"I am Asenath, the daughter of the grandmaster of this

city," she said with a half-smile as she continued walking away. I walked briskly after her again to apologize for our wrong assumptions.

"My lady, forgive us for misjudging your intentions."

"We are exploring the city to understand the gods and goddesses of Nubia and the roles they play in shaping our modern civilization. If you don't mind, can we join you; we would like to learn more from you?"

She paused and thought for a moment as she stared at me and Onan and the crown prince who stood at a distance.

"Your reputation precedes you, your excellency. You have spoken well. I will be delighted to be your tour guide," she nodded in agreement with a captivating gap-toothed grin. Then she approached the crown prince and paid obeisance.

"So, why are you visiting other temples when your father is the grandmaster for the Ra order?" Prince Nublin asked.

"My father is a religious bigot. I have an open mind about these beliefs and enjoy learning about other religions. So, I spend time learning about history, politics, and other religions in my spare time."

"You must have been a lover of books to enjoy learning history." I commended.

"As a daughter of a grandmaster, I was raised to worship Ra, but not encouraged to learn about other religions. I took it upon myself to learn about the history of other religions rather than being narrow-minded. Specifically, I wanted to learn how the goddesses of this land influence their society. I believe women have a lot to offer our society than just being home makers." She affirmed.

We were all surprised at how independent and confident she was.

It was not long before the conversation became a two-way discussion between Asenath and me, while Prince Nublin and Onan admirably watched us interact.

As we walked around the city, visiting other temples, our conversation soon delved into different areas including history, politics, immigration, family, philosophy, agriculture, and so on. After about an hour, Prince Nublin and Onan excused themselves under the pretense that they need to attend to an important function. I discerned that it was an intentional move to allow Asenath and me to connect further.

After a while, we sat near the steps of Horus' temple while I sent one of my aides to bring some food.

"Your friends excused themselves from this conversation, where have they gone?" She asked with a broad grin.

"To be honest, I don't know. I guess they wanted us to connect better." I timidly replied, worried that my friends had upset her.

"Take it easy, your excellency, I was just teasing you." She grinned after seeing me fidget with my signet ring.

It was not long before my staff arrived with a fruit basket, but I was too enamored with her beauty and aura to even feel hungry.

"You should eat some fruits, Mr. Prime minister." She suggested handing me the fruit bowl after packing a plate for herself.

"I am alright. I am just content watching you eat." I admitted while staring at her like someone who had just seen an angel.

"You are such a remarkable individual who seems to know something about everything. How do you manage to learn so much while still running the kingdom?"

"Well, I am flattered. I am eternally committed to learning and development."

"That's so commendable."

"You are truly a remarkable woman as well, intelligent and beautiful."

"Thank you for the compliments. Life will be too boring if we all take ourselves too seriously." She blushed with broad smiles as she gazed into the horizon.

"Are you saying I am too serious?"

"Huh.. huh, not really, sir. The prime minister is expected to be serious, but not always, especially when he's with a remarkable woman he is fascinated with."

"Oh, I see. Did I say you are a remarkable woman who is adept at reading people too?" We both laughed at each other.

Then she continued with more personal questions about my vision for Nubia and how I have managed to handle racial discrimination in the seat of power in Nubia.

"A strong sense of identity and love for people, regardless of their race, has helped me resist and forgive my opponents and detractors for their ignorance. But Nubia still has a long way to go to exterminate the roots of racism in the hearts of her people," I grinned.

"Wow, that's so deep and very important. You are quite something, prime minister."

"Please call me Zeph."

"I like your perspective about racists, like my father, they are indeed ignorant folks who should be punished for demeaning other races. I am sure you know that he is not a fan of your appointment."

"Wow, did you just call your father, His Holiness, a racist?".

"Yes, of course. Don't pretend you don't know that he does not like you."

"Of course, I know. I first met him at the state dinner and earlier this morning on the steps of the Ra temple. He is such an interesting character with strong opinions."

"Oh yes, you can say that again," she nodded in agreement while rolling her eyes.

"You are such an interesting character, my lady. You are so direct and blunt."

"Please call me Asenath," she grinned.

After more than four hours of conversation, she was ready to head home.

"I enjoyed our conversation your excellency," she said with a charming smile.

"Please call me Zeph!"

"Oh, I am sorry, it will take some time getting used to calling the second most powerful man in the kingdom by his first name," she said, a little dimple spotting her cheek as she grinned.

"You are a remarkable woman, Asenath. It's a pleasure chatting with you today. Thank you for spending your precious time to show me around the city."

"You are most welcome, Zeph." she replied timidly as

she turned away.

"I hope we get to see each other again!" I called out.

Then she stopped, thought for a while, and glanced over her shoulder with a big smile,

"Well, I would like that," she replied as she continued walking away.

"Great, how about tomorrow?" I hollered.

"Sure, that will work." She replied before disappearing into a corner street.

After she departed, I fondly reflected on the conversation we had, her brilliance, and her warm personality.

"I can see that you are already enthralled by this lady, lover boy!" Onan teased after sneaking up on me. I was startled.

"How was your conversation? Did you notice the qualities I talked about?"

" I agree with you, Onan. She's such a remarkable young woman, beautiful, smart, opinionated, but quite reasonable. I enjoyed her company."

Onan and Nublin teased me all day citing the way I stared at her on the temple steps. They argued that there was a new spark on my face as I spoke glowingly about her. But I could not deny any of their claims. For the next three days, I tasked Onan to find out more about her and her family and to deliver fruit baskets to her.

On the fifth day of our royal visit , the religious order organized the customary reception dinner in honor of Nobiin and the royal delegation. Even though this was meant to be a dinner, it was widely regarded as a forum for diplomacy and politics. Having heard about Nobiin's displeasure with the reception I had when we arrived in Aniba, the city officials made sure that the sitting arrangement reflects the royal power hierarchy with the prince and I seated next to Nobiin. After the royal protocols and religious prayers were observed, His Highness inquired about the welfare of the religious order before the discussions began.

"We would like to build more temples across several Nubian cities and our newly conquered territories where the worship of Ra has not been properly embraced. We want you to issue a royal decree to this effect as soon as possible," the grandmaster demanded after spending about a half-hour to lecture His Highness about the need to show consistent and sustained devotion to Ra.

"Well, grandmaster, we don't have that kind of resources right now."

"Your Highness, I am shocked that you claim not to have the means to grant this request when you have devoted huge resources to the building of ridiculously high towers for the so-called 'Operations Grow Nubia' which nobody believes in," he retorted in exasperation.

The king was visibly annoyed but chose to make light of his comments. "I am surprised that as the grandmaster of Ra and a senior official in Aniba, you want us to jeopardize the economic prosperity of our kingdom for the sake of building a few new temples even though we already have more than one hundred Ra temples across Nubia."

"Your Highness, you are the spiritual head of this

kingdom, but you continue to defy Ra. I hope you will not bring a curse over this kingdom." His Holiness threatened.

"You threatening me now?"

Seeing that the atmosphere became tense, the prince calmly got up and initiated a toast to Nubia and the religious order.

As the evening wore on with merriment and entertainment, the king inquired about the welfare of the grandmaster and his family, especially his daughters. He went on to specifically ask about the progress of each daughter, a move that got the grandmaster suspicious of Nobiin's intentions.

"Are you or Prince Nublin interested in any of my daughters?" the grandmaster inquired in a softer tone, excited by the royal interest in his family. "Well, one of my sons is interested." Nobiin replied.

"We will be delighted to be royal in-laws, my Lord. My first and last daughters are well-groomed ladies and either of them will be suitable for the prince." the Grandmaster grinned with excitement.

Then His Highness declared that I am his son who is

interested in making a wife out of one of his daughters, to the surprise of everyone in attendance.

After a long pause, the grandmaster declared that he will not marry any of his daughters to a foreigner with a "strange belief" who is not a worshipper of Ra. Nobiin had a long loud laugh at the grandmaster.

"That is okay, grandmaster. It has come to my attention that Zeph is interested in your oldest daughter, Asenath."

"Asenath? Unbelievable?"

"Is Asenath married now?"

"Not yet, my Lord."

"Perhaps she and Zeph are made for each other considering that they both maintain 'strange beliefs' as you had mentioned. In fact, they had a date today which really went well."

I was surprised that His Highness had already learned about my conversation with Asenath and my budding interest in her. For His Highness to announce my date with Asenath means that Onan and/or the prince must have spilled the beans. Turning to both across the dinner table, I gave them a hard and annoyed look, but their facial expressions suggested that they were both unaware of Nobiin's maverick move. The grandmaster was also caught unaware and speechless for a while and spoke in anger when he finally responded. "My Lord, I can now understand that your reason for this visit was to find a wife for Zeph rather than spend time here. It's disappointing that you are still not devoted to Ra. I hope Ra will not strike our lands with disease and famine for this nonchalant attitude of yours. I have no objection to the union should my daughter, who is stiff-necked and stubborn, decide to marry the prime minister.

There was a palpable silence in the room as everyone wondered what the king's response would be. "I will forgive this emotional outburst of yours this time," His Highness announced as he got up.

"Please make sure you arrange to have Zeph and Asenath spend quality time together for the next few days before we head back," he concluded before departing for his chambers shortly after. Then I turned to Prince Nublin and asked how his Highness would have known that I had an interest in Asenath even though I had not considered if she is marriageable. Also, I wondered how he could only come to that conclusion without my knowledge.

"Well, the king has eyes and ears everywhere, but I can confirm to you that I did not say anything to the king." Prince Nublin reaffirmed. "Perhaps, the king's security detail informed him of that development," he reasoned.

After mulling things over, I approached the grandmaster, who was being congratulated by the guests, but he was in no way cordial and respectful when I formally introduced myself and asked for permission to talk to Asenath, but he was not in any way receptive to my overtures.

"You can visit her any time. After all, she does not even listen to me anyway," he snarled before walking away to attend to other matters.

The next day, I visited the grandmaster's family home to speak to Asenath, but she refused to see me. After waiting for a while, she sent word that she was no longer interested in my friendship. I was disappointed, partly by her rude demeanor to a senior royal official and partly by the fact that I was beginning to like her.

"Well, tell Asenath that I am not done with her and I will be here with my entourage all day until she's ready to talk to me," I insisted.

After about one hour, Asenath emerged from her chambers with a sullen look, upset at me.

"I had thought you are a man. How dare you use your political clout to force a marriage. I was beginning to like you until now. No one can force me to do anything against my will, not even the grand supreme commander who is my father. You can be the prime minister, but I am Asenath and no one can control me." She angrily vituperated while pounding her chest. Everyone on my entourage was surprised by her abrupt rudeness and her fierceness as she flippantly expressed her frustration at what she perceived as a manipulation. Her sisters and cousins, on the other hand, watched her rude behavior and apologized on her behalf. Despite her rude violation of royal protocols, I enjoyed seeing Asenath in her elements and admired her boldness as she flippantly expressed her mind before a royal entourage.

"Wow, what a drama! It's good to watch you unhinged, Asenath." I quipped.

"It's not funny, Zeph. I am upset that I was not consulted before you made decisions for me," She replied after regaining her composure.

At this point, I asked everyone to excuse us.

"Asenath, I am surprised that you assumed that I had used my connection with His Highness to force you into a marriage. There is no royal decree mandating you to marry me. You are free to marry whoever you want or stay single if you like. I had just met you three days ago, but I must confess that I enjoyed your company. I was as shocked as you are when His Highness announced my interest in you. I did not even know how he got to know that we met."

"Are you sure the crown prince and your friend did not

pull any strings on your behalf?"

"Yes, I can confirm. None of my friends said anything to His Highness."

She heaved a sigh of relief and was silent for a while.

"Alright, Zeph. I am so sorry that I overreacted and did not give you the benefit of the doubt before concluding that you had masterminded things."

"You are forgiven, Asenath. It's always wise to give people the benefit of doubt.

"Alright, sir. Lesson taken." She nodded while wiping her tears.

"I can see that you value your independence and detests being controlled against your will. I am sorry the proclamation of His Highness puts you on the edge."

"Alright, you are forgiven as well. So, where are we?" she asked as she sought to understand the status of the relationship.

"I must say that I like you. I appreciate your independence and open but frank approach to things."

"The feeling is mutual, Zeph. I have always thought highly of your meteoric rise and the excellence in leadership you have brought to the national affairs, despite all the oppositions you have faced."

"I would like to see you again preferably over dinner tonight and we can tour the city afterwards if you like." I replied while holding her hands.

"Are you formally asking me out, Zeph?" she smiled.

"Of course, something like that." I affirmed with a forced smile as I focused on her finger.

"Alright. This evening works for me as well".

"My aides will bring the chariot to pick you up later this afternoon around 5:00pm if that's okay."

"No, that won't work. If you're serious enough to ask me out, then you have to pick me up yourself." she demanded.

"Alright my lady. I will be here at 5:00 pm."

During the following days, Asenath and I spent more time together, touring the city, visiting the countryside, and dining together. We found similarities in our view on a wide range of topics, including philosophy, parenting, leadership, politics, race, and religion.

"Is it true that your family died when you were young?" she asked as we sat on the steps of the Ra temple.

"Honestly, I don't know. I have not seen them since I was kidnapped and brought to Nubia about 17 years ago."

"So, you have been living as an orphan for these years? You are tough, I must say."

"The truth is that I miss my father and my siblings. I hope to reunite with them someday if they are alive." "Have you ever searched for them?" she asked.

"Not really. The affairs of the kingdom have prevented me from even traveling out of Nubia." I admitted.

Just before we departed Aniba, Asenath and I met again. During our conversation, I formally confessed my interest in her. However, her father's hatred for me largely loomed at the back of my mind. "There is no way the man will allow an immigrant to marry her first daughter" I thought to myself.

"I don't want to marry you without your father's genuine

blessings. How can you help me get him in line?" I asked.

"You are an honorable man, Zeph. You could have ordered a marriage against my father's wish, but you are still seeking his blessings even though he has no iota of respect for you. You have won my heart and my loyalty. My father will come around in time. I can reach out to my grandmother whom he respects a lot."

As we ended our discussion over dinner that night, Asenath got emotional about my return to Buhen.

"When am I going to see you again?" she asked with a lingering sadness in her eyes.

"You can come over to spend some weeks in Buhen if you like. My new villa is being built. You can come over and help pick the right interior décor for the villa if you have some time."

"I would love that. But I want to know when next are you able to visit Aniba?" She asked as tears pooled her eyes.

Then I leaned over the table to wipe her tears with my handkerchief and held her hands.

"I cannot promise when next I would be in Aniba. The weight of running the nation can be so crushing. But there is one promise that I can make."

She lightened up eager to know what type of promise I wanted to make. There was an abrupt silence as we gazed into each other, our eyes communicating a million things more than our mouths could utter. It was clear to us both that were meant to be together.

"Asenath, you know very well what I am about to say. The truth is that you have been on mind since I set eyes on you on the temple steps. You are beautiful, witty, playful, and independent. More importantly, you make me laugh every time. As you probably know, I am a lone, brown immigrant boy who happens to be the prime minister of Nubia. This brown boy wants to marry you and promises to love you, stand by you, and care for you all the days of his life, if you will agree to marry him." I nervously explained as I fidgeted with her fingers.

At this point, Asenath was overwhelmed with emotions as her eyes became misty. After she regained her composure, she smiled through her tears, her voice thick with tears of joy.

"Zeph, I love you too. You are a patient and loving man. Despite being a powerful man in the kingdom, you are not a man who uses his position to oppress others. I look forward to spending the rest of my life with you."

We were both overjoyed as we held hands and vowed to love each till eternity.

As customary, I ordered gifts of all kinds, spices from Ethiopia and gold from Kush to be sent to Asenath's father. After the dinner, she accompanied me to the royal guest house where we broke the news of our engagement to His Highness and our entourage. His Highness, the crown prince, and our royal delegation were elated by the news and we ended the night in celebration. Onan and I escorted Asenath back to her house later that night.

After a year-long whirlwind romance, Asenath and I were united in a lavish royal wedding befitting a prince. Since I had no family, His Highness and the queen stood in as my parents. The wedding was well-attended by the upper echelons of Nubia and the members of the religious order. Foods and drinks were served to residents of Buhen, a targeted gesture to improve my public image. It was the happiest day of my life seeing Asenath, whom I have come to love, become my wife. But I wished that my family was around to witness that day.

CHAPTER 10

Shortly after my wedding, the long-awaited season of prosperity began. The weather conditions became favorable to our daily affairs. By the way, you need to understand that the weather - rain and sunlight - played key roles in shaping every aspect of our lives in those days. The lack of sufficient rain had varying consequences on several aspects of our lives, including irrigation to animal husbandry, construction, textile industry, household use, and so on. On the other hand, too much rain often spelled doom for our construction and real estate industries. During those years of prosperity, we had an unprecedented right balance of rainfall and sunlight. We started the year with some rain in the dry season, which even made cultivation and planting easier. We no longer relied on wells and the Nubia River, which overflowed its banks during the seasons for irrigation and municipal use. Instead, we created water troughs to channel its overflows into different cities and towns in Nubia. The waters were sufficient for all the household needs to the extent that we stopped building wells on arable lands for farming, animal husbandry, and other business activities.

Our crops needed little or no organic fertilizers because our lands had unexplainable richness that enhanced crop production. We had bumper harvests earlier than we would have expected. We experienced three to four cycles of bumper harvests the same year instead of the usual two cycles of harvests (middle and late rainy season). Within six months, Nubia had surplus grains and cash crops. Our harvest during the first year was seven times higher than what we used to have. It was like the heavens and the earth kissed and produced bumper harvests in crop production and animal husbandry for us that year. Our neighboring nations also reported similar prosperity in their lands. From the mountains in Ethiopia to the plains of Kush, to the desert lands of Berber, and the valleys of Twa kingdom, all the lands experienced unprecedented prosperity in crop production, animal husbandry, and personal wealth.

Seeing that the prosperity season was upon us, my team and I activated the second phase of national economic strategy– the famine preparedness plan.

One, we kick-started the national agriculture program that involved arable farming on all royal lands (running into thousands of acres) across Nubia. In addition to farmers in the royal employ, we recruited thousands of farmers and servants who worked on these farms across Nubia.

Two, we promoted farming across Nubia by promising farmers that the kingdom will pay double in exchange for their harvests.

Three, our supply chain team bought all the crops

from the farmers and ensured safe transportation to nearby storage towers where the volume and types of produce were documented. Afterwards, the crop scientists and food engineers supervised preservatives and management of the stored grain. Then our botanists and crop scientists continued to churn out new seeds that could yield bumper fruits in a short period. Our mathematicians kept track of the annual volume of crop yield produced across Nubian cities and furnished my team with information on what percentage we are storing. With this data, they estimated how much produce we would need per year during the economic recession. We also used this information to inform the agriculture production target for the following year.

The prosperity across the lands significantly increased the standards of living for people globally. In Nubia, our people went from focusing on survival to aspiring for luxuries and vanities. Our construction and real estate markets flourished as Nubians built more houses and requested for national infrastructural projects. With the newfound wealth, many Nubians sought to live like royals by taking more servants and owning more properties and lands. Many moved outside the cities into the countryside to live in affluence, something only a few Nubians could afford in the past. The prosperity also changed the economic dynamics of our nation. We had more aristocrats and middle-class families than any time in history. These newly elected aristocrats began to vie for positions of power and influence across Nubia. Also, wealthy immigrants took their newfound wealth back to their own countries to enjoy.

However, the unprecedented prosperity posed a few unexpected challenges to our mission. Many rural farmers became rich overnight, and they abandoned agriculture, altogether, for other profitable but less labour-intensive businesses. It was not long before we noticed a significant decrease in our annual crop production. To stem this loss, we incentivized the farmers again by providing agricultural support through mechanization, seedling support, and doubling the price at which we purchase the harvests from the farmers. Despite these efforts, we realized that it was a tall climb to get everyone back to the farm. Instead, we came up with the idea to buy these abandoned arable lands and then lease it back to hired immigrant workers to farm these lands as we have done with all the royal farms.

On the other hand, there was a national shortage of labor to support our initiatives due to changes in our population dynamics. The growth of the middle class and upper class meant that we had few people to fill the menial job positions. Many migrants also returned to their home countries since the grass was no longer greener in one kingdom than the other. Frustrations began to set in while we wondered how we would cope without sufficient human resources. I was disappointed that we were blindsided by the unexpected consequence of the prosperity, despite all our preparations. More importantly, I was worried that the consequences of having limited human resources to support our program might doom our success. We convened a meeting with the national economic team to brainstorm on the sudden gap in human personnel to get our mission back on track. Some suggested going to war with other countries to get more slaves. Others suggested withdrawing all our troops from the front lines in our newly conquered territories. But none of these options sounded right because our neighbors also had their most-prosperous economic season in which they had strengthened their national defense at that time. With no actionable idea for weeks, I became worried. One evening, after a long day of deliberations, I returned home depressed and tired, Asenath welcomed me with open arms and tried to lift my spirits, but I was in no good mood that night. After dinner, we spent some time in the gardens just to unwind for the evening, but she observed that my mind was not there. "My love, you need to let work matters stay at work and be present with me whenever we are together." she prodded.

"I am trying to get this out of my mind, but it's so hard."

"Okay, why don't you tell me what is going on again?" she asked.

"Not this time, my Love. I don't want us to spend this precious moment talking about my work again."

At her insistence, I reluctantly explained the labor shortage we are experiencing and my frustration at my inability to fix the problem for weeks. As we kept on walking in the garden, my wife changed the subject of our discussion.

"Could you share with me a couple of stories of some difficult times you have experienced and how you were able to navigate yourself out of those situations?" she asked while taking her seat near the lake.

"I am not in any mood for stories tonight." I murmured

as she beckoned to me to sit beside her.

Seeing that I was not interested, she discussed how she spent her day. But I could not get her question out of my mind. The memories of the brutalities I experienced on the way to Nubia, the challenges of surviving in the slave market, my troubles in General Aziz's villa, and the tough times, I faced while in prison, flooded my mind. Suddenly, an idea flashed through my mind like sun rays piercing dark clouds. Immediately, I got up and paced up and down near Asenath.

"You just got a new idea isn't it?" Asenath watched in admiration, having lived with me long enough to know that I pace up and down whenever I meditate on ideas. "The solution lies in our correctional services." I declared to Asenath in excitement. "We need to put our prisoners to work." The prison program that I initiated while in the royal prison was still being implemented even years after my departure. I became confident that the best option was to deploy the inmates to support our initiatives.

"Wait a minute, Asenath, did you intentionally ask me that question?" I paused out of sudden realization. Asenath got up and walked up to me, all smiles, as she hugged and planted a kiss on my lips while she ran her fingers across my chest.

"This is what happens when Mrs. Zeph puts her best into all her endeavors," she smiled sultrily.

"I know you are distracted by this problem. All I had to do was to help you look inward and find a solution your own way."

That night I realized what a treasure Asenath is to my

life and how resourceful and gifted she is. It dawned on me that I have been busy running the affairs of the kingdom, but I have not spent sufficient time with her.

"Now that we have solved the national problem, can the prime minister attend to the needs of the queen of Zeph dynasty for the rest of the evening?" she said while resting her head on my shoulders as we walked past a juniper shrub.

"What kind of needs might that be, my queen?" I quipped, my hands wrapped around her waist. After secretly plucking a flower off a nearby shrub, I turned to her and admitted my shortcomings.

"My love, thank you for standing by me as I resolve these national issues. I admit that I have not been really "present" as I should. Starting tonight, I have resolved to prioritize our relationship above anything else." Then I handed her the flower as a token of my solemn promise.

Surprised by that simple gesture, Asenath teared up while savoring the flower: "it's alright, my love. You remind me of our wedding day. You know I value spending quality time with you; this means all the world to me more than any gift. Make sure you keep me in your heart always," she asserted as she melted in my arms after I planted a kiss on her lips. I canceled all my engagements that night to spend time with my wife.

I got up early the next day, while Asenath was still asleep, to organize a surprise romantic breakfast for her. Assisted by Amram, I got her favorite flowers and personally set up breakfast in my private dining room. When she got up, she was surprised by the beautiful flowers I spread across the room. As she was smelling the roses, I tip-toed into the room in aprons to watch her smell the flowers. Seeing a figure at the door in an apron, she continued smelling the flower.

"When did my husband leave for the royal court?" she asked absent-mindedly as she continued to focus more on picking and savoring the smell of the roses, all the while thinking that it was the chief aide at the door.

"Not yet my lady, this is the most important royal court for the prime minister to be right now. Could you please come over here for breakfast?"

"Wow….what are you doing in aprons?" she giggled admiringly. "I did not know it was you. You should be in the royal courts by now," she replied with a big grin plastered on her face.

"Come on, my love. I will leave as soon as we finish breakfast." I replied as I walked her to the dining room. While she wondered where I had the time to set up the surprise dinner, I reminded her of my solemn promise about spending quality time together. Just before we wrapped up the breakfast, my servants arrived to remind me of my schedule for the day and the need to meet with the national economic team.

"I love you, my love, but I have to leave right now." I whispered in her ears as I bid her farewell. In turn, she gave me a big warm bear hug as I left for the royal court.

In my meeting with the economic team, I shared the idea of redeploying the inmates to fill in for the shortage in the needed human resources. Most of the officials on the economic team frowned at the idea initially, but everyone agreed that the idea can be tweaked without endangering the public. We brought in our royal policy analysts to tweak the idea and finally came up with a policy that would leverage the human capital in our correctional services to support our economic program while ensuring that dangerous criminals don't get back to the streets. Through this policy, which was approved by His Highness, we were able to plug the personnel shortage gap in the short term to get production back on track.

As we were turning the corner with the labor force crisis, Onan alerted the team to another major crisis that needed our attention – the anti-royal sentiment that was already brewing among Nubians. Fueled by the religious leaders who sought to credit the gods with the booming prosperity of Nubians, the royal family's public image tanked among Nubians. Anti-royal sentiments, conspiracy theories, and anti-immigration sentiments were preached in the temples. The religious leaders propounded a conspiracy theory that Nobiin was already in bondage because the "witch immigrant" prime minister had cast spells on him. They dissuaded many Nubians from listening to our message because my appointment as the prime minister was an existential threat to the future of Nubian kingdom. Instead, they encouraged Nubians to stay devoted so that the gods will not withdraw the prosperity they enjoyed. The religious leaders enjoyed so much influence as many Nubians flocked to the temples to worship and sacrifice to the gods. Unfortunately, these messages, which appealed to many conservative Nubians and aristocrats, fueled anti-immigrant sentiments and violence on minority groups across Nubia. The public support for "Operation Grow Nubia" campaign took a serious dent before we understood the extent of the damage being done by the religious leaders. Considering that the grandmaster of Aniba who was leading this campaign was also my father-in-law, I was between the rock and a hard place on how to manage this crisis. I had thought that my father-in-law would be decent enough to have stopped undermining my leadership, but his hatred for me had not subsided since I married his daughter. Asenath was devastated when he heard how much her father had continued to denigrate me and undermine the royal family in his quest for power and influence. She suggested that we deal with her father carefully without estranging him. She traveled to Aniba to meet with him in the hope of settling this acrimony once and for all, but he would have none of her pleas for peace. He blamed her for being a sell-out and puppet of the royal family. When that failed, I traveled to Aniba to meet with him, but he refused to meet with me in person and would not welcome me to the temple or his family home. Instead, my father-in-law and other religious leaders of the Ra sect continued to cast aspersions on my reputation and that of the royal family. They stoked fear among the people by promoting several conspiracy theories about our predictions. They claimed that we sought to turn Nubia into a secular nation where everyone is at the mercy of Nobiin. Those conspiracies thrived among the public, many of whom felt the royal families are no longer relevant since they are wealthy too. This was a challenge that my team and I did not expect to rise at that season. Our approval ratings were lowest during the season of prosperity and we had no clue how to handle this crisis.

After consulting with His Highness and the royal advisers, we invited the religious leaders to the palace to discuss the growing tension for the good of the kingdom and our people. At this summit, the delegation of the religious leaders, led by my father-in-law, accused the king of being the root cause of the problem because he would not accede to the request for more temples and has furthered his pro-immigration policies. Rather than listen to Nobiin's explanation, they demanded that the king amend his ways by becoming more religious, approving the building of more temples, and rolling back his immigration policies, or else they won't tone down the rhetoric. It was evident, to all of us present, that the religious leaders had no intention to negotiate. They basked in the glory of their new-found fame and influence at the expense of His Highness. Nobiin was frustrated by the religious leaders' arrogance and deliberate attempt to provoke harsh response from him.

"I cannot believe that you would level such significant accusations against me when my administration had spent the last five years working to strengthen the economy," he exclaimed, but the religious leaders flippantly dismissed his view point. Instead, he accused them of setting the kingdom against him and his family and promised them that he would not forget this act any time soon. The religious leaders, in turn, scoffed and jeered at his threats and frustration. Seeing that neither side would budge, the meeting ended in deadlock and the religious leaders departed.

"These anti-royal sentiments being propagated in Nubia is part of my brother's grand scheme to destabilize this kingdom." His Highness alleged after admitting that he had been blindsided by his twin brother's craftiness.

"My Lord, I would advise that you do not play into the hands of the religious leaders by moving on your brother. Instead, I have an alternative idea."

"Let's have it, Zeph." His Highness and the crown prince responded as the former paced up and down the throne room.

"Let's double down on the accusations they leveled against you by opening our borders to temporary foreign workers to support our national programs. Since many Nubians feel that these menial jobs are below their status, they would not raise any dust about our immigration policies. After all, they are busy focusing on pleasure and luxury because of their newly found wealth. This would annoy the religious leaders, but they won't be able to stop our progress. We shouldn't be worried about the priests and their anti-royalty campaign any longer, their threats will fizzle out in a few years once the famine hits." They both agreed to the plan, but the king did not let go of his determination for revenge.

"I must deal with my twin brother and sister at the right moment; they won't go unpunished." he affirmed.

That same day, we drafted up the policy, which was signed by the king, to open the Nubian borders to immigrants. They were recruited to work on the farms and the tower construction sites. This further annoyed the religious leaders and even strengthened their case with the people. Despite the priest-led protests and public outrage against this policy by other special interest groups, we focused on our goal to store grains as much as we could. By the end of the fifth year, we had exceeded our target stored produce needed to sustain the nation for the entire decade of economic famine. Nevertheless, we continue to produce and store grains to the extent that we lost count of how much grains we have stored.

Personally, Asenath and I also experienced joy as we welcomed our first son, Isseh. Having lived by myself for so long, the arrival of Asenath and baby Isseh in my life, gave me a sense of stability and a strong appreciation for the value of family while being far away from my father and siblings. With the arrival of Isseh, my persistent longing for my family in Libron subsided. About three years later, we were blessed with another son, Framy, who was a splitting semblance of my father. Framy's arrival coincided with the latter part of the years of prosperity when my influence began to grow internationally.

As we approached the end of the decade of economic prosperity, my team and I focused more on the global implications of the pending famine. We were worried that Nubia would be overrun if the neighboring nations run out of food. So, His Highness sent Prince Nublin and me to our allies and neighboring kingdoms to warn them about the pending economic recession and the need for them to prepare. Unfortunately, many of them did not take us seriously. Instead, they asked us to focus on solving our internal issues, such as the political and religious unrest in our kingdoms. Some of them were suspicious of our true intent, thinking our visit was to discern their weaknesses. We returned to Nubia disappointed by the poor reception we had.

Seeing that we might have to go alone with our plan to prepare for the pending economic crisis, we initiated an emergency plan to handle the likely immigration surge that might result should the famine ravage our neighboring nations. This plan involved working with the military council to develop strategies to handle this. Upon the recommendation of one of our military generals, we identified several strategic places that might be targeted during an invasion. Our grain storage infrastructures topped that list. So, we situated soldiers and spies near all those storehouses across Nubia. We, also, invested in our military personnel and weaponry, brought our troops back home, and redeployed them to areas near the borders. At the end of that decade, I knew in my heart that the following years would be tough and challenging.

It was not long before the frequency of rainfall reduced drastically in comparison to what we used to have in the pre-prosperity era. The water reservoirs dried up, so we resumed drilling wells instead. We had an unprecedented global pandemic of a rare strain of blight disease which affected all crops and our vegetations. The national crop production levels dropped by almost 30% during the first year of famine, leading to food shortages and inflated food prices in Nubian cities. Other nations had more than 50% drop in crop production levels that year. Several other sectors of our economy (international trade, textile construction, fashion, and a few others) were adversely affected resulting in untold economic losses globally. Yet, many Nubians survived the first year based on their reserves. Our botanists, crop scientists, and virologists swooped into action to study this blight disease which affected most of the plants and crops, but they couldn't make any headway in those early days of the crisis.

As the economic situation grew dire, the religious leaders inspired the religious faithful to become more devoted. They reassured their followers that the drought of the first year was just a flash in the plan designed by Ra to draw them back to the temple. They promised that the years of prosperity would return the following year if Nubians would repent and be devoted more to the gods. The message resonated with the people who took their meager resources and trooped to temples to make sacrifices, but they could only fool the people so long before things got worse. By the beginning of the second year, the national crop production level even dropped much further. Personal wealth dwindled drastically to an all-time low, causing many middle-income Nubian families to declare bankruptcies at unprecedented rates. The recession wrecked more havoc on the world. News of hunger, famine, and loss emerged from different kingdoms globally. Many Nubians panicked when they heard the news of the famine-induced devastation in other kingdoms. It was not long before people realized that the religious leaders had deceived them to enrich their temples. The Nubians took to the streets to denounce the lies of the religious leaders by protesting before the steps of the temples where they asked for a full refund of their money and resources they have sacrificed to the gods during the past decade. Some of the hoodlums even burned down some temples in the countryside. The priesthood order in Aniba reached out to the royal courts for security to stem the increasing violence against religious leaders, but His Highness refused to intervene. He insisted that the priests should return all the things they have taken from the people. After speaking with the royal advisers, I pleaded with His Highness to listen to his advisers and send the military guards to the religious temples, arguing that his inaction will further embolden violence especially in this period of economic depression.

"If they burn down the temples today, they will come for the royal family at some point if you don't act now. By the way, not all religious leaders are guilty of deceiving the people. Why punish the innocent and faithful ones?" After much persuasion, he agreed reluctantly to send military guards to restore order in that region.

The protesters refused to be appeased when they were dispersed from the temples. Instead, they brought the protests to the steps of the royal court. Rather than call for violence, the people demanded to see His Highness for days. They wanted to pledge their loyalty to Nobiin's family. Realizing that the people have seen through the lies and manipulation of the religious leaders, His Highness felt a sense of justification after several years of being vilified by these leaders. When he eventually met with them, he addressed them by explaining the dream he had about 10 years earlier and how he decided to appoint me as the man to lead them through the seasons of prosperity and famine. He reiterated his commitment to the security and prosperity of every Nubian as he took a swipe at the religious leaders for portraying him as insensitive. He described the plans his administration had put in place to save the kingdom and assured all Nubians of food security during this economic crisis. As concluded his speech, he introduced me as the "savior" of Nubia who will steer the nation through the crisis. I used the opportunity to inspire people by sharing my "grass to grace" story while dispelling the myth that I am less of a Nubian because of the color of my skin. I announced to the people that the decision about how and where to buy food will be made available to Nubians and assured them that we will all survive if we pull together rather than embrace division. The people were inspired and quietly dispersed to their own homes, assured that they will survive the crisis.

Unfortunately, the news of King Nobiin's proclamation that Nubia had more than enough grain soon reached beyond the borders of Nubia. Within a few weeks, people of other lands congregated on the borders of Nubia. The Nubians took to the streets again to ensure that the government puts them first before welcoming immigrants. After almost a whole day of protests, I addressed our citizens and assured them that Nubians remain our priority during the crisis. I also took the time to explain why it is important to support and welcome those who seek refuge within our borders, and our neighbors and allies, during this global crisis, and the implications for the prosperity of Nubia.

Despite all assurances we provided, the news of the famine devastation in surrounding nations continued to terrify and paralyze Nubians to the extent that all they could think about was survival and hibernation. When we announced that Nubians will buy food in exchange for money, the people resorted to panic buying to stock up on food. It was not long before our people ran out of money. This meant that all the money in circulation had returned to the national treasury, leading to an unprecedented collapse of the Nubian financial system. We could no longer rely on the principles of the free market to save us in those perilous times. So, in consultations with the national economic council and His Highness, we implemented a trade-by-barter system that concentrated power in the royal family. First, we asked the people to sell their livestock in exchange for grains, but the famine got even dire to the extent that the people exhausted their livestock. There were protests in the public square about increased mortality especially among the poor and subsistence farmers who had no assets or livestock to purchase any food.

After days of protests, Nobiin finally addressed the people as part of the efforts to calm the public.

"Zeph and his team will make sure you all have food. He is here to save lives. Whatever he asked you to do, you should do it."

A few days after, people gathered outside the royal courts again to protest the famine and lack of basic necessities. This protest was led by the priests, aristocrats, and the common people. I was devastated by the situation and demanded to meet with the labor leaders who explained the dire situation: "It's obvious that the global financial system, including ours, have completely collapsed and our people have run out of livestock to sell in exchange for food." We deliberated with the labor leaders, aristocrats, and other opposition leaders to find a lasting solution that will save lives and not destroy the economy. After a week-long deliberation, we agreed that Nubians will exchange their ancestral lands for food portions for the remaining years of the economic crisis. Each family will have the opportunity to buy back their lands once the economy rebounds by working for the royal family for a pre-specified number of years. Immigrants and other foreigners in our lands will commit to signing a contract that will keep them working for the kingdom for a pre-specified number of years in exchange for guaranteed food.

However, this policy won't favor the religious priests and their leaders who are on the government's payroll. Seeing that this policy will result in most religious leaders losing their lands, dignity, and independence, Asenath tearfully requested that I find ways to save the religious class from this policy. She explained the consequences of the Land Use Act on religious freedom and the various religious sects in Nubia. So, I extended an olive branch to my father-in-Law before finalizing this policy. I asked him to meet with the king to discuss and make peace within a month when the new Land Use Act will become effective. I was hoping to pull some strings with royal family members and senior cabinet members when he shows up at the royal court, but he refused to make peace with the royal family. Asenath, in turn, mobilized her siblings and family friends to prevail on her father to get off his high horse, but the man insisted that he would not beg anyone. Asenath later traveled to Aniba to speak to him.

"You need to come off your high horse, papa. You lost gallantly because you closed your mind and chose the wrong side. Your son-in-law whom you hated has shown you nothing but compassion, despite your racist character and denigration of his personality both in public and in private. You decided to organize a coup against a sitting king and lost your conscience in the process. Now you've lost everything. It is on you, papa!" Asenath stated pointedly.

"I still maintain that he has not done anything for me, and I refuse to be at his mercy," the grandmaster defiantly lashed out at his daughter.

"Very well, papa. I can see that your pride has blinded you from seeing clearly. Not only has Zeph been a good husband to me, but he has also been a father who has a large heart by treating me with love and kindness. He holds no grudges against you and sent me here to convince you to make peace with King Nobiin. I am sorry father, but Zeph is a bigger man than you would ever be." She yelled at her father in exasperation as she departed after several hours of pleading with him. When she got back, she narrated her father's insistence on not making peace with the king. It broke my heart that my father-in-law will destroy the legacy of his religious sect in Nubia because of his stubbornness. However, I watched helplessly as Asenath mourned the situation with a rare mix of anger and sorrow for weeks.

A week before the new Land Use Act would go into

effect, Onan arrived at my villa to inform me that the grandmaster and other religious leaders were at the royal court to plead for the future of the religious order. Onan, Asenath, and I were excited and left for the royal palace to find the grandmaster and his order bowing on the steps of the throne hall; they would like to meet with His Highness, but he refused to grant them an audience. The crown prince and I mobilized other royal officers and royal advisers to convince His Highness to meet with the religious leaders, but he insisted that he would not meet with them. The news of their arrival soon reached the people of Buhen who started to gather near the walls of the royal court to demand the execution of the religious leaders for swindling the people. To control the situation, we stationed the royal guards to maintain peace. For the following days, Asenath, Onan, Prince Nublin and I sought out everyone who could prevail on the king, the crown prince, the queen, his daughters, his grandsons, but he would not listen to anyone's plea. The priests, on the other hand, stood there on the steps in humility still asking for mercy and peace. They insisted that they would not go until they see the king. I was surprised that my father-in-law would be humble enough to join the wait on the king.

Eventually, when we ran out of ideas on how to bring His Highness to the negotiating table, I became worried about what "no-deal" would look like. It might mean the massacre of the priests on their way back to Aniba by the angry protesters who were still aggrieved about how the priesthood order deceived them. It might mean the destruction of temples across Nubia if the situation escalates. It might mean the beginning of a religious civil war. The possibilities were just endless. I wish the king would see reasons with me, I muttered to myself.

Frustrated by the deadlock after days of lobbying, we were all exhausted and resigned to the fact that we had done our best. Asenath arrived in the royal court a bit later, about four hours before the deadline. She found Onan, Nublin, and I seated on the steps of the royal palace as we kept an eye on the protests near the gates of the royal palace and the other eye on the steps of the Throne Room Hall where the priests were kneeling.

"My love, I know that you have exhausted all options to fight for me and those priests. We have done everything humanly possible to save the priests. It is not in our hands anymore. It's been two days now and you have not had any food. I brought some snacks and fruits for you." Asenath entreated as we sat there disappointed at the turn of events.

While Prince Nublin and Onan munched on the fruits, I was not hungry. Instead I was hopeful for a miracle or a change of heart by His Highness.

"No, there is one more humanly possible decision Zeph could make." Onan thought aloud.

"What else can we do?" I asked.

"Zeph has not directly pleaded the case with Nobiin. He was as hurt by this situation as Nobiin, considering that his name was dragged in the mud, for years, more than anyone else. If Zeph approaches Nobiin to plead on behalf of the priests, then he might get him to listen." Onan suggested. We all thought that was a brilliant idea and decided that I should approach the king. The prince also shared some extra royal etiquette tips as I prepared to enter the throne hall.

"Make sure you worship from the entrance nonstop until you reach the steps of the throne and stay on your knees throughout as you address Nobiin." he advised.

After entering the throne hall, I bowed in worship repeatedly until I got near the throne.

"Your Highness, you have not, for once, treated me as your servant, but more like your son in running the affairs of this kingdom. Your wisdom and ideas have saved this kingdom from countless disasters. I am approaching you to reconsider your decision not to meet with the religious leaders from Aniba. Regardless of what has transpired in the past, these leaders are still our people. Watching them die in the hands of the protesters when they leave without meeting with you does not speak well of your commitment to saving lives."

"Stop, Zeph!" His Highness teared up.

"Have mercy, father." I pleaded while I explained the implications of not embracing peace in this situation.

"How do you forgive the same group of people who conspired to see your downfall, dragged your name and reputation in the mud, and liaised with the enemy to assassinate you?"

At this point, I was confused. I tried to process these words in my mind.

"I don't get you, your Highness. None of these folks are capable of conspiring to assassinate me, or are they?" I muttered loudly unaware that he heard me.

"Yes, the grandmaster, your father-in-law." His Highness responded as I processed the revelation.

It was at that point that I realized that my father-in-law was part of the cabal that sought to topple this administration.

"Wow, my Lord" I sat on my limbs with a jaw-dropping gape.

I was numb and speechless for a while, unable to fully process what I had just heard. Then I got up and bowed to the king again. With tears running down my face, I asked him to give them the gift of forgiveness.

"It was forgiveness that got me to forgive my family… it was because of forgiveness that I could let go of the abuse I experienced in the slave market…it was forgiveness that made me to ignore my detractors. It was forgiveness that got me to make peace with General Aziz and his wife after they lied against me and unjustly incarcerated me. There is power in forgiveness, sir. You need to give them that same gift tonight."

After sitting in his presence for about an hour without any response from him, I knew that the decision was beyond me. I thanked him and excused myself from his presence.

"I will meet with them and give them a gift of forgiveness as you suggested," the king announced as I got near the entrance.

"Thank you so much, your Highness. Long live the king." I dropped to the floor and paid obeisance once more.

Immediately, I rushed out to announce the good news

to the prince, Onan, and Asenath who were pacing around the waiting room adjacent to the throne hall. When they all heard the king's decision, they all returned to the throne hall again to thank His Highness. Then we ordered the protocol officers to invite the priests into the throne hall in preparation for their meeting with Nobiin.

We all waited for the king until he arrived at the 11th hour, less than one hour before the Land Use Act would go into effect. After everyone worshiped, my father-in-law stood up, on behalf of the religious leaders, to tender their apology and to formally request an exemption of the priest order from the Land Use Act.

"Shut up," the king snarled as a hush fell on everyone in the Throne room. He explained that he would not have honored them with his presence considering how they tarnished his name, dishonored the royal family, and attempted to usurp his administration, to the surprise of everyone. Then he announced the only condition for which he would order the exemption of the Priesthood order from the Land Use Act. He wanted the religious leaders to explain their roles in destabilizing his kingdom.

The grandmaster reluctantly got up, after consulting the other religious leaders. He explained how the league of religious leaders in Aniba was convinced by the king's twin brother that his Highness was not interested in supporting the religious order. "The Ra temple in Aniba became the venue for bi-annual meetings for the group, which included the Nobiin's twin brother, his sister (the Berberian queen), the queen mother and the king of Berber kingdom. It was at these meetings that we hatched the assassination plans against Nobiin and Prince Nublin."

At this point, the entire audience of royal officials and other advisers were shocked and murmured.

"What is papa talking about, Zeph?" Asenath asked.

"We relied on the royal guards for King Nobiin's twin and brother, spies and assassins from the Berberian Kingdom, but many of our assassination attempts were foiled for reasons we could not explain. When we realized that Zeph was the anchor for Nobiin's economic success, he became a prime target of our assassination attempts. When we learned that His Highness was to visit Aniba, we made plans to assassinate him, Prince Nublin, and Zeph altogether on that trip. Our original plan was to poison his Highness, but he refused to eat any food for the entire visit. The assassins we sent to eliminate them were found murdered in Menhit temple alley." From the corner of my eye, I could see Prince Nublin ground his jaw in anger. Asenath, on the other hand, gripped my hand tightly. I did not have to look at her to know how shaken she was by the revelation.

"What I did not see coming was His Highness's plan to negotiate a marriage with my family, which put me between a rock and a hard place. I did not agree to the union of Zeph and my daughter, Asenath, because I knew that the cabal would view this as a conflict of interest and perhaps a betrayal of their trust. The cabal demanded an undivided loyalty to the cause or else, I would become a victim myself. However, it was too late because my daughter fell head over heels in love with Zeph. So, we continued with plans to assassinate Zeph even after he became my son-in-law. However, all attempts were foiled by an unknown force. Our last attempt was to destabilize the country by inciting the people against King Nobiin, but, as you all know, now this plan also backfired. My Lord, we are very sorry for these atrocities. We pray you can forgive us." The grandmaster explained to the utter shock and disappointment of everyone.

Everyone was shocked at the level of atrocities committed by the religious order. More shocking news to the audience was the revelation that members of the royal family members - His Highness's twin brother, sister, and the queen Mother - were behind all the assassination attempts and instabilities. Asenath sobbed uncontrollably after hearing the atrocities her father committed against the nation and her husband.

"Zeph, I know nothing about father's plan and his deal with the enemies," she tearfully explained while trembling all over.

"I know…I know." I replied, patting her hand gently while lost in thought.

The audience murmured as they discussed these revelations among themselves for a while. Then His Highness motioned for a silence.

"My people, I can see how shocked you all are about these revelations. The truth of the matter is that I knew about all their plans early on and formed an elite team of spies, "the Team", about fifteen years ago. This team continued to track these miscreants and foiled their plans. I had waited patiently hoping that they will have a change of heart, but they continued in their evil path. I knew about the incessant visits of the queen mother and my sister, the Berberian queen, to Aniba. I knew about the fact-finding missions of the Berber kingdom to learn about our military and economic secrets." The king listened. Everyone was shocked at the king's revelation.

"A few moments ago, I had a meeting with the Zeph who came in to plead on behalf of the Priests for exemption from the Land Use Act. I asked him how he could come in to plead for the same people that sought his downfall and execution. He gave me a one-word answer – forgiveness. He asked me to give everyone the gift of forgiveness. So, I ask you all, how do you forgive these atrocities?" Nobiin asked. A hush fell on everyone in that hall when they heard about the atrocities committed by the religious leaders and the coup plots against the king by members of the royal family. The priests were all shocked by the actions of their leaders but expressed their appreciation for Nobiin's leniency.

At this point, the king approved the exemption of the priesthood order from the Land Use Act and issued several royal decrees. "As of tonight, my twin brother, and the Berberian queen have been banished from the kingdom effective tonight never to step on Nubian soil ever again. The queen mother is also banished from my presence henceforth; she's to live the rest of her life in her quarters. Our diplomatic ties with the Berber kingdom end effectively tonight for their roles in attempting to destabilize this kingdom. None of their people will be able to buy grain in Nubia, henceforth. The senior leadership of the priesthood order is hereby disbanded." Then he turned to the grandmaster. "I should have called for your execution tonight, but I will spare your life because of the love I have for Zeph and how good Asenath has been to him. You are hereby sentenced to house arrest until your death."

Following the return of the priesthood delegation to Aniba, my father-in-law and his accomplices were stripped of their religious titles and excommunicated permanently from the order. My in-laws had to live with disgrace, humiliation, and battered reputation for years after that incident. It would take my wife several years to come to terms with the disappointments of that day and the betrayal of a father dearly loved by his daughters, but we had to move on because Asenath and I had the confidence of Nobiin and the royal family.

All the lands of Nubia became state-owned lands. The royal critics lambasted this decision as King Nobiin's attempt to perpetually enslave all Nubians, but we did not have time to trade insults with critics seeing that people were dying in neighboring countries. This plan ensured that all Nubians had food throughout the famine. We also relocated several Nubians who live in the countryside into the cities to ensure that they are close to food storage towers. As part of our international strategy to strengthen our nation, we opened our borders to people of other lands to come and buy food.

Throughout the famine, Nubia became the breadbasket for the whole world as several nations trooped into Nubia to buy grains. In the interest of national security, foreigners could only enter Nubia to buy food directly from me in the capital city and with my approval. This ensured that we could fully assess the intent and mission of anyone buying food from Nubia. Our military agents also carried out undercover missions and thwarted several attempts to invade Nubia and attack our storehouses.

However, we could not find any scientific breakthrough to the blight disease that destroyed most of our vegetation until five years later. The breakthrough helped Nubia and our neighboring nations to resume our farming and crop production in the seventh year of the economic crisis. Nubians were assigned lands, away from their lands, to farm and grow crops. In return, we instituted a 20% tax on all the yield from the land. With these strategies, we were able to steer the ship of a nation to a peaceful haven. Nubia became the first nation to emerge from the devastation of that decade of economic recession and agricultural pandemic. Although our economic system was decimated, Nubia emerged as the most powerful nation and the seat of the first civilization after the crisis. We were able to turn the lessons learned during the famine into actionable wisdom that was foundational to the prosperity this kingdom has enjoyed till now. My legacy would go on beyond the reign of His Highness and his son, king Nublin, whom I love very much and their descendants till today.

CHAPTER 11: EPILOGUE

My story went on for hours and it was already past dinner time by the time I finished. As I began to wrap up, Limnea raised his hands.

"Excuse me, papa, I have a question." "Go ahead my son, I cannot believe that you are still listening with all attention." "I've been listening attentively papa even though I found your story to be too long and winding."

Everyone roared in laughter.

"Ok, to my question. Did you get any medals for leading Nubia through those bad times?" he asked. "Yes, my son. His Highness showered me and members of my economic team with many gifts, including promotion to senior royal positions. My reputation and influence also grew internationally. My dear friend, Onan, was appointed as the inaugural Director of the National Intelligence Agency which consists of an elite team of spies. The research park where some of the finest ideas that saved Nubia during those dark years were hatched was renamed as Center for Innovation and staffed with some of the best scientists in the world. The Center was also responsible for military intelligence, infrastructural development, and international relations. Both Onan and Akhousta were named the inaugural co-directors of this center while Nobiin, crown prince, and I served as the co-chairs of the governing board for the center."

Next was Eran who wondered what happened to Uncle Onan's love affair with King Nobiin's daughter. Almost everyone wanted to ask the same question.

"Yes, Onan finally got married to his heartthrob, Nobiin's daughter. He had a successful medical procedure that corrected his ailment. Onan and Minaeka had seven sons who remain my godchildren till today. My friend, Onan, passed almost ten years ago."

"Oh, I am sorry to hear this, grandpa. You must have missed your friend a great deal." Eran replied.

"Yes, I do miss Onan, a lot!"

One of the older sons also got up and asked a more tricky question.

"Papa, you have described an inspiring story of your suffering, heartbreaks, challenges, and success to us. What would you consider to be the actual secrets to success?"

"My child, if you listened carefully, you would have picked these points from my story," I answered pensively, staring at the nearby worship altar where we sat. As I thought about my journey from Libron to the corridors of power in Nubia and to that moment, a few important principles that helped me along the way began to emerge.

"Okay, let me be clear that some of the principles I am going to share with you are not in any way an exhaustive list of things you need to do to be successful. Also, I was not intentional about succeeding at the outset, my goal was survival and earning my freedom. Over the years, I have learned that these are important principles for success regardless of who you are, where you are, or what your dreams are."

"One, the past is beautifully imperfect at best. Leaving the past behind is one of the most difficult to do when you arrive at a new place or when you are in a new season. The uncertainties and challenges that come with adapting to a new place can be daunting to the extent that you just want to take solace in the memories of the past. I had my fair share of homesickness in my early days here. I missed my father, my brothers, and the entire family. For others, the excitement of arriving in a new country might soon be overtaken by the challenges of adapting to the realities of the new place. Unfortunately, many tend to cling too much to such nostalgic feelings to the extent that they fail to maximize their potentials in their new environment."

"Two, a commitment to life-long learning gave me an enduring success. One of the realities that you face when you arrive in a new place or a new stage is the need to learn, unlearn, and/or relearn everything. Even though I was a teenager when I arrived here, I had to commit to learning the language, training myself in many new things I did not learn while growing up in Libron. For example, I did not know I have to be trained on how to comport myself before dignitaries until I got here. The situation might be different for others who arrive in their new country at an older age, with bigger families, or even with other perceived limitations that might make them feel it is too late or that it is impossible to learn new things and adapt to the new place. Regardless of your age and situation, it is important to be intentional about learning the language, the culture, mannerisms, etiquettes, fashion, relationships, and ways of life of the new place. For those of you born and raised here, a commitment to life-long learning will make you relevant in the marketplace especially in this era of fast-changing technological advancement and information deluge. Many of you have asked me why I dedicated several rooms in this villa to maintain a library. Well, let's just say that my meteoric rise in Nubia can be attributed to continuous improvement and learning of everything and anything. From learning how to grind the mills, to book-keeping, business, fashion, politics, history, and so on, I kept expanding my knowledge base even till now. You stop growing, dreaming, and attracting opportunities once you stop learning."

"Three, identify friends, mentors, allies, and/or sponsors. My commitment to learning was supported by Master Banga, the household manager who took me under his wings and taught me many things. Learning and continuous improvement don't just happen when you ostracize yourself from others. You need to identify allies, sponsors, and friends who are committed to seeing you succeed. As I have mentioned to some of you, segregating ourselves from the Nubian society is damaging to our growth and prosperity.

Such policies rob us and our children of the opportunity to identify allies, mentors, and sponsors who can point us to the right information or opportunities for growth. I would not have been successful in General Aziz's villa nor appear before King Nobiin without the training, mentorship, and opportunities that Master Banga, Onan, the Prison Director, and many others who helped me along the way afforded me. We need to maintain an open mind and be willing to welcome new relationships even with people who might not share the same beliefs or background with us. We must avoid falling into the trap of labeling everyone as racists especially when their views are contradicting to ours; not every issue is a race issue. There are genuine God-sent individuals who will prepare you for the future. For example, our ancestors did not just become successful by keeping to themselves, they forged alliances, trading relationships, and friends with new people in the land where they migrated. Your journey in life becomes very easy when you identify allies, mentors, sponsors, and destiny helpers who are designed to give you the necessary support and opportunities to achieve your dreams."

"Four, you can still stick to your identity and values. A common misconception held by many, when in a new territory, is the fear that integration with the mainstream society implies a complete loss of their identity and values. Hence, we tend to develop man-made rules of conduct, which are passed down from generation to generation, to safeguard our values. It's indeed possible to integrate well into your new society without compromising your faith and identity as an individual. Having served the royal family for the better part of my life, I have not compromised my faith, but my colleagues and superiors have come to respect my faith and religious beliefs."

"Five, dare to dream bigger than your wildest imagination. When I arrived in Nubia, my only ambition was to stay alive enough to find a good person to buy me as a slave. I was overjoyed when the bill of my sale was finally signed by Master Banga but after spending several weeks in Aziz's villa, my dream metamorphosed from survival to earning my freedom. I worked hard and longed to earn my freedom, like him. By the time I stood before King Nobiin, my vision was to steer Nubia through the global recession and so it went on. I encourage you all to dare to dream bigger than your current situation or environment. Your vision might be small at the beginning, but don't limit yourself to a small dream. Don't let your environment limit your dream either."

"Six, maintain a life-long commitment to excellence. Another important secret of my success is my life-long commitment to excellence. I developed the habit of striving for excellence in all my endeavors regardless of the challenges that I face. Becoming a person of value is one way to distinguish yourself among the crowd and to attract numerous opportunities. Like bees swarming the nectar, people and institutions generally gravitate towards competent individuals who can deliver value to help accomplish their goals. The more value you deliver, the more relevant you become, and the more successful you become. As for me, my commitment to value delivery made me the go-to person for three administrations in the royal court and made me relevant to the nation for decades. Becoming a person of value means investing in personal development, competence, and learning new skills every time. So, I would encourage you all, regardless of your occupation or daily endeavor, that you find ways to enhance your skill set and how to contribute to your clients and the organizations you work for."

After answering the questions from Limnea, Eran, and Philia, I was about to end the discussion when I noticed several other teenagers and young adults raised their hands to ask questions. While I was glad that the young ones are opening up by asking questions, what was to follow wasn't something I had prepared for. Rather than ask questions, many of these teenagers narrated several uncomfortable experiences with racial discrimination and related several sad stories of being bullied. Others narrated the struggles and cultural confusions they faced as they tried to reconcile the two different cultures they have been living in. It was heart wrenching to see several teenagers and young adults open up to narrate the emotional burden and cultural confusion they were facing unbeknown to their parents. Many felt lonely and misunderstood while others suffered from an identity crisis.

However, many parents were unsettled as their children got up and openly shared their frustrations with the lives they lead. In fact, some elders in the audience sought to silence those who openly shared their experiences for embarrassing their families publicly. It was not long before the back-and-forth conversations between many parents and their children evolved into heated arguments. As things started to get out of hand, I had to intervene and motioned for silence.

"My people, what are we doing if our children cannot freely discuss the issues that bothers them?" I asked in exasperation. "These children are our future; they won't obey because we gave them rules and regulations to follow, we need to be more open to explain the "why" and not just the "what". As elders and parents, we need to be sensitive to the daily realities of our children, else, we would lose them even before they become independent. We need to provide a multi-prong, multigenerational, comprehensive, and practical approach to prepare them for the world out there."

After listening to these stories for more than an hour, I realized that I do not have all the answers to their questions raised. So, I admitted to the parents and everyone present that I don't have all the answers. "I am not an island of knowledge, my children! The challenges of my time as a young man are not the same as the challenges being faced by my grand- and great-grandchildren who are still dealing with these issues today. We will need more than just an old man's wisdom. We need the collective wisdom of the young and the old. This came as a shock to all present because they had thought of me as the all-knowing sage with an impeccable record and unparalleled accomplishments nationally and internationally. The teenagers and the young people stood up to applaud this idea as they felt much impressed that an adult was both bold and humble enough to openly admit that they did not know everything. Seeing that it was late, we decided to spend the next day brainstorming strategies for handling such complex issues that these children were experiencing.

The next day, we had a breakout session where anyone and everyone could ask questions or comment on issues. It was such an interesting discussion session watching three generations of my family deliberate on practical strategies for dealing with the peculiar challenges facing our people. By the time we were done, the communique of this session included several action points for members of our community as well as the Nubian government.

One, racial discrimination is a two-faced monster. As immigrants, we are quick to point out the racial discrimination we experience in Nubia, but we often neglect our tribalism and discrimination against children from mixed races and (grand) sons/daughters in diaspora. We are equally as guilty of racism as the black supremacists we detest! If we are to completely root out racial discrimination in Nubia, it must start from our Libronian community.

"Hey grandpa, rumor has it that your wife, grand aunty Asenath, was also victimized and not welcomed by our people because she's black-skinned. Can we call for an end to the victimization and discrimination of non-Libronian spouses such as my mom?" one of the mixed-race teenagers boldly asked. There was a complete hush on the audience as everyone was shocked that a teenager would reveal this dark side of our history.

"Yes, my daughter! You have raised an important point, and I commend you for your bravery. My dear wife, Asenath, of blessed memory, had her fair share of discrimination from our people, but the irony of the whole thing was that my brothers and even my father also married non-Libronian people. The only difference this time was that she was a black woman" I gently responded while carefully picking my words."

After reflecting on the experiences of Asenath, I seized the opportunity to condemn, in the strongest terms possible, the victimization and discrimination against non-Libronian sons- and daughters-in-law and their children.

"This has to stop now and forever. How can we face the challenges out there when we discriminate and tear ourselves apart while our children live in confusion?"

Then I turned to the non-Libronian spouses there and addressed them in humility and understanding as someone who has seen his spouse deal with the same pain.

"My sons and daughters, you are highly valued members of our community. What defines you is much more than the color of your skin. You add value to your spouses and children. Even though you arrived as strangers, you have embraced our ways of life and our belief in the Almighty God. Regardless of the colors of your skin or your looks, you have inherited the blessings of our forefathers just like the rest of us. I can relate to your pain and frustrations having watched my beautiful wife, Asenath, struggle with rejection from our people for most part of our married life. I want you to know that you are part of this community. I honor you and your contributions to our community."

Many of these men and women sobbed as I tendered my unreserved apologies on behalf of my community that day. The elders of our communities also apologized on behalf of our community and promised to eliminate those negative stereotypes that have marginalized non-Libronian spouses for decades. That night, the seed of reconciliation and healing was sown.

Two, we agreed that parenting styles need to be modified. Having listened to the issues raised, it was obvious that the autocratic style of parenting that gives orders and regulations to children without explaining the reasons behind those orders was not working for this generation of children and young adults. With several disgruntled teenagers and young adults who feel their parents are out of touch with the realities of their generation, it was clear that the conservative philosophy of complete segregation from the Nubian society is not working.

Then a middle-aged woman got up and asked.

"Your excellency sir. We are tired of having strained relationships with our children. Do you have any advice on how we can handle unruly children?"

"My daughter, the problem is not really about the children's behavior, but it is more about your style of parenting. As you have heard them today, many of them are going through challenges that they cannot share with us as parents because the parent-child relationship we share is not based on openness and trust. Instead of giving them listening ears, we tend to just give them rules and regulations as passed down by our fathers without understanding the realities and challenges of their times. We cannot afford to let our children coast through life, emotionally handicapped and victims of our society's inequality and systemic racism. It's high time we mended broken walls and reconcile with our children. To successfully parent your children, I encourage you to engage them in discussions by creating a safe environment for them to share their thoughts, ideas, and opinions, regardless of how childish or naïve it might be."

Three, we identified the need for mentorship in our communities. "Asides from the direct relationship that parents have with their children, our community should be committed to raising these children. The extended family and elders in our community constitute an important bloc of support systems that can reinforce our values and our identity as a people. Our teenagers and young adults need role models who can mentor them on how to navigate the challenges they face in communities, at the marketplace, or in government. Those of us who have retired have enormous responsibilities to help the younger generation."

"Hey, grandpa, can teenagers and young adults serve as mentors for the younger children?" Philia asked.

"Absolutely my child! Serving as mentors and role models is fantastic. It also prepares you for your future."

Some of the business leaders in our communities also promised to provide volunteer and apprenticeship opportunities for our children. Other professionals including, shepherds, supply chain managers, transporters, and those in government, all committed to providing mentorship opportunities for our teenagers and young adults. Even stay-at-home moms volunteered to teach them traditional culinary skills. Everyone that night realized that they have a role to play.

Four, we brainstormed on several strategies to engage the younger generation and the mainstream Nubian community. The children revealed that the Nubian community viewed the Libronian community as a closed sect that cannot be trusted. They made it clear that I was still the only member of our community that was trusted by the Nubian public. Other elders who are municipality government officials also confirmed that our community has a bad reputation among Nubians. I found this very concerning for the future of our people. As we talked through the issues, the young ones came up with brilliant ideas. One of the young adults there suggested that we should open our annual cultural celebrations to Nubians and invest in public relations activities that will repair the dented image of our community in Nubia. Another young man suggested that young adults should consider exploring volunteer roles in local government and royal palace. Another young daughter suggested that our children be allowed to volunteer across Nubia. But some elders in the audience kicked against adopting such ideas.

"This is against our tradition." They claimed.

At this point, I stood up to address the older generation.

"My sons and elders of our community, I am very disappointed that you are shutting down the brilliant ideas that our illustrious sons and daughters have brought up all in the name of tradition. The more we fail to engage these children, the more we endanger the future of our people."

"How do you mean, your Excellency?" one of the elders in the audience asked.

"One of the golden highlights of this meeting, for me, is the exchange of ideas among the four generations of our people. What have these traditions done for us except to estrange us from our children? If you, as elders of the community, continue to make the case of complete separation from the Nubians, how would you justify that our ancestors formed alliances with many nations in their lifetimes? To jettison brilliant ideas because they came from children or because of traditions is not right."

After pleading with these elders, they saw reason with me and supported the ideas brought about by the young ones. To refine the ideas, we created working groups that would investigate practical ways to engage the Nubian public and royal leaders.

Five, we brainstormed strategies for equipping our children to deal with racial discrimination in the marketplace. We came up with several ideas based on input from the children. First, we identified the need to ground our children's identity in the knowledge of our history and our lands. As we discussed this, I reminisced about how our fathers employed the art of storytelling to ingrain in us our identity as a people.

"We need to rediscover the power of storytelling." I pensively declared as everyone paused to hear me.

"Storytelling is a form of art that our fathers employed to share their history, legacies, and secrets from one generation to another. We have now replaced this with books and scrolls which many of this new generation of kids do not even have the patience to study. We need to employ storytelling to engage our children's short attention span across the kitchen table, in the backyards, on the farms, and in our temples. No one can tell our story better than we do. If we do not tell our story, we lose the opportunity to shape the identity of our children and an outsider might twist that story to shape their identity for another purpose."

As we continued deliberations, Isseh stood up to address the group: "My people, one common theme that ran through my father's story of unparalleled exploits is his life-long commitment to excellence in value delivery. Through the constant pursuit of excellence in personal and national affairs, father made himself indispensable for more than seven decades of public life. Even after retiring from public office, they would not leave him alone; they still troop here for advice anyways," he announced as everyone roared in laughter.

Then he continued: "Seriously, another way we can break racial barriers and prove our worth to Nubians is through excellence in all endeavors. Now, we are only known for our livestock production. Considering that our occupation is detested by Nubians, they are ignorant of how important livestock is to the entire national economy. One way to put ourselves in the national spotlight is to embrace excellence in how we deliver value across the supply chain. As the biggest livestock producer, we are also the largest suppliers for the food, fashion, agriculture, and service industries. If we embrace excellence in our product delivery, we can monopolize the supply chain for these industries for years to come. We can build on our successes by expanding into other industries and building expertise in occupations other than livestock production. For example, our women are known for their embroidery of linens for our cultural dresses. Is there a possibility that we can leverage this unique embroidery technology to start a new clothing line that will produce new apparel for mainstream Nubians? That's a business opportunity to engage our sons and most importantly our daughters!"

The idea was appealing to the entire group, especially the younger generation, but many elders voiced their concerns against the ideas.

"Isn't this going to encourage our children to abandon livestock farming which has been handed over to us by our ancestors? We need to thoroughly assess these ideas before embracing them." one of the elders hesitantly replied.

This comment was met by a lot of boos by the younger generation. Isseh respectfully disagreed with this comment by referring to our family's history.

"My dear elders, according to the history passed down to me by my father, our ancestors were rich in livestock, gold, and lands through their livestock and other businesses they had. My grandfather dedicated his life to livestock farming, but that should not prevent us from venturing into other businesses," he calmly explained.

The younger generation applauded Isseh for such an insight'.

"Wow…I have never heard someone speak about our ancestors the way Isseh just described them," one of the teenagers commented.

"I wonder why the obsession with livestock farming. Not everyone is designed to be a farmer," another teenager murmured. These rebuttals did not sit well with the elders.

"If Isseh wants to school us about our family history, he's welcome to a debate. We insist that we will not allow anyone to dictate how we should raise our children based on a minute fraction of our family history. We are a nomad family of herders and nothing will change that," another elder declared.

As I watched the back-and-forth discussions between the elders and the younger generation, I feared that this discussion was pitching two generations of our people against each other. While reflecting on this situation, it occurred to me that this is the type of kitchen table conversation that many in our community have avoided for years.

I decided to wade into the discussion despite my worry about being perceived as taking sides. "My dear people, I believe that both sides of this discussion have raised valid points that merit our attention, having listened to both sides of this discussion."

"Your excellency, I am disappointed that all you have done so far is to side with these children against us. I wonder if this has been your original motive for bringing us here." one of the elders questioned, to the surprise of everyone.

"My dear son, I am not supporting anyone here. I sincerely believe that our community will move forward if we listen to everyone. It is important not to abandon our livestock business through which we maintain a national monopoly because of the realities of the new age. At the same time, not every child in our community is equipped and prepared to end up in the livestock business. Having listened to my story, you can easily infer that I would not have made it as a shepherd had I stayed in Libron. But coming to Nubia helped me to realize and maximize my gift and calling in administration. If we stick with the livestock business alone, we risk future vulnerability to political censorship and victimization. However, we become less vulnerable and more influential as a community if we diversify our portfolio and expertise into other strategic areas of Nubian society. We can take our livestock business model and associated expertise into fashion, construction, politics, technology, and agriculture, military, and other areas. Embedding our expertise in these areas further strengthens our influence and contributions to Nubian society. I understand the fear of losing our identity and tradition, as a community, in a fast-paced society and the resistance to change our modus operandi in such changing world. It is to this end that I submit that both perspectives are complementary and not antagonistic. We need the wealth of experience from the elders, the adventurousness of the young people, the conservative and pragmatic perspective of the elders, and the optimistic and futuristic mindset of the new generation to break into new frontiers and move our people, our community, and this nation into the next phase of God's agenda for this kingdom." I explained

"Rather than take sides, can we find ways to work together as a group?"

Then I turned to the younger generation and addressed them as well.

"Dear young people, the elders in our community are not here to stiffen any progressive move you may have. Instead, they bring a unique and pragmatic perspective that can ground you in your identity and heritage. Instead of these endless debates, why don't we all come to the table with a sense of humility to learn, negotiate, and reach consensus on these issues."

At this point, everyone realized the futility of the arguments.

"Folks, the sage has spoken; and he is right. We have disagreed, but now we need to find common grounds without looking down on anyone's ideas," one of the elders replied.

Just as we were wrapping up these discussions, my aide came by and whispered that it was almost lunch time.

Looking up to me with his eyes full of worry, "Grandpa, my tummy is rumbling, I need to eat something soon" Eran exclaimed as he massaged his belly, a gesture that drew laughter from the entire audience. Seeing that mothers in the room affirmed that other toddlers and younger kids were tired, we ended the discussion with lunch.

As we sat at lunch and held hands to share a blessing over the food, I reminded my people of our journey to Nubia and how much we have enjoyed God's favor here in Nubia.

"I believe that the good Lord has brought us into this land as immigrants, not just to consume the riches and wealth of this land, but to be a light in the darkness; to be salts that season tasteless delicacies; to be people of influence who can make this land much better than we met it. It was not an accident that the almighty God brought us here, the most powerful nation on earth. Regardless of the challenges that we face, we are survivors, strong, and indomitable; we are the descendants of Libron. However, we cannot be effective in realizing our goal of becoming a people of influence by living in our bubbles and not fully embracing this beautiful land, its culture, and its people. We have been endowed with so much and have many responsibilities to this land. We owe it to ourselves and the people of this land, who welcomed us with open hands, to give our best and join them to raise this land to its highest ideals. It is not enough to wish for change, we need to live out the change we desire as immigrants every day. Finally, we can only accomplish this by embracing unity, multi-generational cooperation, and integration of contrasting ideas and perspectives from our people to make this nation the beacon of hope, prosperity, and freedom it is meant to be."

"That's a long speech, grandpa. I am so hungry; can I start eating my food now?" Eran asked while struggling to resist the temptation of eating his food before the end of my long-winded speech.

"Of course, my dear child, you can begin your food now."

This meeting with my community would become the first of many we would hold to deliberate on strategies for mentoring our children, engaging with the broader Nubian community, forming national advocacy groups, and holding consultations with other immigrant communities to promote diversity and inclusion in Nubia. As a retired public official, mentoring multiple generations of my people gave me much joy and renewed purpose in my latter years.